"This never could have lasted," Lou said gently.

"It just felt so blissful, so perfect." He felt Mary's stare. "I've been…lonely, I suppose."

"Since Gracie and Trevor left?"

"No."

He glanced at her then pulled the wheel to the side to avoid a shrub growing in the middle of the rough desert road.

"For years now, I think," she continued. "It took meeting Gracie to realize I was nothing but a shadow of a person. And now, seeing Trevor so happy and fulfilled, it's as though a light has been cast on this deep, hollow well that's my life."

Lou frowned. She talked like he and James meant nothing to her. "You might want to explain, because I've always liked having you at the ranch. James and I depend on you."

"You've both been blessings. A sanctuary for my soul. But what you've liked hasn't been me. It's been good food and cl

"That's a bunch of ho

"Is it?"

He swerved to the side
the brakes. "You better believe it."

Books by Jessica Nelson

Love Inspired Historical

Love on the Range
Family on the Range

JESSICA NELSON,

in keeping with her romantic inclinations, married two days after she graduated high school. She believes romance happens every day and thinks the greatest, most intense romance comes from a God who woos people to himself with passionate tenderness. When Jessica is not chasing her three beautiful, wild little boys around the living room, she can be found staring into space as she plots her next story. Or she might be daydreaming about a raspberry mocha from Starbucks. Or thinking about what kind of chocolate she should have for dinner that night. She could be thinking of any number of things, really. One thing is for certain, she is blessed with a wonderful family and a lovely life.

Family on the Range

JESSICA NELSON

HARLEQUIN LOVE INSPIRED® HISTORICAL

Recycling programs
for this product may
not exist in your area.

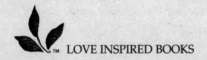

ISBN-13: 978-0-373-28269-2

FAMILY ON THE RANGE

www.Harlequin.com

Printed in U.S.A.

He shall call upon me, and I will answer him:
I will be with him in trouble; I will deliver him,
and honour him.
—*Psalms* 91:15

Dedicated to my sister Josephine, who has Mary's heart. And to my niece Jayla, who is Josie.

Chapter One

June 1920
Oregon

"**B**ag the body and don't forget to ink his prints." Special Agent Lou Riley moved away from the man who had met his demise in the bowels of an illegal liquor operation. He slipped Wrigley's peppermint gum into his mouth and gnawed on it as he thought through his circumstances.

This dead witness meant more time on assignment trying to track down the one who'd hired the foreign bootlegger to do his dirty work.

Prohibition in Oregon wasn't a thing to be trifled with. After a decade of chasing murderers, traitors and thieves in his job as special agent for the Bureau of Investigation, Lou guessed helping the local police track speakeasies and distilleries served him well enough.

Better than the more dangerous spying he'd done until this past year.

He rubbed the back of his neck, feeling the stress of a hard day's work combined with personal pressures. Day before last he'd left his secluded ranch to tackle this assignment. His housekeeper, Mary, had everything under

control at home, but he couldn't shake his unease. Over a
year ago his niece and his best friend, Trevor, had married, and ever since he'd been thinking about the past.
About people long gone. And lately, when he saw Mary, a
strange tension filled him, which was odd because they'd
always had an easygoing rapport in the twelve years she'd
been his employee.

Not that his job ever kept him home with her for long.

Grimacing at the kink in his left shoulder, he wheeled
around and left the dim building. An overcast afternoon
greeted him, heavy with mist and promising rain. He nodded to one of his field agents as he picked his way to the
bureau's automobile.

Summers in Oregon weren't exactly sunny. Not warm,
either. He missed the aridness of his home in east Oregon,
the openness of the desert range. Small cities like this
one tended to weigh him down with memories. Buildings
pressed in on him....

He shrugged the morbidity away.

Every time he went home, saw Mary, he left feeling this
way. Maybe it was her trusting smile or the way her eyes lit
with welcome when he walked in the door. Like someone
else's long ago. Mary's look stirred up memories, blew the
dust of time off them—he stopped himself, stuttering to
a halt near a gutter. He couldn't go there. Not ever again.

"Hey, mister!"

Lou turned slowly at the intrusion, his hand moving
to the weapon at his hip beneath his coat. "You talking
to me?"

"That's right." A shadow slid out from an alley to Lou's
left, heavy Irish accent lilting the man's syllables. "You
the agent in charge down the road?"

"What's it to you?"

"I got information on who was supplying the gig down

there." The man moved closer, and Lou caught a whiff of sour fish as well as a glimpse of green eyes and blond mustache.

"Let's take this downtown. Put it on paper." That pesky muscle cramped in Lou's back again and he fought not to wince. He was thirty-six years old, but he felt sixty today.

"I'll just slip you the information here, quiet-like."

Lou's brows lowered. He looked down the street. His agents were busy coordinating the bust, but something felt off. Every instinct warned him to draw his weapon.

He never discounted his instincts.

Drawing his revolver, he beckoned the man. "Come into the light."

"And get pinned for bootleggin'? Not on your life, mister."

"Then stay right there. I'll get a pen and—"

"This won't take long." The man pulled back suddenly.

Lou's skin prickled.

Shadows closed over where the man had been as he slipped from view. Alert, Lou spun away from the blond and faced the road. A sharp ping split the night before his chest caught fire in a familiar, unwelcome sensation.

Pivoting, he backed into the shadows. Shouts from down the road reached his hearing, but whoever had shot him took off. The sound of the shooter's footsteps was distinctive, a smart uneven clip of metal against cobblestone. Almost like spurs.... The sound faded, merging with other, faster steps.

His shoulder burned. He groaned as the strength left his legs.

This was real bad. Worse than a shot in the leg or shoulder. Body numbing, he crumpled to the ground. He couldn't keep his eyes open. The sounds around him muffled and the last image he saw was Mary's dark eyes, the curve of her lips when she opened the door to welcome him home.

Would he see her again?

Loneliness never killed a person.

Or so Mary O'Roarke tried to tell herself as she mentally prepared for a visit with her mother. Surely once she stated her wishes, her mother would then see reason and quit insisting on living by herself.

Oregon's summer sun rolled above Mary, hot though not quite to its zenith. She slowed her mare outside the Paiute encampment where her mother lived. *Alone*. With no one to rely on. It was not the way an elderly woman should live, and she'd told her mother so many times.

Only now did she have the means with which to help her, and no one could stop her, not even her stubborn employer who owned the ranch where she worked and, until recently, lived. She'd bought an old friend's house next to the ranch, the first home she'd ever owned in all her thirty years, and maybe that might convince her mother to come back with her.

Feeling hopeful, Mary turned the horse in the direction of her mother's dwelling.

The encampment consisted of tents and campfires. The odor of rabbit flesh hung in the air. The government did not appear to care that native Paiutes preferred homes made from various woods and sagebrush, and instead provided them with only the means to make tepees. Mary nodded to those she passed. Some wore the rabbit robes for which her mother's people were known. Others, mostly men, dressed in the white man's garb. Trousers, hats.

She came to her mother's tepee and dismounted. No hitching post for her mare, so she tied the reins to a straggly shrub nearby. Children whispered and giggled, circling but not coming close. A stray dog loped over and the children chased it, their ill-fitting clothes doing nothing to hinder their laughter.

A wistful smile pulled at Mary's lips. She'd longed to have children many years ago. Before the trauma of her past had wrenched her from any chance of a normal life. Perhaps she'd grown too old now, too set in her ways.... She certainly knew nothing about the ways of motherhood. Sighing, she bent near the entrance of her mother's tent.

"It's Mary. I've come to visit."

A rustle ensued. Then the grunt that was Rose's answer. Mary twisted the flap to the side and entered the tent. The interior never failed to elicit a strange sense of distance. This was her mother's life now, a return to her roots, but it had never been Mary's life. The setting filled her with disquiet and a peculiar sense of displacement.

As a child she'd lived in the white man's world. Her father was Irish and while he worked the docks, her mother had used her beauty to bring in money at various brothels. It had been an odd childhood, full of travel and sporadic learning. When she was twelve, her father had abandoned them, followed shortly by her mother.

Tasting bitterness, Mary swallowed and prayed for peace.

"You brought me something?" Her mother sat to the side, high cheekbones cloaked with lined, leathery skin. The map of her broken life.

"Yes, willow and sagebrush bark." She placed the offerings next to the stack of intricate baskets Rose weaved to sell.

They lapsed into awkward conversation. Mostly talk of weather.

"I have my own home," she told her mother at last, warming to her subject. This was why she'd come. To coax

Rose into living with her. At her mother's look of surprise, Mary continued, "I've bought Trevor's house. Now that he's married, he plans to find a place in town for when he and Gracie don't stay at the ranch. I would like you to come live with me."

An old argument, but she tried again, hoping this to be the day her mother might surrender.

"Interesting," Rose murmured, stroking the thick rabbit robe on her lap. "Now you will be alone with your employer?"

"Lou?"

"You have great *besa soobedda* for him."

"A what?" Though Mary spoke some Paiute, she wasn't fluent and disliked when her mother used language she hadn't taught her only daughter.

A crooked smile lifted the corner of Rose's lips. "*Besa soobedda* is love, the sweet emotional bond between a man and his wife."

Mary stiffened as a peculiar heat seeped through her. She'd lived at the ranch for twelve years and never had she entertained such a thought about her employer. Granted, he was charming and funny. He had hired her as his housekeeper when she was eighteen, offering his home as a refuge after she'd been rescued from the notorious slave trader Mendez. Lou's kindness would never be forgotten. But love?

"We have no such love," she denied. "I feel a sister's affection for him." Even as she spoke, she wondered if that was true. When she'd told him goodbye yesterday, there had been the oddest regret creeping through her. Unnerved, she continued, "I should leave if you do not wish to come with me at this time."

"Wait!" Her mother struggled to a standing position, and Mary tried not to cringe at how age and worries had stolen her mother's strength. Perhaps loneliness would not kill her mother but rather another more obvious ailment. She swallowed hard at the thought.

Rose shuffled toward a trunk at the other side of the tepee. Bending, she opened it. "I have something for you."

"I want you to come home with me. I need nothing else."

"This is important."

A small blond head popped up out of the trunk. "Hiya!"

Mary started. "What is that?"

"I'm a little girl." The child clambered out of the trunk and gave Mary a decidedly mischievous smirk. "Are you going to be my mother?"

Startled, Mary groped for words. Finally, she said, "I'm not a mother to anyone."

"Oh, but I need one. Just for a bit, you see, until I go home to my real mama." The girl shot a cheeky, gap-toothed grin up at Rose, who reached down to stroke the girl's head.

The movement snapped Mary from her shocked paralysis. "You have someone's child? Do you know the penalty for such a thing?"

Rose met her accusation with a steady look. "She is in danger. You have a home apart from Lou now. You can hide her."

"No." She shook her head, feeling her braid swing against her back. "No, I can't do it."

"My daughter, I need you." Her mother shuffled forward. "I cannot keep her much longer."

Mary glanced at the child, who'd shifted her attention to the baskets and studiously went about picking one apart. "Who is she?"

"I don't know."

"My name's Josie Silver," the girl put in. "I live in Portland but my mama's not home right now."

"Where is she?" Mary asked. "How about your father?"

The girl lifted her shoulders. "I don't know, and I don't have a papa. I want to stay here."

Mary glared at her mother. "Where did you find her?"

"Half-dead near Harney Lake, one week ago."

She shuddered. "That's horrible. You should've taken her to the authorities."

Her mother grimaced. "I wasn't supposed to be out there."

"Mother."

"Don't berate me. You say you follow Jesus. A woman in town says He helps the poor and motherless. This child is that, and I—" Her mother peeked at the girl and lowered her voice. "I'm begging you to hide her until I send word it's safe."

"This makes no sense. How do you know she's not safe?"

"Her guardian has posted a reward for her."

"You said you didn't know who she is? Return her." Mary frowned. Where was the problem if someone had offered a reward? They already knew the child's mother's name. Confused and feeling lost in the maze of her mother's reasoning, she backed toward the door flap.

"I know the guardian," her mother said quietly. "He is not a man to be trifled with."

Uncharacteristic impatience rushed through Mary. "Take care of the matter, then." She had no room, no time, for a child.

I'm afraid.

The thought slammed into her. Tension hovered at the base of her skull, knotting and twining the muscles of her neck.

Her mother moved closer, bringing her once-beautiful

features near. "I knew him when you were a child. In my past."

Mary's hand flew to her lips, but the movement didn't stifle her gasp.

"Yes." Her mother nodded. "Now you understand. He is a bad man, and I do not know why this child lay in the desert like a starved and wounded animal, but I will not return her. He will come looking, and it will be impossible for me to hide her from others."

"I'll take her," Mary said through numb lips.

It was true she could take the child to her new home, but for how long? The girl couldn't live with her indefinitely. The authorities must be contacted.

What would Lou say about a child near his secluded ranch, a haven he'd created for secret agents of the Bureau of Investigation and not for child rearing?

The little girl stared at her with big eyes, and she winced.

Why should she care what Lou thought? Yes, he employed her to keep his house, but she'd just bought her own home, her first step toward a more independent life. Determination straightened her backbone. If she was going to stop being afraid, to start living again, then she must put Lou and everything he represented behind her.

Could she do that, though?

Thank goodness he wouldn't be home for several weeks. That gave her time to return Josie to her mother and persuade her own mother to come live with her. Because if Lou were home, he'd protest, and she didn't know if she had the backbone to stand up for what she thought was right.

Chapter Two

An uncomfortable dryness at the roof of Lou's mouth woke him. His tongue felt oversize, and his throat worked to swallow. He opened his eyes to find himself in the dark tones of his bedroom. A sense of claustrophobia wrapped galvanizing tentacles around him.

He tried to shove upward, but fierce pain in his chest snatched the breath from his lungs. Forced to lie still, he took shallow breaths while the pulsating daggers near his upper rib cage ebbed. Only thirty-six. It wasn't fair to feel this way.

"Water," he croaked.

Movement to his left, and then a firm hand slipped under his neck. Relieved, Lou allowed his head to tip forward so he could drink from the proffered cup.

The hand took the water away too quickly. After resting his head back on the pillow, Mary crossed his line of vision, disappeared, and then reappeared on his right side.

Hair pulled back in a bun, she might've passed for any Irish lass but for the duskiness of her skin and the high cheekbones that pronounced her native heritage. As usual, the sight of her stunned Lou for a moment.

His lids lowered and he watched as she bustled with

his covers, stretching and straightening. Finally, she patted them, a satisfied look relaxing the line of her full lips. She turned her gaze to him.

Immediately he noted the strange look in her eyes. Normally she appeared serene, gentle, timid even. Today, however, wariness shadowed her gaze, something he'd only seen in her eyes when she dealt with others. Never with him.

He didn't like that something was wrong with her. He would fix it, whatever it was. Frowning, he ignored the burn in his throat to speak. "Something's wrong."

Her eyelids flickered before she turned away. "You're still thirsty."

The water she brought him slid down easy, coating the soreness with cool relief. Cleared his head, too, so he could more closely examine the situation. Something was off. Mary's evasion, that look on her face…

"Help me up," he said.

She set the cup on his dresser and then returned, sitting at the edge of his bed, just out of reach. Her scent, a strange mix of sage and flowers, filled his senses and taunted him.

"I won't help you sit up. You might tear your stitches," she replied. Her pronunciation was technically correct, but an exotic flavor rounded each of her words, courtesy of her trilingual skills.

"How long have I been out?"

"You left the ranch a little less than a week ago. I believe two days into your assignment you were shot and then taken to the hospital. They removed the bullet and telegrammed James."

Her mention of his ranch hand and long-time friend failed to comfort.

"Did they catch the shooter?"

"No one has told me much. James picked you up from

the hospital and brought you here. He drove to town this morning to find supplies to keep your wound clean, but he should be back this afternoon." Her brow lined. "You have been going in and out of consciousness for days now. How do you feel?"

Confused. He felt confused and bothered.

"Sore," he answered shortly. "Where's my M&P?" His Smith & Wesson military and police revolver had kept him company for almost twenty years. He didn't plan on losing it now.

The lines in her forehead deepened. "I put it somewhere safe."

He pushed up, purpose fueling his movement. His vision blackened for a moment as his upper body throbbed with pain, but he ignored the sensation.

"Bring it to me," he managed to say.

"You can't move like that." Mary leaned over him, her features drawn with worry. "You almost died. Someone tried to kill you, and that's why the bureau decided it was best to get you here, to the safe house. You are on temporary leave until you recover."

Lou closed his eyes and waited for the nausea and torturous aches in his body to pass. This couldn't be happening. He needed his job. The last place he wanted to be stuck at was the ranch.

"Let me give you some pain medication." Mary's voice drifted over him.

"No," he said, voice rough. "Not yet. This place isn't safe."

"Mendez is dead."

Lou forced his eyes to open when what he wanted more than anything was to sleep. "He might've passed our location on to one of his buddies."

Twelve years ago, Mary had been kidnapped by a man

called Mendez. She'd been his first kidnapping and, thankfully, had been rescued by government agent Striker, aka Lou's friend Trevor, before Mendez could sell her.

Unfortunately, her rescue hadn't stopped Mendez from becoming a notorious slave trader, known for trafficking women down to Mexico.

Trevor spent the next ten years as a shadow, tracking Mendez and rescuing what women he could while hiding behind his nickname, Striker. And Mendez had developed an obsession to pay Striker back for foiling his moneymaking kidnapping schemes. Out of fear, and knowing Mendez wanted to use Mary to draw Striker out from his anonymity, she'd been hiding on this ranch until two Christmases ago, when Mendez had found her again. He'd attempted to kidnap Mary but had accidentally taken Lou's niece, Gracie, instead.

Thanks to Gracie's ingenuity, she'd escaped and had been found by Trevor. Mendez and his men had died of poisoning unrelated to their kidnapping plans, but Lou couldn't shake the feeling this place wasn't safe anymore. He didn't want Mary to see the depth of his worry, though. She had enough burdens to carry.

Feeling exhausted yet unwilling to surrender consciousness, he met her gaze. "Trevor and I buried Mendez. You don't have to worry about him. But our cover is gone…." He paused for breath. He'd been shot before, stabbed, even, but never had he felt this tired.

"Take the medicine." A note of stubborn finality crept into her voice. "I will speak with you about this later."

Lou blinked hard against the tide of sleep pulling his lids closed. Mary wavered in front of him, holding out some foul-smelling concoction. She pressed the spoon against his lips, and he grabbed her wrist. Keeping his gaze pinned on hers, he swallowed but didn't let go of the delicate bones beneath his fingers.

Her eyes widened, and a blush spread across her face at his touch. She tried to pull away, but he tightened his grip.

"Thank...you." He struggled to speak without slurring, to give her a reassuring smile.

"You shouldn't talk right now." She lifted her other hand to his brow, smoothing his hair with warm, firm fingers. "I hear the wagon. James will be in at any minute."

It seemed only a second to Lou until he heard his ranch hand and old friend James in the room. "Got him laudanum. Some Oregon grape root, too."

Mary rose and disappeared from Lou's view. He stifled the urge to shout and demand someone help him up from this bothersome bed. They came back, James smirking down at him.

"Had to go and get yourself shot, boss?" He swiped the hat off his head and rubbed the gnarled mass of hair above his ears. "Leave us with all the ranch work while you catch them bootleggers, and now look at ya."

"Can you watch him for me?"

"I don't need watching," Lou told Mary crossly, annoyance temporarily strengthening him. "Get a message to Hayworth that I need to be moved. Maybe to headquarters." Surely his superior would approve a move under the circumstances.

James bent over him and squinted. "You sayin' the ranch ain't safe?"

"Not with me here. These people mean business. If Mendez found us, chances are someone else...will...too." Lou struggled for breath, hating the weakness of his body. If he'd just gone with his gut instead of standing in the road like a yellow-bellied pansy, he might be flushing out criminals at this very moment.

Now he was trapped here. Forced to see Mary every day, when every second just looking at her made him remember more and more of his past. It didn't used to be this way. He didn't like how things had changed.

He aimed to get out of here before things spiraled out of control.

"Let us take care of you." Mary swished over, bringing medicine with her. "Here, gently now."

Lou took the medicine, unable to fight the droop of his lids any longer. Mary's and James' voices became distant murmurs, then faded away.

He wanted sleep, but instead images from the past flashed through him. His mother and father. His brother with his wife. His niece, Gracie.

And Abby.

Sarah had named Abigail after her mother. He moaned, thrashing his head, willing the images to leave. To stop assaulting him.

His chest burned, but he couldn't tell if it was the wound or his heart.

More laudanum. That was what he needed.

"Mary," he whispered.

Nothing.

"Mary." He tried again, forcing his windpipe to push out more air. A creak followed his plea, but he didn't smell her.

An odd sound cut through the air. Like a…giggle?

He cocked an eye open. With the medicine swimming through his blood, the room tilted to the side. The doorway wavered, and for a second he thought he saw a thatch of blond hair beneath the doorknob.

"Abby," he breathed. A hard rush of pain splintered through his chest, cutting off his air and making his eyes burn. Just one more look. After all these years, he wanted to see her one more time.

He waited. A second later the door creaked again, and Abby poked her head through. She shot him a wide smile that showed off teeth with a gap between them the size of Texas. Had he missed her losing teeth, then? It seemed she'd just started cutting them.

Sarah said she ate everything in sight. A smile curled up inside Lou like a soft blanket over his heart. "Abby, come here. Give Daddy a hug."

Her giggle sprinkled through the air, light and fuzzy, followed by a sweet rush of darkness that took him to a warm and gentle place.

Lou Riley was seeing dead people.

Unable to shake the morbid thought, he opened his eyes. Bright morning sun poured through the window, highlighting the suspiciously clean lines of his room. Mary had been in again, dusting and cleaning. He groaned, wincing as a nasty throb of pain jolted through his temples.

His chest felt better, though. He tried shifting in the bed. His bandages crinkled with the movement, and a definite soreness invaded his muscles. No fever, no infection, which was a good thing. He'd be glad to discontinue this medicine, glad to get his head turned straight, glad to put an end to the dreams plaguing his sleep.

"There you are, sleepyhead." Mary floated into the room, her hair a shiny ebony in the morning light. Her features appeared smooth and even, a hint of worry not evident. He must be doing great.

Despite his aches, he grinned at her. "Right where I've been the past week."

"Oh, not that long." Blushing in response to his flirtatious smile, she set a tray on the bed.

Lou sniffed the air. "Pancakes?" he asked hopefully.

"Yep."

He took a closer look. "Is that a...rattler?" He glanced at Mary. The burnished rose color of her cheeks deepened.

"I was experimenting with shapes. A little artistic license. I'm not sure how that was placed on the tray." She frowned and didn't meet his eyes.

Interesting. He took the plate she held out to him and loaded up. Days of no food had made him famished. His stomach hurt just looking at it all. But that snake... A frown took possession of his mouth.

He settled against his pillow, carefully moving the plate to his lap. "You know, my mom used to make me and my brother animal-shaped pancakes."

"Really?" Mary fiddled with the sheets on the bed.

"Oh, yeah." He nodded, never taking his gaze from her face. An uneasy suspicion was taking root. "Moms do it for kids all the time."

"Not all mothers," she interjected.

"Creative moms." He amended the sentence with a flourish of his fork. "Speaking of kids, you might want to lighten my laudanum dosage. I've been seeing things."

Mary moved toward the dresser, her back to him. For a moment, Lou was distracted by the waves of hair that fell like a silk waterfall against her shoulders. He'd forgotten how dark her hair was, thick, and blacker than a sky bereft of stars.

In all their years of knowing each other, he didn't think he'd ever touched her hair before. In fact, he made certain not to unnecessarily touch her. To give her space and to help her feel safe. His general policy regarding women involved distance. Women were lovely creatures, interesting, a tad difficult, but getting mixed up with a woman took more stamina than Lou was inclined to expend.

Relationships meant pain. He'd learned that early on.

Clenching and unclenching his fingers, he willed the itch to touch Mary to leave.

"What have you been seeing?" she finally asked.

He studied her, noting the stiffness in her shoulders. "Things that shouldn't be here."

"Oh?" She pivoted toward him.

The look of obstinacy on her face might've made him laugh if he didn't realize it meant something he wouldn't like.

"A kid," he said flatly.

She didn't respond at first. Then a serene mask settled over her face. Her armor. Seeing it confirmed his suspicion that she was hiding something. A lead weight settled in his belly, feeling almost like disappointment.

"What's going on?"

Her eyelids flickered. "You haven't been seeing things. There is a child here, found abandoned by the lake. But she's not staying long," she rushed on. "I've made efforts to find her mother and hope to hear something soon."

He groaned. Impatience and a different kind of pain burned through him. He wanted to leap off the bed and make her see reason. His limitations, this inconvenient injury, might prove to be his undoing. "The girl can't stay. This place is too dangerous for a child. Take her to the sheriff."

He waited for Mary's reaction to his words. As usual, she withdrew. He could sense the retreat, see it in the way she backed up, eyes shuttered, face expressionless.

How many times had he seen this look of hers? From the moment she'd been brought to the ranch, bruised in spirit, a desperate eighteen-year-old in need of rescuing, he'd known she was different. Vulnerable. He'd taken her under his protection, watched out for her even though he'd only been twenty-four and dealing with his own sorrows.

Lou ground his teeth, trying not to scowl and failing. She met the look with a guarded demeanor.

"I know you're angry." Her voice came out tiny, quiet.

"I'm not angry, but it's important for that little girl to be home. I can find her family within a day."

"No." She moved forward. "You have to stay in bed. Rest and recuperate."

Suddenly the door to the room whipped open. James stood in the doorway, hair askew and whiskers bunching.

"Josie's gone."

Mary whirled, her hand to her chest. "You were supposed to watch her!"

"The little whippersnapper slipped out of my sight," James grumbled. "She wanted cocoa."

Mary picked up her skirts before casting Lou a worried look. "I have my own home now. You can't tell me who's allowed to stay there."

He narrowed his gaze. It sounded as if she was referencing her mother, the only person she argued with him about. Otherwise she never spoke up, never acted feisty. His niece, Gracie, must've influenced her more than he realized.

It was a nice change from her natural timidity.

Almost smiling, he made to speak but was interrupted by a harsh knocking from below. The sound reverberated up the stairs. Every muscle in his body tensed. No one should be knocking on a secluded ranch's door.

"Get me my derringer." He pointed to his dresser, where he hid a backup.

"Where?" Mary moved toward the dresser.

"Behind, on the floor."

She reached down and picked it up, then brought it to him.

Their fingers brushed when she set the heavy weapon in

his hand. She was warm, gentle, and she shouldn't be exposed to danger. His grip tightened as he drew the weapon from her and slipped it beneath the sheets.

Her eyes widened, never leaving his, irises dark with strain. "I have to find Josie."

Lou nodded. "James," he said without looking at his employee, "answer the door. Mary, find the girl and keep her safe."

They rushed out, and Lou leaned back with a grunt. His head hurt. At least the butt of his gun lay solidly in his palm, cool to the touch, reassuring with its heavy weight and the promise of security.

He looked to the thick door, which remained cracked, and listened for sound from downstairs. If Mary and James needed him, he'd be useless. Did he even have the strength to stand? Shifting in his bed, he gingerly sat forward.

A rush of dizziness pressed in on his head, and the edges of his vision grayed. Groaning, he lay back. How could he have let this happen? He should've stayed away from the prohibition problems Oregon had. But he loved challenges, and aiding the local police gave him something to focus on.

Frowning, he cradled his gun and watched the door.

A rustle sounded. Voices drifted up, low tones, calm sounding. Maybe it was just a homesteader passing through. A lot of his neighbors were leaving their small ranches, abandoning them to the wild desert of Harney County.

The rustle caught his attention again. Ears perked, he held his breath.

A ball of pink rolled out from under the bed and into his line of sight.

Chapter Three

Lou jerked back, causing shards of pain to splinter across his chest. Gut tight, he eyed the little girl as she stood and brushed off her fluffy dress. Her hair was a mass of blond curls that framed a round face, complete with a dimple and a decidedly crooked smile.

"Hi, mister. My name's Josie." She skipped to him and shoved her hand in his face. "Nice to meet ya."

He ignored her hand, giving her the darkest glare he could muster.

Her eyes were a deep blue, almost violet. He'd mistaken her for Abby, but now that she stood before him, in the light of morning, he could see the differences. Abby's eyes had been a bright blue, like his.

A lump clogged his windpipe. Her hair had been dark, like her mother's, and straight as a horse's mane. This girl before him wore a smile that showed off rows of teeth, complete with gaps. Abby hadn't lived long enough to get all hers, let alone lose any.

Because his mouth felt drier than Oregon's Alvord Desert on a summer noon, he couldn't speak, could only wordlessly watch this little person, the kind he'd stayed away from for more than a decade.

"Are you okay?" The girl poked his arm, her touch a hot brand that seared through his skin, straight to his heart. "You look scared. I promise I won't hurt you. I just need a family for a little while." She flashed that dimple at him again and winked.

Caught off guard, a rusty chuckle broke loose, sounding like an old gate he used to hear creaking in the breeze outside his childhood home.

"Who's your father?" he asked.

"I don't have one," she said simply. She rounded the bed, grabbed the water off the bedside table and carefully brought it to him. The look of concentration on her cherubic face did something funny to Lou's middle, almost made him want to smile again. When she reached the bed, she brought the water close to his mouth.

"You sound thirsty. Sometimes my dog is thirsty, too. I always bring her water."

"Thank you." He took the cup and sipped, mind working overtime. Surely a family was looking for this girl. She looked clean and bright, rosy cheeks, healthy hair, unbothered by whatever had happened to bring her here. "You know you'll have to go home."

Josie tilted her head, her never-ending dimple bugging the tar out of him. The girl was too cute for her own good. She'd cause trouble, no doubt about that.

She appeared to be mulling over his words. "I don't think I have a home anymore," she finally said.

No father and no home? He found that hard to believe.

Footsteps in the hall turned Josie's head. There was something familiar in the cadence of the steps.... He couldn't place what. Then the low rumble of men's voices reached him. James sounded ornery and gruff. He didn't recognize the man's voice, though it held a definite Southern lilt.

Someone from the bureau, then? They could help find Josie's parents, or at least put her in an orphanage. The thought of an orphanage unexpectedly filled him with regret, a physical punch that stole the breath from his lungs.

He shot Josie a glance.

Her fingers bunched into her dress, and she stared at the door like a deer caught in the sights of a rifle. The flush that had reddened her cheeks earlier had fled, replaced by an unnatural pallor that pulsed dread through Lou's veins.

"What's wrong?" he asked.

Josie turned eyes too terrified to belong on a child his way. "He's a very bad man," she whispered.

The voices outside the door rose in argument. At any moment the door could open. Lou positioned his gun under the sheets and jerked his chin toward the edge of the bed. "Get under, and don't say a word."

Mary peeked around the door frame of the downstairs study. After racing through the house, searching for Josie, she'd hidden in the study while James spoke with the man at the door. The visitor sounded urbane and sophisticated. She'd caught sight of a pressed suit and slicked-back hair as the men went up the stairs.

Was it someone from the bureau? Why else would James bring this stranger into the house? Heart pounding, she moved around the corner and into the empty hall. The rising sun splashed light against the dark floor she'd waxed yesterday morning.

She loved this home, had lived here for all of her adult life, but it was time to grow up. With time, Trevor's house would feel like hers. She picked her way to the stairs, listening to the low sound of masculine voices.

As she moved upward, the voices escalated. A sense of urgency propelled her to the noise. She reached the top and spotted an unhappy-looking James with the stranger, standing outside Lou's door.

"I was just fixing to show this man out of the house," James said, his tone a warning.

Oh, no. The man must have forced his way upstairs and she was sure James didn't carry his weapon in the house. But he did have one stashed in the guest room....

Wetting her lips, she smoothed her dress and started their way. "Gentlemen." She forced her lips into a smile, shivering inside when the man swiveled toward her. His eyes were the same purple color as Josie's, but where the child's were alive and bright, his looked dark and forbidding.

Evil.

An inner warning she'd developed as a young girl encased her body, chilling her to the core. This man intended wickedness, of that she was sure. Smile pasted to her face, she drew near Lou's door, sliding her body in front of the knob. She needed to distract him.

James gave her an imperceptible nod of approval before turning to the stranger. "This is Mary, our housekeeper. She the one you've been looking for?"

The man's gaze traveled the length of her, a leer in his eyes if not on his lips. Dread pooled in her belly, and she had to force herself to meet his stare, to be calm in the face of his unrelenting perusal. This man fed on control. It made him feel powerful.

She'd met enough like him in her mother's former life to read the sins on his face.

Finally, the man looked at James. "No, the woman I'm looking for is much older. I was told you housed a Paiute, but evidently this lady isn't the one." The man gave her a slow, ugly wink. "I could offer you a better job. Higher pay." His gaze flicked over her work dress. "Nicer clothes."

"Perhaps you know the woman's name for whom you search?" she managed to say, though her tongue cleaved to the roof of her mouth.

"I only know she took something of mine, and I want it back."

Mary gulped, despising the fear that froze her veins and rooted her to the floor like an ice statue.

James broke the tension by clapping a hand on the stranger's shoulder. "Well, now you've met Mary and she's not the one, so why don't I get you some vittles and drink before you get on your way."

"Will you reconsider my offer?" The stranger directed his question to her.

She couldn't speak, could only shake her head.

"Very well. A pleasure meeting you, ma'am." He inclined his head, but she had no intention of reciprocating. None at all.

A hard look passed over his face when he realized her snub. James strode down the short hall to the stairs, beckoning the man to follow, but he paused in front of her, lips a thin line against his pale skin. "You're a scared little lady." The corner of his mouth tilted. "I like that."

Her heart stilled in its beating, paralyzed, until he pivoted and sauntered after James. Then it resumed a frantic pounding that flushed blood through her body so fast her knees grew wobbly and she thought she might vomit.

Get control. She had to be stronger somehow. Take charge of the situation. There was no way on earth she'd let Josie return to that monster. If she had to keep the girl in hiding her entire life, then that was what she'd do.

Inhaling several deep breaths, she sagged against the door, letting her body calm and forcing her face to relax. If she went into Lou's bedroom right now, he'd know with one look that something was wrong.

The last thing he needed was action, and knowing him, it would be his first instinct. If he discovered this man was looking for Josie, what would he do? The question filled her with uneasiness.

Somehow she had to work harder to locate Josie's mother. See if she was a more fit parent than the malevolent stranger she'd just met.

Squaring her shoulders, she straightened and let herself into Lou's room. His window faced south, exposing a bright sky scattered with fluffy clouds that spoke nothing of evil. Only of good. Of a loving God who'd rescued her from men like the stranger who'd just visited.

A cleansing calm spread through her. She walked to Lou, who lay on the bed watching her, an alert expression on his handsome face.

"Who was the visitor?" His eyes, those shining orbs that had caught her attention from the moment they'd met, glinted at her.

"A stranger." She gingerly sat on the side of his bed, careful not to bump his body. "How is your wound?"

"Burning, but not as much as my gut. Something's wrong, and I want to know what."

"The man was looking for a Paiute woman. He said she took something of his."

"Josie," Lou stated, giving her a hard look, not his usual smile.

"The man didn't specify but I'm assuming so." Stomach quivering, she clasped her hands. "My mother—"

"The woman who abandoned you?" he interrupted, his face darkening.

"She found Josie near Harney Lake, half-dead. Since I have my own home, she asked me to hide her until things were safe."

"Safe from what?" Lou tried to push up from the bed

but stopped, a grimace crossing his even features. "Never mind. You have no business keeping her and you know it. That's called kidnapping."

"No," she protested shakily. "I've telegraphed the Portland police, and they're trying to locate her mother. My mother claimed to be familiar with the father and said he's put up a reward for Josie, but when I rode into town the other day, I saw no such thing."

Lou settled back, the whiskers on his chin drawing Mary's attention. He needed a shave badly. Her gaze traversed the face of a man who'd protected her for so long. Now that time had passed. Now was the moment for her to stand proud and strong. To rise as a woman in charge of her own life.

She could not allow him to take Josie away. This matter belonged to her.

But as she studied him, she realized that despite his good looks and charming smile, he was still exhausted and in need of her care. The epiphany brought a tender warmth to her chest. "I will make you a special meal tonight."

"You will, huh?" Familiar crinkles appeared at the corners of his eyes. "Josie might have something to say about it."

Mary's warm feeling dissipated. "She will not be an issue. You will not have to see her."

"Too late." He gestured to the floor. "Come on out, Josie."

Scrambling ensued before the towheaded girl popped out near Mary's feet. Stifling a surprised squeal, she frowned at the girl. "I've been looking everywhere for you."

Josie squirmed, eyes cast down. "I just wanted to meet Mister Lou."

"We met, all right."

"She's staying with me," Mary put in, worry welling up at Lou's tone. He sounded distant, more removed than she thought possible. "You have no part of this decision I've made."

Her statement seemed to incense him. He grew agitated, rustling the sheets as he attempted to sit. The stubborn man was sure to hurt himself, but she made no move to help him. "The sooner you lie still, the sooner you'll heal."

"Do I really have to leave?" Josie asked in a plaintive, little-girl voice.

"Yes."

"No." Mary glared at Lou. She opened her arms, and Josie ran to her, snuggling in, her hair smelling like the lavender Mary had rinsed it with this morning. Smiling, she tightened the hug.

"We're going to find her a safe place, but first, you need to realize that she knows more than she's telling." Lou's tone caught Mary's attention. She looked up into his serious face. "Ask her, Mary. Ask her who the man at the door was."

Chapter Four

Children complicated matters.

And that was why Lou didn't want them around.

He hated lying in this bed, waiting while Mary sat beside him with that stoic look stuck on her face. Deliberating. The little girl buried her head in Mary's embrace, ignoring Lou and his demand.

Josie was in a heap of trouble. He could tell that much. None of her own doing, of course, but her safety was a priority now. He wanted things to return to normal, and he didn't want to worry about this little girl. Somehow it was up to him to get this mess straightened out.

"I will ask who this man is when the time is right," Mary said at length. Her arms tightened around the girl.

She already felt protective. He admired that, but she'd get her heart broken. He frowned, knowing he felt the same way, too.

"Josie."

The girl made a muffled noise and didn't look at him.

"Josie," he said again, lowering his voice and injecting some sternness into it.

She shuffled around, hair mussed about her face, eyes bright. Her little lips puckered into a pout. "What?"

"Will you tell us who that man is?"

Mary stroked the girl's forehead, her skin a rich color against Josie's blond curls. Josie blinked at him. "I don't wanna."

Chagrined, Lou told himself to be patient. This wasn't a case. Just a little girl who needed to go home, who needed to be safe. Especially before his concern for her turned him crazy. Or worse, drowned him in the sorrow of his losses.

"We want to help you find your mommy," he said with his most winning smile. It worked regularly on women of all ages and didn't fail with the girl. Obviously charmed, her dimples flashed.

"My mommy doesn't feel good. I'm not s'posed to bother her."

"Sweetie, she probably misses you," Mary said.

"She sleeps too much." Josie's dimples disappeared.

"Do you know your address in Portland? A phone number?"

"You sound grumpy, Mister Lou. I think you need a nap."

"I agree." Mary gave him a look that was the equivalent of sticking her tongue out at him. It made him almost want to smile.

She'd changed from the frightened young woman brought to his door years ago. She'd pulled her hair to the side, exposing the lovely bone structure of her face, the deep mystery in her eyes.

He mentally shook himself. What was he thinking?

She was practically a sister.

He glared at the subject of his errant thoughts. "Are you making me something to eat?"

"You just ate pancakes."

"I'm still hungry."

"I will, Mister Lou," piped up Josie. "Be good and I'll bring you some soup. Right, Miss Mary?"

"How about meat?" he asked hopefully. The gurgle in his stomach wasn't getting any quieter. A man needed something to stick to his ribs.

"You'll get what's best for you." Mary shot him a quiet smile as she ushered Josie out the door.

"Wait," he called out.

She paused at the door, but Josie ran off. He heard the pitter-patter of her feet, and then she yelled for James in a voice that could wake a corpse in its grave. Even though seeing her pained him in ways he didn't want to explore, he couldn't help the reluctant tilt that grabbed his lips and wouldn't let go.

"She's something."

"Yes, she is." Mary cleared her throat. "Was there anything else?"

"Just keep talking to her. Soon as I can get up I'll take her into town. Find her a safe house."

"She's my responsibility, Lou. I'm praying about what to do."

He arched a brow at her and she had the grace to flush.

"I'm sure God wants me to find her family," she said. "In the meantime, I want to take care of her."

"God doesn't need to be brought into this. Do the right thing."

"I will." Eyes flashing, she shut the door harder than necessary.

He sighed and relaxed against the pillow, just now realizing how tense his muscles had become. How long did he have to stay in this sickbed? Why, the last time he'd been wounded he'd been down only a few days and then a new case cropped up and he'd headed out.

But a week had passed this time, and he still couldn't

sit up without feeling dizzier than a bootlegger spending
too much time in a speakeasy. If he stayed here much longer… He didn't think he could take much more of Mary's
God talk. Let alone seeing Josie every day.

This wasn't a good place for the little girl. That man was
looking for her, and he'd be back. They needed to find her
mother and a different place so no harm would come to her.

And then there was Mary. After being kidnapped, sold
by Trevor's mother, Julia, surely she should see that God
didn't care anything for her or her life. It was a lesson he
himself had learned the hard way. He just hoped the whole
situation with Josie didn't deal Mary too harsh a blow.
Maybe he'd warn her somehow. Soften the news.

Smothering an oath, he shifted position. Why should
he warn her? The idea suddenly struck him as pompous.
Who was he anyway?

Just a federal agent who wanted nothing to do with
God, women or kids. And now he was stuck with all three.

Never had Mary met a more grumpy man than a bedrid-
den Lou Riley. Gritting her teeth, she carried his breakfast
tray up to his room, Josie tagging behind her.

"After this can we go see the horses? And the cows,
too? I've never touched a cow. Can I touch a cow, Mary?
Just one time?"

"We'll see," said Mary. *We'll see* had become her answer to Josie's constant questions. Was it safe to let a little girl near the cows? She'd learned to ride horses at a
young age, but probably not as young as Josie. The girl had
proudly told her and James last night at dinner that she was
five years old, almost six. A smile tugged at Mary's mouth.
She looked down at Josie, who was marching past her on
the steps, stretching her little legs to skip a step at a time.

"Be careful you don't trip on your new dress," she reminded her. The past few nights had been spent creating a wardrobe for Josie. She'd loved every stitch.

"I'm not gonna trip." Josie stood at the top, arms folded proudly across her chest. "Can I take Mister Lou his breakfast?"

"You'll stay in the hall."

"But I miss him."

Mary balanced the tray on her hip while fumbling for the doorknob. What should she say to such a sweet comment when it was obvious Lou felt uncomfortable with Josie? "I'd really like to get the kitchen cleaned up so we can go outside. Maybe you could sweep the floor?"

"By myself?" Josie's face brightened. Her arms swung back and forth, and then she started hopping on one foot.

"Absolutely." Mary grinned. Could children see past a distraction? Josie didn't seem to. "You did a wonderful job practicing with me the past few nights. It's time to put your skills to use."

"Yay!" She spun, twirling the skirt of her spring-green skirt. She leaped down the stairs so quickly a little hiccup of fear filled Mary's throat.

When Josie disappeared from view, safe from the treacherous descent, Mary tried the doorknob again. The door swung open, and she sidled in. "Breakfast."

"Lots of bacon, I hope." Lou stared at her from where he sat propped against the headboard. The sickening pallor that had tinged his skin the first week was now gone. He looked much healthier.

And too handsome for his own good. Or hers.

A rush of longing pulsed through Mary. She missed Lou's ready smile, the twinkle he usually handed out so generously. The longer he was cooped up, though, the more it felt as if he disliked her.

Even now he wouldn't meet her eyes. Perhaps it was

better this way. Better to break off her dependency on him before he left again on a new assignment. Gaze downcast, she focused on getting the food settled on his side table. Clinking filled the room, and the sound of their breaths, quiet and steady.

So be it, she thought grimly.

Ignoring him, she went to the curtains and pulled them open. Sunlight poured in, a giant wave of light that bathed the room. The sound of rustling followed by Lou sipping his coffee pounded against her ears. Normally she loved silence. Reveled in its clean reliability.

Not now. Lou didn't know how *not* to talk. The silence in this room clouded her peace, its unnaturalness filling her with disquiet. She risked a glance his way, her heart thudding in her chest.

He was watching her.

Hair disheveled, eyes like sapphires in the morning light, his gaze trained so deeply on her that a pleasant shiver cut to her very core. She swallowed hard and broke the connection.

"You stare at me," she said, gaze trained on the wall behind him.

"Do you mind?"

"It is…odd." *But not unwelcome.* The realization startled her. She turned her back to him, whisking to the closet and pretending to look through his clothes. "Are you in need of anything laundered?"

"Mary—" Lou's voice broke off on a ragged note.

"Yes?" As if against her own will, she found herself facing him across the room. She was too aware of the pulse slamming through her veins, too aware of terror, and something different, something unnamed, working in her throat.

At that moment, James poked his head past the open door and gave a gruff throat clear before looking at Lou.

"Telegram," he said. He shuffled in and flipped a small white envelope onto Lou's lap. He glanced at Mary. "You got a young'un dusting up a bunch of dirt in the kitchen. You know that?"

Oh, no. Darting the men an apologetic smile, she raced out the door. By the time she reached the kitchen, she felt calm enough to dismiss Lou's strange perusal from her mind and focused her attention on the sprite standing in the middle of the kitchen, a cheeky grin on her face.

Mary stopped at the entrance, her gaze scanning the room. Everything looked fine. Shining floor, broom propped against the wall. She relaxed.

"Well, it looks as though you've done a marvelous job. How about we visit those cows?"

She followed a rambunctious Josie out the door. Together they trekked toward the stables and barn, stopping to pick flowers on the way. Josie's blond curls glimmered as she hopped through the sparse grasses and shrubs. Desert flowers, in various stages of bloom, drew the little girl's attention and her high-pitched giggle sparkled like glitter on the breeze.

The sun warmed Mary's face, while the sage-scented air seemed to lift the worries from her heart.

Be anxious for nothing, but in everything, by prayer and supplication, let your requests be made known to God.

In this moment, she chose not to fret over Josie and her lack of family. Nor could she allow Lou to take the joy from what she wanted to build in this place. A peace she'd prayed hard for filled her soul.

Who knew what God intended? Josie's laugh rang clear and charming. Perhaps He didn't plan for her to be alone the rest of her life after all.

Chapter Five

❧

"Take me into Burns."

James ignored Lou's demand, bending over the bed to check his pulse and blood pressure. Before coming to the ranch, James had been a physician who'd succumbed to the lure of alcohol and lost all he held dear. He'd recovered from his addiction but never practiced medicine again, except for times like this when his skills came in handy.

All night Lou had studied the telegram he'd received, ready to take action as soon as he could rise without being beset by dizziness. Or guilt.

Had he made the right choices? He wasn't sure, but changing the things he'd set in motion didn't seem possible now.

James set his stethoscope on the bed, frowning at Lou.

"What?" he asked shortly, temper rising at the look.

"Going into Burns is a foolhardy task."

"I've got things to do. Get the truck ready to go."

"Trevor say you could use it?"

"Grab the car, then."

"I ain't drivin' your fancy Ford." James's whiskers bunched in a scowl, but his eyes were keen.

James seemed to know what was going on but wanted

to stop Lou anyhow. Odd. "I need to telegraph the Portland office and arrange for travel."

"Can you stand yet?"

"I can." He'd tried last night and succeeded, if only for a few seconds. Not James's business, though. "In a few days' time I'll be ready for the trip. My vitals are fine, and I'm going stir-crazy in this house."

James nodded at the telegram, which he'd propped on the side table. "That the reason?"

"They have a lead on my shooter."

"What about Mary? The girl?"

"Mary stays here. I'll take the girl—" A crash interrupted him, shaking the house with its force.

James jumped up. "Hoo boy, that girl is in some trouble."

"Where's Mary?" His pulse notched up. Crazy child causing all sorts of trouble.

"She went to town. Stay in bed." On that command, James shuffled out of the bedroom as fast as an old man could hobble.

Determination filled Lou. Mary was in town, leaving the child here? With little protection? No, sir. Not on his watch. He might be have difficulty being around kids, but that didn't mean he'd ever let something bad happen to one. He swung his legs across the mattress. They felt heavy and unnatural; his vision swam, but he pushed through until his legs hung over the side of the bed and his hands were planted against the edge of the mattress. Head hanging, he closed his eyes and fought dizziness.

He could do this. Although his stomach bucked against the movement, he waited the feeling out, allowing his body to readjust to his change in position. The wound in his chest throbbed dully, but the pain wasn't incapacitating.

Hadn't he made it through the war? Memories crashed

through him: the noise and the smoke, the gut-searing terror of knowing tomorrow might never come for him. And yet he'd completed various espionage activities, shadowed criminals, hunted killers. Only to come home and get gunned down at a low-level speakeasy. The irony was ridiculous.

Very slowly he opened his eyes. The first item he focused on happened to be Mary's Bible, resting on a folded blanket near the door. Groaning, he looked away.

God and Lou hadn't been on speaking terms in a long, long time. Not since God had failed him, taking his child and his wife. Leaving him alone. Unaccountably, his gaze flitted back to that silent black book. Its pages had once been a lifeline for Lou.

No longer. Now they dredged up a past he resisted, a past he thought he'd buried.

Years-old grief clogged his throat.

As his eyes stung, little feet pattered into view, stopping right next to the Bible.

"Mister Lou, I brought you something."

He lifted his head. Josie looked a mess this morning, her hair a frightful nest of twigs, snarls and... Was that paint clinging to her forehead?

"Leave me," he said, but when the little girl's face crumpled, he immediately felt regret churning his stomach. Or maybe it was the swaying floor. "What do you want?" he managed to say.

"I brought you cookies. Sweets make me feel better, and you're looking awful peaked. Sometimes I hear you yelling, but you don't sound mean, just sad."

Lou eyed her, noting the brightness of her eyes beneath the clumps of goo and mess straggling around her face.

"Here." She stepped forward, thrusting a cookie beneath his nose.

The scent rose to greet him, a thick mix of chocolate and some kind of nut. Praline, maybe? He took the cookie, watching Josie as he did so. "Mary's a good cook, isn't she?"

"Yeppers. Much better than Doris."

"Who's she?"

"My old cook."

Maybe sensing Lou's change in mood, the little girl hopped around his room, her dress flouncing. It was a mass of pink ruffles and ribbons, a frothy creation that under normal circumstances should give anyone a toothache.

Munching on the cookie, he slowly straightened and was relieved when the room didn't shift around him. Maybe a little sugar did the trick. Could be a trip into town would happen after all.

"Where'd you leave James?" he asked, watching as Josie twirled in front of his bed.

"He ran outside yelling. His face was purple, like a flower. He needs cookies, too." She cocked her head, fingers trailing over the silk of her dress. "Do you think I look like a princess?"

Lou choked on his cookie.

Hacking and coughing, he brushed the crumbs off his knees while he tried to regain his senses. He'd never heard something so preposterous. A princess? Yet, as he studied her, with the morning light streaming in ribbons across her features, highlighting her hair, making her eyes twinkle with hope, a strange emotion clutched at him.

He cleared his throat. "You're the prettiest princess I've ever seen."

A grin wider than the desert outside his window spread across Josie's face. Before he knew what to expect, she launched herself at him. Pain radiated through his upper body, and he felt useless as she entrapped him. His hands rested on his knees while she hugged him, her little-girl arms feeling impossibly frail as they wrapped around his neck.

Before he could stop himself, he realized his hands were patting her back. Hugging her back. He dropped them to his legs.

"Josie," he said, spitting a wayward hair from his mouth and pulling away, "you stink."

She stepped back and, folding her arms, pouted at him. "Princesses don't smell."

"They do when they mess with things. What'd you do downstairs?"

"She knocked over a can of paint from that big case I'm trying to move." James stood in the door, glowering at Josie. "You'd best come clean up before—"

"Do I have to?" She wheedled a pretty smile toward Lou.

The stinker. Unbidden affection surged through him. "A princess always takes responsibility for her mistakes."

"Oh, fine." She stomped out the door, her little shoulders ramrod straight.

James chuckled. "You need anything before I follow that whippersnapper?"

"When is Mary returning?"

"Soon."

"Send her up. We've things to discuss."

James nodded and left. Lou stared at the door, hating how the empty feeling in his stomach got worse when everyone was gone. He rubbed at his neck, almost feeling the imprint of Josie's arms around him. Would his little Abby have been so affectionate? Yes, because hugs had been common in their home.

Love and warmth and family. All gone.

The hollow in his chest deepened into a gaping void

that wrenched through him, a chasm in his soul he could never escape. This pain worried him more than any shoulder wound. Why did Mary have to be so stubborn? Even more, how could he have let himself get shot?

He wanted to blame Mary.

He definitely blamed the shooter.

Because of them, he was starting to remember what he'd fought so hard to forget.

And the memories burned worse than any bullet ever did.

After Mary left the Burns general store, she paused on the walkway to let the morning sun warm her. Around her, people nodded at her as they ran their errands. No one stared. This was a good town.

She let her head drop back a bit so the summer rays could touch her cheeks and chase the chill from her soul. After the few errands she'd finished, she'd yet to find a flyer with Josie's name or face on it, let alone someone who could share information on the homeless child. No response from the Portland police, either.

It seemed the girl had appeared out of nowhere, with no kin to claim her. Except that man with the violet eyes…. She hadn't the courage to ask if anyone spoke with him. Shaking the shudder away at the thought of him, she resumed walking toward where she'd tethered her mare.

"Mary. Mary, wait!"

A woman's voice broke Mary's walk. She whirled and grinned as Alma Waite bustled over.

"Oh, you dear girl. How have you been?" Miss Alma's bright hazel eyes winked up at her before the elderly woman gathered her in a honey-scented hug.

"I'm well, thank you."

"You should visit more. I'm in need of pies and cookies for the Independence Day celebration."

"I shall make you some. I've been a mite busy lately." Mary released Miss Alma and moved beneath the shade of a storefront. Might Miss Alma know of Josie's parentage? While the woman who'd brought Mary to faith years ago knew everything about everyone, she wasn't a gossip.

"Well, we've missed you." Miss Alma tittered as she dug through a bag at her side. "I bought yarn and threads for you. That Grant woman has finally left the sewing circle and we've a hole now…one we'd like you to fill. Ah, here they are." Triumphantly she shoved the bag at Mary.

She took it, feeling a blush warm her cheeks. "Thank you. I shall think on your kind offer. How much are these?"

Miss Alma waved a hand. "Pishposh. They're a gift. I worry about you. Alone on that ranch."

"I have James and Lou—"

"No female companionship at all. It's not healthy. At least we used to meet for church…." Miss Alma trailed off as Mary shifted uncomfortably.

Since Lou had gotten shot, she hadn't been to church. Was it two Sundays she'd missed?

"My sweet girl, is there anything I can do for you?" The elderly woman, who had more fire in her than a rowdy pony, sported a soft look upon her face.

Mary hugged her again. "We're fine. I'm actually looking for some information, though." She thought of the man who'd come calling and decided to hedge a bit. "My mother found a child, and I'm having trouble locating the girl's parents."

"Oh, my." Miss Alma's hand went to her ruffled breast. "Why, I haven't heard a thing. Where did your mother find the child? Does she need a place to stay?"

"No, no, she's safe," Mary replied, flustered by the

questions. "Perhaps you might keep your ear to the ground, as it were, and if you find out anything, let me know?"

"Of course I will."

They said their goodbyes, and Mary watched the lady who'd saved her life bustle away. Not her physical life, but her emotional one. Childhood chaos aside, she'd been a mess when Trevor first brought her to Lou's. Miss Alma had nursed her back to health and introduced her to God, to a Jesus who saw past skin and circumstance to the very heart of a person. Who loved despite a person's flaws or parentage.

Feeling cozy from memories, she wheeled to the right and headed toward her horse. One more stop and then she could go home.

Home.

Humming her favorite hymn, Mary set out for the Paiute encampment. Sunlight warmed her shoulders and bathed the path before her in brightness. If only her own path could be so clear. With Lou injured and Josie running wild, she wasn't sure what to do.

And there was that way Lou had looked at her the other day—intent, dark. Her belly flip-flopped at the memory. She shook herself.

No matter what occurred in the next few weeks, she must disentangle herself from Lou, from the ranch, from everything that made her dependent on him.

The encampment loomed before her, scents reaching her as she came closer. Her mother's tent had no smoke, but that didn't mean she wasn't home. It was a warm day after all.

As she stopped before the tepee, an older man appeared from behind the tent's flap. He peered up at her, eyes black in the light.

"I am looking for my mother. Rose." That had been her

name in the past, but Mary didn't know if she'd kept it or reverted to a traditional name.

"Rose not here." The flap fluttered closed as the man disappeared.

Around her, kids laughed and a dog barked. Sweat trickled down her neck as she roasted beneath the sun, trying to process the man's words. Not there? Had she left on her own? Or had the man with the violet eyes found her?

Whatever faults her mother might have, Mary didn't want harm to come to her. Maybe he meant she'd gone to a general store, perhaps to sell goods?

She debated pestering the man again or riding back to town. Her sense of decorum made the decision for her. Sliding the reins over her mare's neck, she turned the horse back to town.

Once there, she discovered no one knew of her mother's whereabouts. How strange. She glanced at the general store, where she'd caught up with Miss Alma, who'd reinvited her to the sewing circle. When she asked about her mother, the women in the store shrugged and said she'd been to town early in the morning to sell her baskets. They hadn't seen her since.

Feeling a heavy sigh forming, Mary led her mare down the road going out of town and in the direction of the ranch. Ahead, a lone horse hitched to a pole stomped his hoof. The mare whickered and edged to the left, bumping Mary.

"Come on, girl." She soothed her with a pat on the neck as they moved farther left, away from the nervous stallion at the post.

Raised voices ahead slowed Mary's gait. Male voices, sharp and angry. She remembered that sound altogether too well. Cringing, she hugged closer to the horse, hoping to sneak past. It was her hope the men were too involved to notice her.

Here, at the outskirts of town, there was no telling what riffraff lingered. She wet her lips. She could always jump on the horse and gallop away, but that would certainly draw attention. Drawing a deep breath of horse, dust and sunlight, she trudged forward, wincing when one man's voice rose particularly loudly.

From beneath lowered lids she scanned the area and saw nothing amiss. Tilting her head, she looked to the left. The space between two buildings resembled an alley. It was dark and deep, the perfect place for an argument. She shuddered and kept going. She'd just passed the opening there when the sound of a grunt followed by a thick thud startled her mare.

The horse jerked and the reins slipped through her hands, burning her palms. With a clatter of hooves and a flurry of dust, the mare left her standing slack-jawed in the road.

Instinctually her arms rounded her rib cage. Miss Alma's gift bumped against her hip. She hurried to the opposite side of the road, hiding behind a stack of onion barrels. She glared at the speck of her horse on the horizon, no doubt heading home. She must find a new one, and soon, before the mare worried Lou and James needlessly. But who could she ask?

Miss Alma might still be in town. Surely she'd give Mary a ride for part of the way, or possibly send a message to the ranch somehow….

Mind made up, she stepped away from the barrels and promptly stopped. A man appeared at the edge of the alley across the street. He stood tall and narrow, and something about his posture sent a shiver of foreboding through her.

Pivoting, she headed toward town. Footsteps sounded behind her. She picked up her pace, knowing only a few yards farther the streets teemed with shoppers.

The footsteps increased, faster than hers, until she felt a presence beside her and smelled the overpowering odor of cologne. Pulse clanging in her ears, she looked up and met the gaze of the violet-eyed stranger.

Chapter Six

Lou was sitting by the window when he saw a mare race into the yard. The horse pranced nervously near the porch before galloping toward the stables. An empty saddle went with her.

Biting back an oath, he rose from his spot, palming the wall until his vision became normal and the dizziness passed. His legs felt rubbery, but somehow he made it to the post of his bed. James had helped him earlier to the window. Now Lou wished he'd left some crutches in the room. He could barely breathe.

Taking a deep, steadying breath, he shuffled to the opposite bedpost, the one closest to the door. *Don't fail me,* he urged his body. Finally, his neck clammy and a sheen of sweat pebbling his forearms, he made it to the door.

"James," he shouted. His voice sounded like a croak. Scowling, he tried again. The sound of footsteps padded up the stairs. Little feet.

He'd never been so glad to see Josie. He rested his head against the door frame and waited for the girl to appear. Sure enough, she plopped herself right under his gaze, a big smile on her face.

"Hey, Mister Lou. Whatcha want?"

"Get me James," he said.

"Okeydokey."

She pattered off, but the image of her guileless face remained, taunting him with memories. Swallowing past his dry throat, he allowed himself to slide to the ground.

In moments, James was clumping up the stairs, his breaths heavy and labored. Lou saw his feet stop at the head of the stairs. "That whippersnapper said you was dying."

Squinting, Lou looked up at the man who'd been with him for so long, a former doctor whom Mary had taken from a life of homelessness on the streets of Burns and brought to the ranch for healing from too much drink.

He tried to keep his voice steady and careful. "Mary come back yet?"

James heaved, bending at the waist and meeting Lou at eye level. "You sayin' you sent that stinker runnin' like a herd of wild mustangs was after her, and you ain't dying? You jest want Mary?"

"Did she take a horse?" Lou continued calmly, training his gaze on James.

James growled and straightened. "She did."

"Check the stables, see if her horse returned."

"Now, how'm I supposed to know which horse she took?"

"Find out." The snarl took more energy than Lou thought it would.

"What's going on?"

"Is Miss Mary missing?" A little voice trembled from the stairs, snagging Lou's attention and putting an ache in the vicinity of his heart. He couldn't meet her gaze. Something had happened to Mary and he hadn't been there to protect her.

Just like Sarah.

Sourness coated the roof of his mouth.

"Don't you worry, Josie. Everything is going to be okay." He jerked his chin at James. "Pull out my car. We're going to town."

For once, the old man didn't argue about driving a fancy Ford.

Soon, they were on their way to Burns. Lou stared out the window, his whole body aching, his worry amplifying every pain. Getting down the stairs had proved to be a terrible chore, one that had required lots of stops and support. He grimaced at his reflection, knowing he looked haggard and not caring one iota.

His strength might be on the low side, but James said the wound looked to be healing nicely. Only a few more days and he ought to be able to hunt that shooter down, if the bureau or local police hadn't found him already. He'd check on that in town.

He felt his lips tugging farther downward. Where was Mary? If anything happened to her.... He clenched his legs, letting his fingers dig into his thigh, needing a different kind of pain to take his thoughts from what his life might be like without her in it.

Even though, according to the telegram sitting in his room, in a few months' time he might never see her again. Guilt joined the worry, creating a ruckus in his head.

"You're quiet," James remarked from the driver's seat.

"Not much to talk on."

"She's probably fine. We'll find her. Give her grief over this whole thing."

"Watch out the window," Lou said. "She could be laying somewhere, hurt."

A rattler could've spooked her horse, and though Mary had been riding a long time, she didn't have a close bond with any of the horses. They wouldn't think twice about leaving her.

"I hope Josie behaves for Horn," said James.

They'd left the girl with their neighbor, though she'd been unwilling. Only the presence of a fresh batch of puppies had seemed to mollify her.

"I'm sure she'll be fine. Seemed happy enough with those pups."

"You heard anything on your shooter?" James dodged a shrub growing in the middle of the road.

The movement jolted Lou, sending an arcing pain through his shoulder. He winced, waiting for it to subside. "Nah. They think he's related somehow to that speakeasy we busted." Enforcing prohibition laws didn't necessarily fall into the bureau's jurisdiction, but they'd found some creative loopholes to catch criminals. Whatever it took to capture the bad guys, Lou was for it.

They didn't make any more small talk the rest of the way. A sick feeling persisted in Lou's stomach. As they drove into Burns, he felt a new resolve take hold. They hadn't found Mary on the way, which meant she should still be in town.

He was going to chew her out good.

Feeling grim, he shuffled behind James, a crutch under his good side's arm and James on the bad side, supporting him. They entered the police station. James's gait was stiff, and Lou was ready to punch something.

The feeling worsened when he saw Mary sitting on the bench. With her hair pulled back, neat and clean, and her profile strong, she looked neither worried nor scared, but serene.

A burst of adrenaline exploded inside Lou, rushing through his body with the power of a locomotive. He growled.

She startled, turning to face them, surprise plastered all over her face. Her mouth made an oval shape, and then she broke into a smile.

Heat shot through him, anger and fear melding into an emotion so powerful he could barely hold himself to where he stood. Yet he resisted, forcing a calm he didn't feel, holding back when he wanted to yell and stomp the way Josie had when he'd taken away the cookies she'd filched yesterday morning.

Mary must've sensed his mood because she stood slowly, casting a look to James before meeting Lou's eyes.

"You're angry," she stated, and the sound of her smooth voice flavored by exotic syllables only heightened his turmoil. "I can explain."

"Get in the car."

Her features changed, becoming impassive. "Thank you for coming to get me."

He jerked his head to the door and watched as she glided past, head high, shoulders straight. She hadn't learned that posture from her mother, or from Julia, Trevor's mom. No, that walk was all Mary. Proud, graceful, aloof… Another growl erupted.

"Let's go," he said.

She made it to the car before they did. They found her in the back, staring blankly out the side window and not meeting their eyes. Once they'd cranked his tin lizzie and hit the road, Lou still found it hard to speak. He knew from past experience that yelling at Mary solved nothing.

Not that he liked to yell, but when she stared up at him with those deep brown eyes, passive and quiet, it stirred him up, made him itch to get her to respond to him, not to ignore him the way she did others.

* * *

"What happened, Mary?" James interrupted the horrible silence that had filled the car since they'd picked her up. She could feel tension radiating off Lou and it scared her stiff.

She swallowed hard, afraid to speak, afraid Lou might explode.

He'd never, ever lifted a hand toward her, not even during their most volatile argument years ago when she'd asked to let her mother come live with them. Intellectually, she knew he wouldn't hurt her.

But emotionally… Sometimes she dreamed of the men who'd visited her mother. Sometimes she woke from nightmares, drenched in sweat, trying to rid her mind of the paralyzing fear that overtook her.

"Speak yer mind. I'll boot this shot-up agent out of the car if he yells, okay?" James cast a crooked smile back at her. She attempted to lift her lips, though the pit of her stomach ached.

She glanced at the back of Lou's head, marveling at the blondness of his hair, how it had grown too long and remained straight and fine. Not like her own thick locks. She'd inherited the Paiute ebony color but Irish curl. At least that was what her mother had always said.

She frowned. No one had seen Rose. It was as though she'd just disappeared. Kind of how the man with the violet eyes did when the police chief interrupted them on their walk toward town. Her eyes fluttered closed for a moment as another wave of relief swept through her.

"Mary girl, are you okay?"

She opened them and looked at James. "There was an assault in Burns."

The car jerked. "What did you say?"

Confident she could keep her voice steady despite the

unrest raging inside, she nodded. "I was leading my mare out of town when I heard scuffling. A tethered stallion nearby was restless, so I brought the mare to the other side of the street. Two men in an alley were arguing—"

"You should have rode out of there," Lou interrupted. His voice was gravelly and raw, completely unlike the talkative man she'd come to know through the years. Somehow this gunshot wound had changed him, and she wasn't sure why.

"I didn't want to alert them to my presence," she responded defensively.

"You did the right thing," said James.

His backup emboldened her. "As I tried to hurry past, there was a sharp sound, not a gunshot, but something striking a hard object. The horse startled and ran off on me. You should train them better," she couldn't help saying pointedly to Lou.

"So, that's it?" James asked. "Why didn't you borrow a horse and get on yer way? We've worried over you, Mary girl."

She felt a flash of remorse, followed by unexpected warmth. Though she'd been housekeeper for these two men for twelve years, they'd all kept to themselves, minding their own business while maintaining an unspoken loyalty to each other. Since Josie had come, things had changed. The girl, or perhaps the familial situation, had tempered loyalty into a new bond, something stronger.

"You shouldn't have worried," she answered. "Once the sheriff stepped out to speak with me, all was well."

"What happened with the scuffle you heard?"

The grate of Lou's tone surprised her, but he was an agent, trained to pick up on minute details. She had been foolish to think she might hide anything from him.

Still, she hesitated to tell him for fear of what he might do.

"Girl, you'd best spit it out." James waggled his eyebrows at her, perhaps trying to induce a smile.

But violence did not inspire smiles. Heart heavy, she looked at her clasped hands, debating whether to snag the lumpy-looking blanket on the floor to cover their coldness. "There was a man in the alley," she finally said. The memory of that thud shuddered through her and she pressed her fingers more tightly together. "Beaten."

"Is he dead?" asked Lou.

"The physician is not sure he'll make it."

"Who found the man?"

"Not me. But I pointed the way."

"You just walked into the sheriff's office and told him a man was in an alley beaten to a pulp."

Irritated by Lou's casual, almost sardonic tone, Mary frowned. This was the part she did not wish to share. She glanced out the window, at the rising mountains in the distance and the land she called home. "After the mare bolted, I walked toward the interior of Burns, hoping to catch Miss Alma to ask for a ride to Horn's spread." Their neighbor lived only miles away. "But as I walked, footsteps sounded behind me. Then caught up to me. A man desired to make conversation, and I obliged until we reached the heart of town."

"What man?" Suspicion dripped off Lou's words, thick and heavy.

"He does not matter. The sheriff will find him and I pray charge him. A man like that should not be allowed to roam."

Lou shifted in his seat but did not turn to look at her.

"Are you in pain?" she asked gently. "I picked up a few things in town."

"No," he said, voice tight. "I want to know more about

this man following you. Do you think he knows what you told the sheriff? If this man thinks you're a threat—"

"I'm safe at my new house." At least she hoped that to be true. Lately, Lou seemed anxious, and she did not know if his rattled emotions came from being confined to bed or if there was another reason, something secret.... She swallowed at the thought. "The man... I've met him before. He knows where we are and can come at any time to your ranch, but he does not know of my new home."

"What do you mean you know him?" Lou swiveled and pinned her with a piercing blue glare.

"Remember the stranger who visited last week? He is one and the same."

"What's his name?"

"He never said, but he has violet eyes, like Josie."

"He might be her guardian." A thicket of hair fell over Lou's brow as James bounced across the uneven terrain.

"He didn't ask for a little girl," Mary retorted. She did not care for the accusing look on Lou's face, as though she had done something wrong or immoral. "This man is dangerous, and I don't believe he has any right to Josie."

Lou sighed and ran his palms down his face. "James, you heading to Horn's to pick up Josie?"

"Fixin' to veer off now."

"Good. If we haven't heard from the authorities about Josie's family in a week's time, we'll take her to Portland ourselves. I have unfinished business there. The ranch isn't safe for Josie. That man was there once and now he's been sighted in Burns—"

"It's too soon." The protest rolled off her tongue before she could stop it. "You'll reopen your wound."

Lou grunted. "I'll be fine. Someone must be looking for her. James wired the bureau for me days ago, and they think they've found Josie's mom. If not, we'll track down another relative."

They knew? Even the police hadn't been in touch with her. She slumped down. It was for the best. It had to be.

Movement on the floor startled a gasp out of her.

The blankets reshuffled and out of their haphazard mound popped a blond head. Josie scowled up at Lou. "I'm not going back and you can't make me."

Chapter Seven

Why did the man have to be so stubborn?

Mary's legs itched to pace, but she squelched the urge and forced herself to sit quietly as Lou moved across his living room floor. Only days after Lou had picked her up from the sheriff's and announced that Josie was going home, he insisted he was well enough to travel into Portland.

Truthfully, he'd made it down the stairs on his own, but that did not mean he was fit for travel. She eyed the way he shuffled across the floor, noting the pallid tone of his handsome face because he insisted on venting his frustration by moving about. No, he needed more time to recover.

More important, Josie did not wish to live with her family. Specifically her uncle, who she'd confessed to being the stranger who'd visited. The little girl's alarm fueled Mary's own dismay. Surely a man wanted for the kind of assault he'd dished out on the man in the alley should not have the care of a child. Not to mention the way he'd ogled Mary....

"Did you hear me?" Lou stopped in front of her, a frown on his full lips.

She lifted her gaze to his. "I did not hear."

His hands sliced through the air in an impatient gesture. "Pack a bag. We're leaving tomorrow morning. If you don't pack, you're not coming. I've received information that reports Josie's mom has returned to Portland."

"It is a large city," she said slowly. "Do you suggest we knock on each door?"

Lou grinned, the movement lighting his face and tugging at her heart. Here was the smile she'd missed, the crinkle around his eyes and curve in his cheek. "That, my dear, is taken care of. We've an address, and I already sent a telegram requesting a meeting with the mother."

She picked at her skirt, unable to bear looking at the triumph splayed across his features. This would be the end, then.

"Mary, aren't you happy?" He dropped down in front of her. She saw the wince that flashed across his face before he masked it. Eyes alight, he peered at her. "She needs her home. Her mother. This place is no good for a child. I'm going to make sure she and her mother are protected."

He was right, of course. Allowing Josie to stay only fulfilled her desires. A lonely desert with scattered neighbors could not possibly meet a child's need for companionship. She stared down at her hands, which she'd clasped in her lap.

Lou sighed. "I wish you'd talk to me. Communicate."

"I have nothing to say."

"Say we're doing the right thing here. That you want to give a mother back her daughter."

Her head shot up as a bolt of anger darted through her. Her nerve endings tingled with the prickly feeling. "If this mother wants her daughter, why has she not been scouring the countryside for her? Posting pictures and letters? I have seen little evidence that Josie is wanted."

A gasp came from the front door, followed by pattering feet as the little girl raced away. Mary cringed.

"She needs to stop eavesdropping," Lou said in a grim voice. He rose very slowly, and Mary could tell he'd fatigued himself.

She wanted to run after Josie but didn't know what she'd say. The truth was, no one but that dreadful man had looked for the little girl. And Mary wanted her to stay. To be family.

Lou was still looking at her, seriousness shadowing his expression. Why did he want Josie gone so bad? Why did he shy away from the little girl and even seem afraid of her at times?

"And if I do not wish to travel with you?" she asked, watching him carefully. "You will be forced to care for Josie yourself. To see to her needs. To be her sole caretaker."

"If you don't pack, then you won't go. That's all there is to it." He stood, turning away so she could no longer see his face.

Empathy battled with frustration. She could go with him now, but that would leave Josie in a bad place. The thought of leaving the little girl hurt too much to dwell on. If she refused to go, what could he do to her? Not much, she surmised.

Mind made up, she stood, straightening her skirt with the movement. He shuffled around, shoulders straight despite the obvious pain striking his features.

She leveled her gaze on him, refusing to let him see how horrible she felt that he was in such distress. "I will not go until you can move without pain."

"That so?" he said quietly. Challenge filled the blueness of his eyes and an unwelcome ping of excitement zipped through her. These weeks together were revealing a side to her nature she hadn't suspected existed. A side that seemed to enjoy his challenges, to revel in tension.

The thought was discomfiting, at best. She returned his stare, even though her stomach roiled and her palms slicked.

After a tense minute of silence, she spoke, her voice clear and even, much to her relief. "I must find Josie. She should not have heard our conversation." It hurt to think her words had caused Josie pain. She, who tried so hard to be quiet and speak wisely, had been undone by her unreasonable, blasé employer.

"I'm coming with."

She swished forward. "You can hardly walk. Lie down and recover if you wish to return Josie."

"That girl's leaving tomorrow." As Mary passed, Lou reached out and gripped her arm. His touch imprinted her skin with heat.

"Why do you care so much? She's just a little girl." Slowly, she removed her arm, amazed she felt no fear at his handling but rather wary at what she did feel: a nervous tension that had nothing to do with fear.

"This place isn't safe for her." He gave her his profile.

"So you've said, but why? It is unlikely that man would think she's here." She studied the stubborn line of his nose, the shape of his square, unyielding jaw. Somewhere a little girl cried for a home she'd lost, and here she stood, interrogating a man who didn't seem to care.

Annoyed at herself, she let out a huff. "Never mind. It's obvious I'm not the only one who has trouble communicating."

Aiming that last comment at the doorway, she stalked out of the sitting room and then hurried down the hallway. James was rocking on the front porch when she burst out the door. An uppity wind brushed past, tangling her skirt and hair in its wake.

"Have you seen Josie?"

"Went thataway." He pointed in the direction of Trevor's house. Her home.

"Thank you." She darted off the porch and ran to the house. Halfway there, she had to stop and gasp for air. This was her fault. Maybe Lou was right. Maybe Josie needed to be with her mother. Perhaps there was a reason the woman hadn't searched for her daughter. Josie had mentioned illness.

Then again, some mothers, for one reason or another, couldn't expend the energy to find their children.

She frowned and kept walking, trying to ignore the whispery accusation toward her own mother who'd dropped her off with Trevor's mom at the age of twelve and never looked back. Not until it was too late and the emotional damage had been done.

Her breath hitched. Taking a moment to inhale and exhale, to remember God and how He'd protected her, was not only good for the lungs but good for the soul.

As she inhaled the cleansing scents of pine, sage and desert brush, her pulse slowed and her vision sharpened on the little house that grew larger as she drew near. A curtain flickered in the window.

Feeling deep chagrin, she kept her legs moving until she'd reached the door. Opening it, she stepped into the house. The living room smelled like cookies. Sugar cookies. Tinged with the underlying aroma of wood floor polish. A comforting welcome.

"Josie?" She shut the door behind her. "Sweetie, please come talk to me."

"I don't want to talk." Her mulish voice drifted from the sofa. A blanket covered a misshapen lump but didn't quite reach the stockinged foot peeking from beneath its edge. "I'm going to run away."

Unsure, Mary stayed rooted near the door. Should she take the girl to task for talking in such a way? Or should she go hug her…? Indecision was a heavy coat she couldn't seem to shrug off, so she just stood there, kneading her fingers against her skirt.

If only she owned an instruction manual for parenting.

Finally, Josie flipped the blanket off. Her blond curls stood at attention, static fuzzing them up into a rat's nest. An unruly giggle snickered past Mary's lips.

Josie's eyes narrowed. "Go away."

"This is my home."

"Then I'll go." Huffing, she threw the blanket to the floor and gave Mary such an ugly glare that another laugh sprinkled out from somewhere.

"You're laughing." If possible, the glare turned uglier.

"Oh, honey, I was worried." Instinctually, she dropped to her knees and held out her arms. "I'm so glad you're okay."

"But no one wants me, so what do you care?"

"When I was a young girl, no one wanted me, either." The confession came unbidden. "It is a lonely, horrible feeling to be unwanted."

Josie eyed her arms and Mary held her breath.

Slowly the girl walked over. "Why didn't anyone want you?"

"I was inconvenient."

"What's that mean?" She settled on Mary's lap, the child's warm weight shooting giddiness to a place in her heart that had been neglected far too long.

"It means I wasn't easy," she said against the aroma of Josie's hair. "I want you, sweet girl. Raising a child is hard work. But it's also wonderful joy. I was very blessed that

God sent me a friend when I was a wee bit older than you, and He showed me I was loved." Trevor had been family for a long time. Despite her loneliness, she prayed he and Gracie were enjoying their trip to California.

Josie snuggled beneath Mary's chin, her arms rounding Mary's back as she pressed closer.

"No one is inconvenient to God," Mary murmured. "He loves you so much and no matter what happens, you must know that He wants you. I will pray God sends you a friend, sweetie."

The girl wiggled, pulled back and met her gaze. "Will you pray he sends me a family?"

"Made it down the stairs, I see." James hovered in the sitting room doorway, chewing a stem of unfortunate grass. "You still ain't fit for travel."

Lou sighed, his recent talk with Mary bothering him too much to let him care what James said. The hand knew his medicine, and no doubt the man was right. "Looks like we'll be waiting one more week."

"Sounds good." James came into the room and plopped down on a couch, the grass twisting between his teeth. "Miss Alma cornered me in town this morning."

The huff James emitted coaxed a grin to Lou's mouth. "Don't tell me you don't like her attentions, old man."

"The woman smells good, it's true, but she's plain nosy. Always trying to ask me over for lunch, or worse, to visit that little church she and Horn got going."

"She give you any food this morning?" He was feeling a bit hungry and it might be a good distraction from the memory of how Mary had felt when he'd grabbed her arm. Warm. Fragile.

"It's in the icebox." James interrupted his meanderings.

"You mean the refrigerator?"

"Whatever you youngsters call that newfangled contraption." James's completely white whiskers twitched on the word *contraption*.

With a start, Lou realized the ranch hand was getting older. He had at least twenty years on Lou, which meant he must be pushing sixty.

He eyed his employee. "If you need help with ranch duties, let me know. I'll hire on a few extra men."

"I'm fine. 'Sides, thought you were selling it?"

Startled, Lou glanced at the door before realizing his nonverbal slip.

James cocked a brow. "You didn't tell Mary yet?"

His gape annoyed Lou. "It's not set in stone. She's got her house now, and it shouldn't matter what I do."

"You're her source of income. And mine, come to think of it."

"I know." Lou growled. It was a problem, one he was determined to find a solution to. "The ranch is having a hard time making money. The cooler weather is doing in ranchers all around us. I talked to Doc about you joining on as assistant in Burns since the town is growing so much. He seemed amenable to the idea."

"It'll be hard to get Mary a job, seeing her skin's dark."

"The people in Burns are familiar with her. I don't think she'll have trouble, but no matter what, I'll make sure she's taken care of." Even if he went broke doing so. She deserved the best, and he'd make sure she had it.

"And how about her feelings on the matter? She's uncomfortable around people. Given her history—"

"She'll be fine," he interrupted. He couldn't escape the subject of his housekeeper no matter where he went, it seemed. "She takes stuff to town all the time. Miss Alma will watch out for her, and I'll take care of the financial end."

"Speaking of that woman, she's invited Mary to some kind of lady event on Saturday. So's you best stay here till then." James flashed him a pointed stare before pushing himself out of the seat and heading for the door.

"What time?"

"Noon."

Great. Another week trapped at the ranch when he could be tracking down his shooter. After returning Josie first, of course. Though he was trying to draw that out until he heard a little more about her family. No matter how uncomfortable she made him, no way would he put her in a dangerous situation.

He shook his head, got to his feet. He didn't want to think about Josie or Mary. He just wanted to return to the way life was before.

Simple.

He headed to the door, feeling weak but not dizzy. The fact that his legs carried him to the hallway without buckling was reason to say thanks to the Creator…if they were on speaking terms.

And they weren't. Mary could keep her God for all he cared.

The God he used to serve…

He slowed near the stairs, breathing heavier than he'd like. Maybe he'd rest a bit on the porch. Get some sunlight and fresh air. Take his mind off matters too weighty for a beautiful summer day.

He shuffled to the door, let himself outside and found a spot on the steps in a patch of sunlight that immediately seeped into his bones and spread through him in a liquid spill of relaxation.

Decisions, decisions. He closed his eyes and leaned against the railing. What was he going to do? The ranch's secrecy had been compromised, but even worse, the weather proved that trying to ranch in this desert was a futile effort. Scents caressed his face. Would he miss this place? It had served its purpose, but he didn't need it anymore. Yet he hesitated. Mary seemed more than ready to move on. Now that she had her own place, she'd probably have her mom move in.

That foolish mother who'd abandoned her daughter to run off and search for a man. Granted, she'd been looking for Mary's father, but that didn't excuse things, to his way of thinking. And then there was Mary's kidnapping and the huge part her mother, unbeknownst to Mary, had played in it. He frowned. Mary was asking for trouble by inviting that woman to live with her.

Could she handle any more betrayals? His gut hurt just thinking about it.

The memory of Mary's arm beneath his palm, warm and small, heated his cheeks. She hadn't seemed afraid of his touch, didn't cower the way she had the first few years she'd been hired on as housekeeper. Not that he'd touched her often.

Nah. She was like a little sister. That was it. Someone he cared about and wanted to protect.

Even if she seemed determined to escape protection by moving into Trevor's old house.

As he rested, a sound tinkled in the distance, reaching his ears on the breeze. The laughter grew louder, uncontrolled giggles that swept over him in a swirling dance and left him listening for more.

He opened his eyes, shading his vision with a hand against his forehead. Nothing to the front of the house. Cautiously he stood, scanning the periphery of the house, but he still couldn't distinguish the source of the sound.

A strange and painful yearning had started in his chest, right below the vicinity of his wound. As shrieks floated on the afternoon's breeze, lingering in the scents of summer, the warmth of sun, Lou found himself drawn forward, away from the safety of the porch and toward the laughter that seemed just beyond his reach.

He poked past shrubs and sparse grasses, toward a lush little valley that lay behind the house. The tiny indentation of land was always filled with wildflowers and grass in summer. A verdant patch, one of the many that had fooled neighbors into thinking the Harney desert area might make good land.

As he walked to the sound, a wedge of guilt niggled at him. Mary should know he figured on joining the ranks of sellers. He just needed to find the right moment to tell her. Had planned to before getting shot. Though he didn't farm, cattle sales had been declining for a good number of years now. There was no reason to keep this place anymore.

He ignored the guilt and kept up toward the valley, the growing laughter hooking him as thoroughly as the bass he used to catch with his brother when they were kids.

As he neared, his steps slowed, the sounds he heard filling him with a mixed kind of joy and pain. It was moments like this, in the sun-drenched air, that he wished desperately to hear Sarah's laugh one more time, to see the crooked toothless grin Abby had given him the day he'd left on assignment.

Before he'd come home to find— Nope, he wasn't going there. Forcing the memories to the side, he reached the edge of the valley.

Only feet away, Mary and Josie twirled in rhythmic abandonment. His breath stuttered to a stop, then rushed in as adrenaline began knocking through his system.

Josie's blond curls bounced and glistened, moving with the sound of her giggles as she spun through the flowers, around and around, a purple bloom clutched to her chest.

Mary was spinning, too, and when his gaze landed on her, he couldn't look away.

Her hair was down, flowing, a midnight veil taking flight as she spun. The dress she wore clung to her body, molding against lithe legs and rounded hips. Her face tilted to the sky, eyes closed, lips parted, her arms rotating with her body.

And then the little scene was over. Both girls collapsed on the ground, laughing on their backs as their world no doubt tilted perilously from one side to the other.

Lou swallowed hard, backing up. He felt like an interloper. An intruder on their carefree fun. The image of Mary burned in his mind. The woman he'd considered a sister...

The lump in his throat seemed to magnify and with a sudden decision he pivoted and marched back to the house. But the speed of his walk did nothing to erase what he'd seen. What he felt.

One thing was for sure: whatever he felt toward Mary was far from brotherly.

What was he going to do about that?

Chapter Eight

Mary found out about the invitation to the quilting bee approximately two hours before she was to arrive. Lou showed up on her doorstep as she and Josie slid the final batch of cookies into the oven. Damp tendrils stuck to her neck from the hair she'd pinned this morning but that had escaped in strands during baking.

She wiped her hands on a towel as Josie ran to the front door.

"Mister Lou," she shouted, her voice's pitch making Mary wince.

To his credit, Lou didn't back away but managed to give the girl an awkward pat on the head. Then he turned his startling blue gaze on her. Since the other day when they'd argued over when to take Josie to Portland, he hadn't brought up the subject with her again. In fact, she'd barely seen him.

It was almost as if he was avoiding her. Frowning, she finished rubbing a towel over her fingers before setting it on the little table she'd inherited from Trevor.

"Do you need something?" she asked Lou.

"Nope, not on your day off." He gave her a crooked grin, lounging against the wall near the still-open door.

Sunlight from the rising sun surrounded him and a strange catch crowded her throat.

Josie scampered past Lou, stopping in a square of light. "Can I go outside, Miss Mary?"

She nodded her assent and the little girl was gone.

"Miss Alma wants you to join a ladies' group today. I'm sorry that I forgot all about it until James reminded me. If you get ready now, we can be there early," said Lou in a penitent voice.

"We?"

His arms crossed. "I'm going to drive you."

"A horse would serve me fine."

"Not for me. There are things we should…discuss." He pinned her with an electric smile, his gaze sliding from her eyes to her mouth.

She wet her lips. "What things? I have said that which needed to be said."

He left where he stood, his smile widening as he advanced. She backed up, though what she felt in her belly was not terror but a rather more alarming emotion.

Edged against the wall of the kitchen, she could go no farther. Lou trapped her, moving so close she smelled the mint of Wrigley's on his breath.

"I saw you yesterday." His fingers crept to her neck, and his touch was feather soft against her skin.

She suppressed a shiver.

"With Josie, in the flowers. And I realized that—" A pained expression crossed his face. His words cut off, and his hand left her neck, leaving her skin cold and lonely.

"Realized what?" she asked, her voice as tremulous as the state of her knees.

His gaze shuttered, growing distant as he backed up. "If you want to go, be ready within the hour." He spun and left her against the wall, more shaken than she'd been in a long time.

Nerves aflame, she set about gathering her quilting supplies. She put them in a basket and then made a smaller basket for Josie. As she calmed, her mind turned to the event ahead.

Miss Alma had always been generous and kind, a woman of great wisdom. But she couldn't help wondering how wise this outing might be. How would the other women react to her presence? She had no desire to be subjected to the ill-mannered treatment her mother's people often experienced. Even though the people of Burns had been good to her in a distant way, she'd never actually interacted with the townsfolk in a companionable, talkative setting like a quilting bee.

But the trip into town *would* give her another chance to inquire about her mother's whereabouts.

Lou arrived promptly at eleven. James scooted out of the passenger side of Lou's automobile, but her employer remained inside, a scowl visible on his face.

"I'm here to watch Josie. Where's that wild thing at?" James chomped his tobacco.

"She's here somewhere." She tore her gaze from Lou and turned to the house. "Josie, it's time to go." She stepped toward the corner of the house. Maybe Josie had scampered out back. "I'm taking her with me. You don't have to watch her, James."

"Figured I'd take her shooting."

Mary whirled. "I think not."

"But he promised." Josie popped out from the corner of the house. "I don't wanna go sew. That's boring."

Mary sighed and closed the front door. She stepped onto the grass, moving toward the little girl, whose face was set in a stubborn yet adorable pout. "Every girl should know how to use a needle, Josie. It will come in handy."

The skill had kept her out of the brothels.

Josie's head tilted. "Do I have to?"

Mary looked at James, who shrugged. There appeared to be a slight curl to his lip, as if he was amused. Well, that was that, then. She would not force Josie to quilt. Times were changing and women had more options these days. Even she'd taken shooting lessons from James and had bought her very own pistol.

"Very well. Please be safe."

"Really? I can go?" Josie squealed and vaulted into Mary, her arms chained around her waist. "Thank you!"

Touched, she looked down into Josie's eyes. "You're welcome."

A high-pitched blast cut through their hug. Lou on the horn.

"Okay, girlie. Let's get on." James patted Josie before capturing Mary's gaze with a serious look. "Remember, these ladies invited you. They want ya there."

"Thank you, James." She vowed to remember that. She watched as Josie followed James across the expanse of ground between her new home and Lou's ranch house. Their chatter hung behind them, fading from hearing as they grew more distant.

She turned to the car. The baskets she clutched suddenly felt heavy and cumbersome. Though the sky burned a bright, sizzling blue, promising a warm day, tension knotted her stomach.

Lou reached across the front seat and opened the passenger door. "Let's go or you'll be late."

Once they were on their way, bouncing across uneven terrain to the road that led to Burns, Mary finally felt as if she could take a breath. Lou had said nothing to her. Perhaps he would skip this "talk" he'd spoken of.

She had no wish to discuss her private life with him. Or with anyone, for that matter.

"You're going to have fun, you know," he said, breaking into her thoughts.

She pulled her basket closer. Josie's sat on the floorboard, unneeded now. "I go only for Miss Alma." And to find her mother.

He cast her a look loaded with curiosity. "You've lived on the ranch how many years? Ten?"

"Twelve," she said stiffly.

He let out a low whistle. "Twelve years. That's a long time. You ever gone to a quilting bee? Never mind. Your knuckles are white on that basket."

Surprised, she looked down. Deliberately she released the basket.

"Now, you bring neighbors things all the time. There's nothing to be nervous about. Just be yourself and they'll love you." Lou gave her one of his half grins. "Charm these ladies and then we'll head up to Portland at the beginning of the week."

"You're not well enough yet."

"I'm fine. We'll take the train. My wound's closed up, there's no infection, minimal pain."

"Josie doesn't want to go."

"She's a little girl. She doesn't have a choice."

"Everyone should get a choice," she choked out. Her hands were back on the basket, and she didn't care. The basket's handle dug into her ribs.

Lou sighed heavily. She glanced over. The rugged lawman had slowly been returning to his carefree, light ways, yet the subject of Josie always seemed to sober him.

"I know you didn't get choices when you were young.

And when you were older, Trevor brought you to the ranch and we asked you to stay awhile. To be safe. But time passed and you never left. Why not?"

Mary stiffened. "This is not about me. Josie is afraid of that man. We do not know that he is her guardian. She shouldn't be left in his care."

"Even though we're leaving her with the mother, I'm still going to make sure she's safe."

"*My* mother found her and risked much to shelter and care for her. Where was this *mother* when Josie was left for dead in the desert? I do not trust this type of mother." Too late she realized that her outburst condemned more than Josie's mom. Her face burned.

There was an awkward silence in the car. She looked out the window, fastening her attention to her beloved rocky horizon. How she adored this place. Dry and vast, teeming with wildlife and plants carrying all sorts of value.

They were almost to Burns when Lou spoke. "I'll pick you up in the afternoon. Save me some of those cookies I know you have hiding in that basket."

She managed a small smile. "I left many on my counter. You may help yourself when we get home."

"Thanks, sweet Mary. You're the best cook I know." His smile broadened.

The action sent her pulse scurrying. To cover, she let out a gentle snort. "I'm the only cook you have."

"I know." Sporting an annoying grin, he pulled up next to Miss Alma's home.

She lived in a cozy, small house surrounded by blooming flowers. Behind the home, land sloped up in jagged crests to the horizon. Mary paused with opening her door.

"Do you see that grassland plateau?" she asked Lou.

"Over there, behind the house?"

She nodded. "My mother took me there to forage when

I was young. Her mother took her, and her mother before took my grandmother. During this season it is ripe with food. Bitterroot. Biscuit root. The food of my mother's people."

"I see women out there in the mornings sometimes. Didn't know they were finding food."

"It is only in these warm months that it can be found, but enough can be gathered to last a winter."

"You're making a point."

"Yes." She held his gaze, wanting him to understand. "My mother taught me of the past. She cared for me—"

"If this is another plea for your mom to live with you, stop now." His expression hardened. "That woman dropped you off with Trevor's mom and didn't look back. At a brothel. I won't ever understand what you see in her."

"I am not asking your permission, nor pleading for anything," she told him sternly, though her stomach twisted like well-wrung laundry. "What she did was ill-advised."

"No. It was wrong."

Oh, he made her angry. Setting her jaw, she jerked the car door open. She bolted out and shoved the door shut, its well-aimed slam puncturing the air and giving her a deep satisfaction. Mule-headed man. Why couldn't he see that forgiveness meant more than harboring ills? What had happened to make him so unforgiving? It wasn't as though Rose had wronged him. She'd left her child with a friend, little knowing the "friend" would end up selling Mary, years down the road.

And yet even that horrific experience had brought her to this place. Harney County, Oregon. To a ranch inhabited by three independent men. To a town that was home to a woman named Miss Alma, who taught Mary the way of the cross.

She stepped to Miss Alma's door. Shoulders straight, basket up. She could face this on her own.

Mary couldn't face another cookie.

She shook her head at the kind lady who'd just offered her another sugar cookie. Miss Alma's house was filled to the brim with women, patterns and treats. The ladies chattered as Mary huddled in the corner chair she'd chosen. Though no one had outright snubbed her, she'd felt the surprised looks when she'd opened the door.

Though she knew one or two ladies, most were strangers. Women who lived in town and rarely traveled outside its limits. No wonder they were startled to see a new face.

Of course, Miss Alma bustled around as friendly as a pup and sweeter than the desserts currently loading her counters.

Mary looked down at the stitching on her lap. She'd traded a few of her own gingham squares for a lovely ivy pattern another lady claimed to have picked up in New York City.

"Ooh, I like that." One of the younger ladies present, perhaps near Gracie's age, scooted close. "Are you making the entire quilt in that color scheme?" The girl's russet hair fell against freckled cheeks and she had an upturned nose that reminded Mary of a curious cat.

"I am considering ivy and greens," she answered.

"Lovely." The girl held out her hand. "I'm Amy Donovan. Gracie is a riding friend of mine."

"Oh…" Mary stared at the hand. Did this Amy really expect her to shake hands like men? Not that she disapproved, the movement simply surprised her.

"Go on, grasp my hand. It's quite fun and perfectly acceptable."

She took Amy's hand and was rewarded with a vigorous pump.

"I'm so glad you came. It gets awfully stuffy in here sometimes. Quilting has its merits, but my aunt, whom I accompany, spends all her time tittering about who said what and who's cut their hair into a bob. I've been missing Gracie dreadfully." Amy's eyes, a pretty brown, widened. "Say, do you ride? This weather is perfect for a good gallop."

"I miss Gracie, too" was all Mary could think to say. No wonder Amy and Gracie had found each other. Chatterboxes, the both of them. Yet she quite liked their loquaciousness.

"When will she be home?" Amy pulled out a long stretch of squares and started working.

"Perhaps in a few weeks." With Josie and Lou both suddenly appearing at the ranch, she hadn't even thought about Gracie and Trevor's return.

"Well, the sooner the better. Sometimes I'm afraid all the ranchers scooting out will leave us with a ghost town."

Mary pricked her finger, despite the thimble she wore. "What do you mean, scooting out?" She sucked the pain from her finger and then returned to her sewing.

"Well, this weather and all. With the Indian summers gone, lots of ranches are up for sale. I heard some homesteaders are just leaving their places without even trying to sell."

"You don't say," Mary murmured. How sad. The high desert of Oregon was a difficult soil for agriculture, though the land grew rich with herbs and roots. One had to know where to search.

"And did you hear of Mr. Baxley?"

"No, I'm afraid not."

"Oh, the poor thing was beaten horribly and died from

his injuries. There was this good-looking man skulking about and I've heard gossip that he's the murderer."

Mary's gaze snapped up. "Is he still in Burns?"

"Oh, no." Amy's head shook vigorously. "Our lawmen wouldn't allow that. Though there's no proof. Only conjecture."

"Everything going well over here?" Miss Alma appeared in front of them. She wore an absurd hat laden with all sorts of funny little things that made Mary smile. They hovered above her happy face and bobbed with her movements. "Mary, dear, those snickerdoodles were wonderful. You must give me the recipe and bring something to the picnic tomorrow. Now, may I get you ladies anything?"

"We're doing just dandy, Miss Alma. Thank you, though." Amy flashed a broad grin, but the elderly lady was already swishing off to the next group of women in her crowded living room.

The rest of the afternoon passed uneventfully, though Mary couldn't shake the troublesome feeling nagging at her. Could she have done more to help Mr. Baxley? And how had the violet-eyed man escaped conviction so easily? Perhaps Lou would know.

At precisely three o'clock Miss Alma's door swung open, and a broad-shouldered Lou Riley filled the door frame. Gasps and titters resounded through the room. A few of the younger girls gaped as Mary gathered her belongings and said goodbye to Miss Alma.

She turned to the door and then paused, her heart stuttering in her chest. No wonder the girls were catching flies. Lou lounged in the doorway, one shoulder propped against the frame, his legs crossed at the ankles, hands pocketed in his blue jeans. His leather hat hugged his head at an angle that mimicked the smirk on his lips.

He swirled a toothpick lazily with his teeth as he surveyed the room. The sun slanted in from windows behind Mary, highlighting the mischievous sparkle that winked in his blue eyes.

The man knew the effect he was having, and she didn't know whether to be amused or outraged.

Finally, he took out the toothpick and straightened. Not a woman stirred. He slid the hat off his head, gave Mary a slow wink that filled her with hot mortification and proceeded to dazzle the women with the kind of smile that turned a woman's heart.

"Hello, ladies," he drawled.

Chapter Nine

"I am not impressed." Mary hoity-toitied her way to the Ford, posture so stiff Lou figured she could carry a basket on her head the way he'd seen women on the continent of Africa do. Or maybe just plain old books like the stuffy girls back East used to practice with.

"With what?" he called after her. He wasn't going to bother trying to keep up while she threw the most abnormal fit he'd ever seen. Maybe this quilting thing had gone worse than he suspected. Though when he'd walked in, everyone had seemed peaceful enough. Miss Alma had even piled him down with cookies to take home, with clear instructions to send James out for a look at her pipes within the week.

"You know what," Mary retorted.

He barely caught the words before they were followed by the solid *thunk* of the passenger door. No matter. He ambled down the driveway, marveling at how much better he felt. The slightest twinge in his shoulder was his only reminder of that bullet.

Soon enough he'd track his shooter down and get some answers.

But first things first.

He kept an eye on the passenger side as he rounded the front of the Ford. A bright sunny day like this called for good spirits and happiness. Instead, he found himself dealing with a grumpy woman who was going to get even grumpier when he talked to her on the way home.

After cranking up his tin lizzie, he yanked the driver's door open and slid gingerly into his seat. Mary wouldn't look at him, her lovely profile a stark reminder of the reality he'd been trying to avoid since the other day.

She was beautiful.

Beautiful.

The word could barely get past his brain. Just thinking it made him feel guilty, as if he might ruin her somehow. Because she'd been almost like a sister to him, or so he'd thought, but now as he gazed at her proud chin and clenched hands, he realized he knew nothing about this woman who'd been his housekeeper for so long.

Nothing except that she'd been thrown aside in the worst of ways before being mistreated at the hands of greedy, criminal men. He felt his mouth tighten as he pulled onto the road. Why would she want anything to do with men ever again? His good humor dissipated.

They drove in silence while he waited for her to speak. When it became obvious she was too stubborn to talk about what was bothering her, he cleared his throat.

"Do you…" He paused. Asking personal questions went against the grain. He'd never done it before. Had always given her the space he thought she needed. But now it seemed he should get involved somehow. Find out who this woman was. He tapped the steering wheel with the base of his thumbs. "Do you want to talk about your annoyance with me?"

"No."

"You seemed upset back there."

"I'm fine."

Irritation crowded his throat. "Sometimes talking helps you feel better. Sharing your feelings."

"I don't have feelings to share," she snapped. Out of the corner of his eye, he saw her swivel toward him. "Why do you care, anyhow? A man who involves himself in nothing that requires emotional commitment? Those ladies are kind and giving. You shouldn't toy with them."

"I made their day exciting."

She looked away.

"And you disapprove?" Yes, he'd complimented them. He'd looked at their needlework and asked questions. At no time had he been insincere, and yet there was censure in Mary's tone. He stared sightlessly at the road, reminded again why he didn't ask questions. Why he didn't get involved.

"I don't.… I'm sorry, Lou." Now her voice had softened. He glanced over and found her staring at him, eyes wide, the deep darkness of them stitching a surprising thread of awareness through him. "I had no call to speak to you in such a way. You've been nothing but kind to me from the moment I stepped foot into your home."

He cleared his throat. "The things I said in there, I meant them. Those ladies are making incredible quilts any person would be honored to own. A woman needs to know she's special, that she has something to offer.…" He trailed off, thinking of his Sarah and the canvases she'd painted. She would never paint again.

"I'm happy you meant those things, Lou. I apologize again. Perhaps I'm on edge because of our situation."

He focused on the road, wishing the forlorn quality of her voice didn't bother him so badly. "No problem at all. I think this is the first time I've seen you frazzled in public before."

"I've never been frazzled, as you say."

"Last year."

"Excuse me?" Her voice rose, but he recognized humor creeping through.

"I recall a particular batch of dough that wouldn't rise for you."

She made a noise that sounded suspiciously like a laugh. He fought back a smile.

"Mary, you've got nothing to apologize for. Besides, we have bigger things to discuss, and I don't want my behavior today impacting any decisions we make."

Her heavy sigh rested between them. "Do you mean Josie?"

"Yep. There was a telegram waiting for me today. From her mother."

Mary said nothing, but the tension in the Ford felt thicker than churned-up cream.

"She wants Josie home as soon as possible," he added. "Claimed she's been ill and thought her daughter was visiting relatives. There's no getting around this telegram.... If we're not on a train within the week, she'll press charges."

"Her story is plausible," Mary said quietly, and he heard the resignation in her voice.

He ached for her, a steady, unnerving pain beneath his sternum. He knew what it was like to lose loved ones. "This never could have lasted," he said gently.

"It just felt so blissful, so perfect." He felt her stare. "I've been...lonely, I suppose."

"Since Gracie and Trevor left?"

"No."

He glanced at her then pulled the wheel to the side to avoid a shrub growing in the middle of the rough desert road.

"For years now, I think," she continued. "It took meeting Gracie to realize I was nothing but a shadow of a person. And now, seeing Trevor so happy and fulfilled, it's as though a light has been cast on this deep, hollow well that's my life."

Lou frowned. She talked as if he and James meant nothing to her. "You might want to explain, because I've always liked having you at the ranch. James and I depend on you."

"You've both been blessings. A sanctuary for my soul. But what you've liked hasn't been me, it's been good food and clean clothes."

"That's a bunch of hogwash."

"Is it?"

He swerved to the side of the road and slammed on the brakes. "You better believe it."

Her eyes widened and her lips parted. The Ford chugged, mindless of the emotional state of its passengers. Over the various odors associated with automobiles, he caught the clean whiff of Mary's scent. That tantalizing, exotic flavor that had so tormented him when he'd been stuck in bed.

Scowling, he leaned toward her. "You haven't been just a housekeeper in years, little lady, so get used to the fact that you mean more to us than some woman doing the laundry. You're special. And you know you could've left at any time, but you didn't. Why not?"

"I—I don't know." Her eyes never left his face, studying him as though she wanted to read the depths of him.

Deliberately he held her gaze. "You've been afraid."

She broke the visual standoff. "Perhaps. Can we go home now?"

He slammed the clutch down, and the Ford jumped forward. "Holding things inside isn't healthy." It struck him how alone she'd been for the past twelve years, how unnatural that aloneness must be. "Don't you want to move on with your life? Maybe not get married, but form relationships? Time slips away too fast and you'll be old before you know it."

"I find your comments ironic. While you've been traipsing all over the world, I've built the friendships I want. It is you who has been alone. As for secrets…" Her voice trailed off.

"What?" he said, more harshly than he'd intended.

"I see the way you look at Josie. There is something you hide from, perhaps run from." She shifted, and he felt that probing gaze again, digging, searching.

He gripped the wheel. "So we both have issues. I'm just worried you'll never have a normal life. You're young, smart and talented. You should use your skills to create a better life." This was the moment he needed to tell her the truth. Why did he feel so badly over it?

"I'm selling the ranch," he said quickly.

There was a sharp intake of breath as she absorbed that information.

"I'm going to make sure you're well cared for," he rushed on. His face felt so hot he could light a wildfire with his cheeks. "You could work for the new owners of the ranch. I noticed a small store for rent in town. Maybe you'd like to open a shop or something." He chanced a look at her and his stomach flopped at the look on her face.

Expressionless and pale.

Why did she hold everything in? This was all his fault. Jaw tight, he stared forward. "You hear me?"

"I hear you. I'll pray and see what God wants me to do."

"God? Really? And you think He'll answer you?"

"You think He won't?" she countered, and a new strength had entered her voice, challenging him, battling the belief that had helped him survive the loss of his wife and child.

"Experience has proved that when a man needs God, He doesn't show up."

"Perhaps you've measured God by the wrong experiences."

His teeth ground. Sharp pain shot through his chest. Suddenly he was overwhelmingly angry, so enraged he wanted to spill everything that had happened, show her just how faithful this God of hers was. But a man didn't talk about things like his wife and daughter dying in his arms. It didn't feel right to share, even though the words pulsated on his tongue, straining to rip free of the cage he'd put them in.

"Lou," she said quietly, "I don't know what happened in your past, but you're not the only one to have suffered pain." A small catch in her voice caught on the word *pain,* leaving it hanging between them, a shattered sound in the noisy automobile.

In that moment, the anger drained out of him, leaving him tired and empty. He opened his mouth, rotating his jaw, trying to loosen what felt tighter than his trigger finger on a loaded gun.

He wanted to explain to Mary, even though she was the type who never nagged for explanations. She was the kind of woman who waited patiently, who didn't press for what she wanted. It was both her strength and her flaw.

The road stretched before them, long and windy, the jagged horizon only hinting at what lay beyond.

"Sometimes it's easier to blame God," he finally said. Because she didn't seem to blame Him for the things that had happened to her, which made him wonder why he did.

"True."

He made to look at her, but a figure ahead on the left grabbed his attention.

"Lou, there's a woman walking on the road."

"I see her." He steered to the right, passing her safely and at a distance. The woman's silver-laced black hair streamed behind her and she wore the traditional garb of a Paiute.

Mary twisted in the seat, peering behind them.

"Stop," she said.

He looked at her. "Now?"

"Yes, stop the car!"

He slowed, but before he'd fully stopped, she opened her door and scrambled out.

Mary darted across the rough road, the sun in her eyes as she raced toward her mother. "Mother," she shouted.

Rose shuffled along, ignoring Mary, even when she skidded to a stop in front of her. She placed her hands on her mother's shoulders, mindful of the fragile frame beneath her fingers. "Where are you going?"

"You should not be here," her mother whispered. Her gaze landed somewhere behind Mary. Wind raked up the dusty road.

Mary squinted against the debris. "Come with me, to my home. It isn't safe for you to walk these roads alone."

"No."

"Please, I can take care of you."

"There is danger in these hills...." Rose's voice trailed ominously.

A cold tremor shivered its way down Mary's spine. Sometimes it seemed danger lurked everywhere. Running from it solved nothing.

And yet the vacancy of her mother's gaze was alarming, to say the least. Frowning, Mary slid her hands away and tried to meet her mother's eyes.

"Where are you going? I will take you."

"He will find us." Her mother's shoulders began to

shake, small ripples of movement almost lost in the dirt-laden breeze. Long strands of hair whipped over her features, lashing at her skin as if punishing her.

Mary didn't want her mother to be punished. Not then and not now. She stepped forward and gathered Rose in a hug, inhaling her earthy scent.

"The ranch is secluded. No one shall find us there." She smoothed hair from her mother's brow. "The little girl, we must take her to her mother soon, but I need help in the meantime. Will you come?"

A sound cut through her words. Lou sidled up next to them, arms crossed, something near a scowl playing about the corners of his lips. "What's going on?"

"Mother needs a place to stay." She tilted her chin at Lou, daring him to defy her.

"She has a place."

"Not now. Something's happened." She glanced at her mother, who still looked as though a wisp of wind might tilt her over.

He moved closer. He stepped in front of her mother, and his closeness urged Mary to move back. The aroma of his cologne penetrated her senses, dredging up good memories. Her first Christmas at the ranch, exotic gifts he'd brought her from his travels.

"Rose, why aren't you at home?"

His deep voice brought Mary out of her musings. She focused on her mother, who stared blankly ahead. Refusing to answer. Stubborn. As she'd always been.

"Mother, answer him. We will help you, but we must know what we face."

Lou made a sound in his throat. "Just leave her. She's probably packing up and leaving without a word. She's got a habit of doing that." He cast a concerned look at Rose before turning his piercing gaze on Mary. "Come on. We've got things to do."

"I can't leave her."

"You can and you should." His hand waved dismissively. "She doesn't want our help. Let her deal with her own problems. We've got enough of our own, plus what she added."

"But—"

"Let's go." His curt tone brooked no argument.

Still, she hesitated. "Mother, look at me. Please."

Slowly Rose's gaze slid to meet Mary's. Dark and unblinking. She'd seen too much pain. Mary's heart hurt with the thought. She held out her hand, hoping her mother would take it. "You are welcome in my home."

"Not if she doesn't say what's going on."

Rose's gaze shifted to Lou. "I will say, but you won't like it."

Mary dropped her hand, letting it curl into a slight ball at her side. A gust swept dirt up from the road, but her mother didn't even blink. She held Lou's look long and tight.

"There is a very bad man," she pronounced. "And he wants the girl."

Chapter Ten

"Tell us something we don't know, lady." Lou lowered the brim of his hat and glared.

"It doesn't matter if he wants her," Mary said, ignoring her bothersome employer. "She's going home to her mother." It was hard, but she forced those words out.

"This is true?" Her mother's brow arched.

"Yes." She nodded to the sack in her mother's hands. "Is that everything you own?"

"Everything that's important."

"What about your baskets? Should we go back and get them?"

"They are all sold. I will go with you, on one condition."

Lou let out a loud, annoying snort. Mary formed a glare and flung it his way. He reached for her arm and none too gently propelled her a few feet from her mother. "What do you think you're doing?"

She pulled from his grasp. "I'm inviting my mother to stay with me. That is none of your concern."

"She's not riding in my tin lizzie."

Though she felt weak inside for fear, something compelled her to retort, "Is that so?"

Lou looked a bit taken aback at her spunk. But not angry. Relief unfurled inside.

"She's got a condition, Mary. That isn't right. This whole situation is wrong and I'm not going to stand by and watch her hurt you again."

"She never hurt me." At his look, she grimaced. "Not much," she amended.

"Regardless, I don't trust any friend of Julia's. She says she's running from this guy who's looking for Josie, but what if she's working for him?"

It was true her mother and Julia had been friends, which was why her mother had left her to live with Julia and her son, Trevor, at the brothel. But Mary had no reason to believe that her mother had anything to do with her being sold to Mendez at eighteen and she certainly wouldn't hold another's actions against her.

"You're too suspicious."

"Nope. I'm not. It happens all the time. Like I said, she doesn't need to be close to you. I'm putting my foot down about her."

He had a very satisfied look on his face that would've made her smile if she wasn't so angry. Her hands fisted, palms slick. She swallowed hard.

"I do appreciate your concern, but you know nothing of why my mother left me with Julia. You have judged with no knowledge." He made to interrupt and she held up a hand. "If you will not give us a ride, then we shall walk."

"You're taking her side?" He had the temerity to look aghast.

"This is not about sides. It is about right and wrong. To leave my mother alone is wrong."

"I see."

"I hope that you do." The words rolled off her tongue, succinct, surprising her.

Lou barked a quick laugh without mirth. "Fine, then. Try to fit her in."

"Are we going to the picnic?" Josie watched as Mary drew a pan of snickerdoodles from her Glenwood gas-and-coal stove. She inspected them, feeling very thankful for the modern range she cooked with. The cookies were perfect.

"Do we have to go to church first?"

"Don't worry, you'll like it." She patted Josie's hair, which hung in the two neat braids her mother had formed while Mary baked. "Miss Alma and I sing wonderful songs, and you're going to meet some of my friends."

Mary didn't attend a traditional church but rather met with other Christians at a neighbor's property. Mr. Horn preached the sermons and sometimes people brought instruments. Mostly those with homes on the outskirts of the desert attended, though Miss Alma often came from town.

"Thank you for my dress, Miss Mary." Josie's eyes sparkled, and Mary couldn't help grinning back. The girl had picked a lovely green to border her white dress. Mary had sewn it together and added matching bows.

"You're welcome, my sweet girl. Ask my mother if she can put your bows on."

"Okay." She skipped out of the room, her new Mary Janes tapping a happy tune.

These snickerdoodles were the last batch. She popped one that had cooled in her mouth, then set about searching for a basket to put them in. She sneaked a few into a hankie for the ride to Horn's and arranged the rest neatly.

Once done, she found Josie jabbering away to Rose, who sat with a smile on her face. The creases in her skin seemed less deep somehow, as though weight had gone from her soul.

Mary smiled and crossed the room. "It's time to go. Are you sure you won't come, Mother?"

"I am certain. Perhaps I'll take a rest."

Her mother woke early now, perhaps because she'd spent more than the first half of her life sleeping through sunrises and well into the afternoon. Mary nodded and guided Josie toward the door.

"We'll be home in the afternoon."

Rose nodded, and her eyes slipped closed.

As Mary shut the door to the house, she heard Josie shriek, "Mister Lou!"

She barely caught the girl by a pigtail as Lou's fancy Ford pulled up to the porch.

"Hop in, ladies." He winked at them. "I'll be your chauffeur today."

Josie squealed with delight. Mary frowned but helped the little girl into the car. She settled where Rose had sat yesterday.

Even now, a day later, it was a strange sensation to know she'd done something out of the ordinary, that she'd risked Lou's disapproval to do what she felt was right. But it had also been empowering and thrilling. For some reason, he'd allowed her to load her mother into his Ford and bring her back to the ranch.

Perhaps he'd felt bad for her at the time. After all, she'd brought up her past, and she knew the things she'd gone through caused him grief. She didn't wish to use her past to get her way, however.

"You coming?" He beeped his horn, making her start. Her basket tilted.

"If these snickerdoodles spill..." she warned.

"Yes, ma'am." He shot her that grin of his.

Mouth tight to cover the ratcheting speed of her pulse, she scurried to the passenger side and loaded up. The trip to Horn's homestead took almost an hour, thanks to the bumpy, rutted road. A horse could handle the trek much faster. Josie and Lou kept up a stream of chatter while Mary attempted to darn an old sock. A useless endeavor considering the uneven terrain. Finally, they arrived. Josie bounced in the back as she waited for Mary to exit the car. As soon as she stepped foot outside, Josie escaped, slipping past her and running toward Horn's place.

Families milled around, unpacking lunches beneath the shaded trees.

"Josie, come back."

"Aww." She sped back, though. A good listener.

Mary handed her the blanket she'd brought. "Could you please find a place for us to sit? And if you see Mr. Horn, let him know I'll be there shortly."

"Okeydokey!" Josie popped a smile and snatched the blanket. She ran toward the other kids, who played near a sturdy elm. She was easy to see from this distance.

"She's going to get dirty quick," Lou remarked.

"I know." Mary smiled. "You may pick us up in four hours or so."

His head cocked to the side. Morning light danced in his eyes. "Thought I'd stay and keep an eye on things."

"Surely you do not believe Josie's uncle will find his way here?"

He shrugged. "Better safe than sorry. If he did, we'd spot him right away. Either way, it's my job to keep an eye on the girl until we get her home safe to her ma."

"Of course," she said, refusing to dwell on the disappointment that filled her at his words. "Come along. You know many of these people, I believe. At least by face."

"But I plan on sticking close to you." He winked again, and a flush warmed her skin. "May I carry your basket?"

She allowed him to take it. Not knowing what to say, she picked her way toward the picnic area. Neighbors had spread their blankets in a grassy area beneath a sprawling elm. Children frolicked in the grass, shrieking and laughing. Josie ran amidst them, her giggles lost within the group.

"They having a service today?" Lou asked beside her.

"Probably a little something." Did he sound worried? She glanced at him and saw that he did indeed look unnaturally tense. "Mr. Horn is easy on the ears."

"Not worried about that."

"What, then?"

"There you are!" Miss Alma's bright voice cut off anything he planned to say next. "I shall take your wonderful desserts. I saw that darling girl of yours. Is she an orphan?"

"No." Was it horrible to wish she was? Battling a sense of guilt, Mary gestured to the basket. "I hope they'll do."

"Of course they will. Now, did you bring James?"

"No…"

"Tsk, tsk. I needed to speak with the man." Miss Alma whisked the basket from Lou, barely offering him a glance before tottling off toward the tables set up near the trees.

"She's a bundle of energy, huh?"

"You really don't have to stay." As soon as the words left her mouth, she regretted them. For how long had she been praying Lou would attend service? Maybe there'd even been a secret hope inside that he'd change his views on God, soften a bit. She'd never had the nerve to pray out loud for meals until his niece, Gracie, had come. That had been how ornery both James and Lou became, though James tended to approach the mention of God in a more intellectual manner.

But Lou closed up completely. All emotion, much like Trevor. As though he'd been hurt. She sidled a look toward him. The breeze ruffled through his hair. He caught her staring and gave her a tight smile.

"I'm staying," he said. "There's no way I'm missing your desserts."

She sniggered. "You'll be going back to work and needing new clothes if you keep this eating up."

"A well-fed man is a happy man."

"I wish that was true."

"Me, too." He sighed and looked toward the horizon. The mountains rose sharply against the sky, steep and dangerous. Much like the feelings spreading through her.

Yet she didn't know how to stop this warmth…no, this fire. She'd always felt tender toward Lou. How could she not? He'd taken her in at the darkest moment of her life. Kept her safe.

But lately…things were changing, and she wasn't quite sure what to make of it.

Stuck in God talk.

Last thing he wanted, but here he was, settling down on the blanket, with Mary only spaces away from him, her scent mingling with the aromas of fried chicken and flowers. Mr. Horn had instructed everyone to take seats so they could have a short preaching before the picnic.

It had been years since he'd attended any kind of Christian event. What had coerced him now was beyond his ken, but he'd just have to starch his backbone and ignore the rumbling of his stomach.

Truth be told, a picnic had sounded bunches better than sitting home by himself. James planned to stay home reading, but Lou preferred action of some sort. He wasn't a reader, never had been.

Josie came scrambling over, hair flying in her face. She stopped in front of him and brushed knotty strands from her eyes. "We gotta sit still now, don't we?"

Lou made a face and she giggled. Plopping down beside him, she leaned her head onto his arm. A lump formed in his throat but he didn't move away.

Horn moved into sight. People had arranged their blankets in rows, just like a church. The man went to the front.

"Morning, everyone."

The group replied with murmurs, mornings, et cetera. An interesting mix of folks here. Mary wasn't the only Paiute. There was also a Chinese man on a far blanket. Miss Alma with her fancy hat and pleated dress sat next to a family who wore homespun clothes and no shoes.

Feeling more comfortable in this mix of people, he leaned back on his elbows and stretched his legs out. He felt Mary's glance but got caught in Horn's words and didn't meet it.

"Troubles come our way. Hardships." Horn cleared his throat. "But God brings us through. He delivers us from the snare of the enemy and fills our souls with peace. I thought today it would be nice to read the nineteenth chapter of Psalms and sing a few songs before we dig into these scrumptious vittles the ladies worked up."

"Pa fried up his special chicken recipe," a young girl called out.

Horn chuckled. "He sure did. Who'd like to read?"

Miss Alma stood. Lou heard the bustle of her voluminous skirts from where he sat.

"I shall," she said. She adjusted the petite glasses on her face and held up a heavy-looking book. Her voice surrounded them and suddenly everything faded but the clarity of her words.

"'Because he hath set his love upon me, therefore will I deliver him. I will set him on high, because he hath known my name. He shall call upon me, and I will answer him. I will be with him in trouble, I will deliver him, and honor him. With long life will I satisfy him, and shew him my salvation.'"

Lou squirmed on the blanket, glad when she was finished. A heavy sense of regret crept through him. For what, he wasn't sure. Miss Alma sat and then, suddenly, Mary stood up beside him. She opened her mouth and sang "Amazing Grace." The others followed until the entire area filled with the sound of voices.

Mary's voice was a husky soprano. He'd heard her humming throughout the years as she worked but never had she sang so lovely, so invitingly, of God and His grace.

The song he used to sing. Years ago. As a child and young man. The God he'd trusted. Mary thought Him worthy of trust. Still…Josie wiggled beside him. He glanced at her blond curls and thought of Sarah and Abby. Their passing had been so long ago. Why did the memories still hurt so much?

He blinked as the singing faded and an odd silence descended on the group. Then Mary began "How Great Thou Art." A chill rippled through his body at her words.

Her face was relaxed, her lips rounding and changing as she sang. Her hands lifted and swelled with her words. She was happy here. At peace.

Because of God.

Deep down, in a place he didn't care to explore, he felt the truth of it. That he'd turned his back on Jesus and everything he'd been raised with and now he felt pain and bitterness. But Mary had embraced what he'd spurned and it had changed her.

He blinked as Josie slid her hand into his. He looked

down at her broad smile and vowed to protect this little girl. Whatever it took. He returned Josie's squeeze and sang with the group.

It had been a long time. His throat worked each consonant and spit them out rusty, but Josie didn't seem to care. When the song ended and they'd all spread out on blankets, he found himself plopping down next to Mary.

"Mmm, you smell good. Like cinnamon and roses. Like snickerdoodles."

She blushed beside him. The grin that had taken hold during the song widened. He leaned back, folding his hands behind his head and crossing his ankles. "What's on the menu?"

"Fried chicken, apple dumplings—"

"Snickerdoodles?"

"You know so." She sent him an exasperated look, but he saw laughter in her eyes.

"Where's Josie?"

"I'm right here!" She hopped onto the blanket, spinning, and then dropping down.

"Your dress, Josie."

But the girl didn't hear Mary. She was staring at a group of kids in the distance. Someone's father, or maybe an older brother, was giving each a turn at being swung in a circle.

"Go over there," he told her.

"She's wearing a dress," said Mary.

Josie sighed heavily, a bit on the melodramatic side. He shook as unexpected laughter bubbled through him. Mary was hiding her own smirk behind tightly pressed lips. He met her eyes and suddenly the laughter dried up.

The chirping of the birds, the sounds of chatter and laughter faded, and all he could see was Mary. Kind, beautiful Mary. Her hair shimmering, her eyes pinned on him, widening when he didn't look away. A strange and almost foreign feeling swept through him. He leaned forward.

"Mister Lou!" Josie tugged on his sleeve. "Will you swing me around like those kids?" She slid between him and Mary, ending what had been an intriguing moment. He shook his head to clear it and then gave Josie a wink.

"I'll swing until you can't stand anymore. Let's go." He followed her to the elm, letting her grip his palm as she skipped beside him. A different feeling filled him, something close to contentment.

When he was gone to Asia, he'd look back and hold these memories dear.

Chapter Eleven

Mary didn't want Lou to sell the ranch.

There. She could admit it to herself. After watching him with Josie yesterday, laughing and relaxed, she realized the life she'd built here wasn't enough. Lou had been right. She needed more than what she had. She was ready for more.

Thoughtful, she pinned a towel on the line, thankful for the sun that dried each piece of laundry. Her mother was in the house with Josie, teaching her to weave baskets. The delicate scents of desert drifted around her and for a moment she closed her eyes as the refrains of yesterday's hymn swept through her heart.

Then sings my soul, my savior God to thee.
How great Thou art, how great Thou art.

Humming, she reached for a shirt and clipped it to the line.

"Mary." Lou's voice rose above her humming.

She turned, shading her eyes from the glare of sunlight, trying to pinpoint his location. She heard him behind her. She whirled, hand to her chest.

"Are you sneaking up on me?"

"Do you have a moment to talk?" He squinted at her.

"I'm almost done. What do you wish to speak of?"

"Plans need to be made," he said gently.

Her spine stiffened. She pinned a bread cloth to the line, avoiding his gaze. "Have you told Gracie and Trevor you're selling the ranch? Don't you need their permission?"

"I have it." He gestured toward the house. "Why don't we go up for lunch and talk a spell."

"Lunch isn't quite ready."

"We'll speak here, then."

She felt his perusal to the marrow of her bones and suppressed a shiver. Lately it seemed as if he'd been looking at her differently, more deeply, as though he truly saw her. She found the interest both intoxicating and terrifying.

Refusing to meet his eyes, she plucked a towel from her basket and stretched it evenly on the line. Lou took a clip from her waist and pinned the cloth.

She wrinkled her nose at him. "If you'd rather do this, I can go prepare lunch. Since you're apparently not busy."

"I'm busy." He shifted closer, and suddenly she became aware of how much larger he was than her, and yet she felt no fear, only an odd fluttering below her ribs that prompted her to step back. She reached for the remaining sock in the basket.

"I can meet you up there." She wanted her voice to remain steady, but it came out wrong, breathy and not at all like her.

Thankfully, Lou turned and paced away, toward the small porch of Trevor's—her—house. Stifling a sigh, she hung the sock and then trudged after him.

Perhaps he wished to speak of the ranch sale or of her mother's presence on this property. Resolve hardened within her and gave life to her steps.

Heart thumping and breath a tad thin, she followed Lou onto the porch. She settled in the chair next to his. Close enough to smell the Wrigley's in his pocket and see the stubble on his chin. "You're in need of a shave."

He cocked his head, catching her gaze with his. "I was going to ask you to do that for me this afternoon."

"Me?" she squeaked.

"Yeah, we're heading out tomorrow morning, early, and I don't have time to get to a barber."

She swallowed her denial. The man needed a shave and a trim, but she'd only given them to James. Rarely had she touched Lou, and now it seemed they were thrown together all the time. It did not bode well for her nerves.

"Josie does not wish to go." She heard the stubborn note in her voice and didn't care.

"I'm gonna be honest with you." Lou peered at her, forehead furrowed. "If we don't take her home, my bosses will be sending someone to do it for us. I've bought as much time as I can but any longer and we're liable to be charged with some kind of wrongdoing."

"That's not right."

"Life isn't about what we feel. You're saying it's not right, but what about Josie's mother? How's she feeling, knowing her daughter never made it safely to relatives?" Lou frowned. "What's gotten into you? I've never known you to be so unreasonable."

Mary recoiled. "It is not I who is unreasonable here. You've wanted to get rid of her since the very beginning."

"I just wanted her to be cared for, out of danger." His eyes were inscrutable.

She stood and paced near the steps, pushing her skirt in front of her knees as she moved back and forth.

Lou stepped in front of her, placing his palms against her shoulders. She stopped, unable to move forward because he'd effectively ended her momentum. Annoyed, she glared at him.

"Remove your hands."

His eyes narrowed. "She's not ours, Mary. You've got to let her go."

No. The word echoed in her heart, a lonely, distant wail that couldn't seem to make it to her lips. She didn't want to let Josie go. She wanted to hold her and love her and raise her. Spin in the sunlight with her a million times more.

His grip loosened, and he crossed his arms across his chest. "This afternoon I need a shave and a trim. Can you do that?"

Numbly, she nodded past the ache that was already spreading through her.

"Good." He paused as though he'd say something more, and his gaze lingered on her face, but she couldn't bear to feel his pity for her.

The alone woman, as he'd said.

She watched as he walked away, his body casting a long, confident shadow against her beloved lands. How many times had she watched him leave? Drive off to fight battles unknown. To rescue those in distress. And never once had she asked him to stay so she wouldn't be alone. It hadn't been her place either, and yet...

This time she was determined to walk first.

Mary rode hard into Burns shortly after hanging the wash. Josie remained with Rose. As for Lou, she planned to cut his hair this evening, but for now she wanted to see about renting rooms somewhere. An idea had blossomed after he left, but she wasn't sure how financially practical opening a bakery might be.

Many are the plans in a man's heart, but the Lord's plan prevails.

The verse resonated within as she hitched up her horse and hurried into the general store.

She found the owner bent beside an old shelf, dusting it. "Joseph."

"Miss Mary." He stood and shared his ready smile. "Did you bring any winterfat? The ladies wiped me clean within the week."

She shook her head. "I am actually curious to know if you've heard of a storeroom for rent. And if you've advice on how to go about getting some."

"Well, now…" He scratched his chin. "I can't say I've heard a thing about that. Maybe the best one you should be talking to is a solicitor? I bought this place years ago and don't reckon I remember which is the best way to go about finding any places for rent."

Mary pasted a smile to her lips though her heart had sunk to her knees. "Very well. I shall try someone else."

"Are you planning on opening a goods store?"

The too-casual question amused her. "Never fear, I shall only bring my herbs to you."

"I don't care either way." He shrugged, and Mary bit back a smile at the untruth.

She left him and walked the streets of Burns. There were, in fact, several rooms within buildings for sale. But which one would best suit her needs? She peered within dusty windows while pondering the situation.

"Yoo-hoo, Mary!"

Turning, Mary looked for the source of the female calling to her. Across the road a young woman dressed in a frilly garment scooted over, clutching her dress in one hand and a parasol in the other.

Amy. Gracie's friend. She waited as the girl dashed over.

"How nice to see you again." Amy's smile spread wide and fresh.

"And you." Mary inclined her head. "Your dress is lovely."

"Why, thank you. I'm attending a wedding. A Monday wedding, which is rather romantic. This gentleman returned from the war and my friend Sally had waited ever so long for him, but he'd been hurt, you see, and had to recuperate. Well, they're finally marrying and it's the biggest to-do."

"That is very romantic," Mary acknowledged, feeling her own heart wither beneath the girl's innocent, starry outlook. "Young love—"

"Oh, they're not young." Freckles trotted across Amy's features with bold perkiness. Rather like their wearer's voice. "She's been waiting years, ever since school days, and it took his going to war for him to realize that she was the woman for him. It helped that she nursed him back to health, as well."

There seemed to be an underlying message in Amy's eyes, and Mary shifted uncomfortably. "I suppose such a thing could bring about a certain closeness."

"It most certainly can." Amy's grin stretched as she swooped her parasol to point at Mary. "I must be off, but wanted to run over and say hello. Also, I had a bit of news about that murderer."

"You did?"

"Yep." She leaned forward conspiratorially. "Turns out that good-looking stranger has been released. The police have a new suspect. I don't know why or how it all came about." She straightened. "Well, then, care to join me at the wedding?"

"No, thank you." Her mind churned.

"Boy, it's sweltering out here." Up popped the parasol. A vigorous wave and then Amy was off in a different direction.

Mary watched her, feeling a strange intermingling of bewilderment and laughter. When Gracie returned, she probably ought to join her on one of her outings with Amy. She rather liked the girl.

A quick glance in both directions proved the road to be empty. She crossed and moments later knocked on a local deputy's door.

"Hullo?" The elderly man poked his head out. The scent of Colgate shaving cream wafted out and reminded Mary that she needed to get home and help Lou before dusk.

Shrugging off the thought, she straightened her shoulders and gave him a serious look. "Sir, is it true that a murderer has been released from your custody?"

"I highly doubt that." The door widened to reveal his bent structure.

Frowning, she held his gaze. "I've been told the man originally arrested for assault, the man I pointed out to you, is no longer under suspicion."

"Don't know how you heard those details but it's true. Mr. Langdon is no longer considered a suspect. We have a man who came forward and confessed. Is that all you needed today?"

Dumbly, she nodded. She turned and walked down the road, back to her horse, mulling over the deputy's words. It seemed rather convenient that a man confessed. *Too* convenient. And incredibly bothersome.

Did Mr. Langdon know she'd pointed him out as a suspect? She could only guess he did, and of course he knew she worked at Lou's ranch.... A shudder swept through her despite the summer warmth.

Suddenly she had an urge to hurry home, to check on Josie and share with Lou what she'd learned. But perhaps he knew. He was a man who, for all his smiles and carefree words, kept secrets.

She reached her horse and mounted quickly. Casting a look down the road, she felt sure the coast was clear and galloped out of town. She passed the Paiute settlement on the way and waved.

The sight of the dogs, the misplaced tents and the run-down people filled her with sadness. But for her Irish father and renegade mother, she might be weaving baskets for an income and living in a canvas tent that would never be her own.

The horse's even movements lulled her into deep thoughts of the past. She'd been thirteen when her mother dropped her off with Trevor's mom, at the house of ill repute she'd owned.

Although she'd known Trevor since she was a wee one, her mother's constant moving had kept them in sporadic touch. When her da had disappeared and the men in her mother's life had started looking at Mary, she'd dropped her off for safety with Trevor's mom and gone in search of Da.

That choice had forged a loyalty between Mary and Trevor that had kept her safe until she was eighteen. Until Trevor's mother had grown impatient with Mary's decision to be the house seamstress and nothing more. Until she'd seen the growing bond between her son and her friend's daughter. Until her jealousy had forced her to do the unthinkable....

Mary blinked and urged her horse to move faster, wishing the hot air against her skin could melt the memories that blistered her heart and twisted her stomach. She glanced at the sky. It must be nearing three o'clock. She would go home, make a meal, help Lou, and then she'd have to speak with Josie to explain what must happen soon.

Would the little girl understand?

Mary felt sure she wouldn't. Every day it seemed the

pressure on her shoulders grew heavier. It had taken Gracie leaving and Lou being home to make her see how much she longed for family. After her self-induced seclusion of twelve years, the need for family and belonging bludgeoned her senses and as Lou had said, twisted her priorities.

It had been wrong for her to try to keep Josie for so long. A little girl needed her mother and for all she knew, Josie's mother had been frantic with worry. Powerless to change anything since she was ill.

Oh, Lord, forgive me.

Keeping Josie from her mother was the biggest mistake Mary had ever made. How could she have been blind to it for so long? Thinking only of her own desires and not another's?

This must be fixed. Tomorrow she would leave with Lou and do what must be done. It was time to put her trust in the God who had saved her from wicked people, who had filled her with peace.

A hawk swooped ahead, gliding through the sky in search of food. Like that bird, God would care for her and tend to her needs. She must believe it.

And it started with thanks, something she'd sorely neglected since Lou had returned with his injury and since she'd been busy taking care of Josie.

The hawk disappeared from view, its majestic red-tipped wings spread in splendor against the azure sky. Mary lifted her face upward, feeling the graze of sunlight against her skin, and began a song to praise her King.

Her voice echoed, rising and falling, filling the desert around her, reaching, she hoped, the God she loved. As she neared the hidden trail that wound carefully to the ranch's secluded location, her voice tapered with the end of the song and she slowed the mare to a stop.

She took a deep breath. Filled her lungs with the scents of sage and pine, listening to the sounds of summer birds calling to each other across the rugged landscape.

As she sat there, another sound filtered through to her hearing, a different sound. A sound that didn't fit.

She froze, patting her mare to soothe the sudden dance she did with her hooves.

The sound came again. A steady clop, like the muted sounds of covered hooves.

Her breaths shortened as panic began to claw up her breastbone, rising and grabbing her, reaching to her throat and clutching it in an unbreakable vise.

Someone had followed her.

Chapter Twelve

Somehow Mary managed to keep calm and continue onward. She dodged the main, albeit camouflaged, trail and instead guided the horse down a steep embankment into a gnarled, woody area. The steep hills and shrubbery provided decent enough cover if she stayed within shadows and kept to the sides of the range, which in some places rose to over a thousand feet.

The ranch was nestled in a deserted area that was almost like a valley. The Steens Mountains loomed on one side, and the surrounding desert provided natural protection against human intruders. When Trevor had first brought her to the ranch, she'd been in shock from the kidnapping and hardly noticed her surroundings. As months passed, though, the encircling natural formations began to be her peace, to comfort and protect her. But they never did warm the chill in her soul.

It took a special kind of person to do that. She smiled as she navigated a particularly rough patch in her detour. Miss Alma's presence had changed the way Mary looked at life and though it took time, eventually she'd been able to trust others and find joy again.

Fear hadn't been her companion in so long that now

when it reappeared, she wasn't sure what to do. Praising God had helped…until she'd heard someone following her.

For the first time in years, her faith was being tested in a large, unanticipated way. She deliberately slowed her breathing, willing her heart rate to follow.

Nothing stood out, though. Just familiar horse noises from her mount. Once she was sure no one had followed her onto this new path, she forged ahead and willed the old memories to stay at bay.

"For God hath not given us a spirit of fear, but of power, love and a sound mind." She uttered the verse beneath her breath. And then she felt strong emotion welling within her, a hot arc of anger that someone dared follow her, that they even dared to make her afraid.

This was *her* home. Josie might be leaving soon, but until tomorrow, she was Mary's responsibility and she *would* keep her safe. Who knew where that stranger had gone who looked for her, but she would not allow him to trespass on her property. If he so much as tried to get in her front door, well…she wouldn't hesitate to use her derringer.

Her jaw set and she lengthened her stride. When she was certain she wasn't being followed anymore, she took a more direct route to the ranch. By the time she reached her home, the sun had dropped to the horizon and a cool breeze scooped and swirled around her.

Josie sat outside the house with her mother, weaving a basket.

Mary rode past, took care of the horse in the stable, then walked home. Josie looked up with a toothy smile. Rose's smile was in her eyes.

"You've been busy," Mary said, grabbing a rocking chair and pulling it near where Josie sat on the porch floor so she could reach and touch the little girl's hair, which glinted in the fading sunlight.

"I have many baskets to sell," Rose answered. Her hands moved steadily.

"You do not have to work anymore."

Her mother's eyes flickered before she looked down at her work. "It is something I've done since I was a small girl at my mother's side. I will pay my way."

Mary wanted to tell her mother that she didn't owe her anything. This home was free. But Josie watched them with bright eyes, and the subject was much too personal to air in front of little ears.

Instead, she shrugged. "My trip to town was fruitful. There are a few store areas that look as though they'd fit my needs." She'd discussed the ranch sale with her mother last night.

"And the cost?"

"I didn't find out yet." She shifted uncomfortably. Though she'd saved quite a bit in the past years, she wasn't sure it would be enough to open a new business, let alone rent a space for a baker. If she was going to own a business, it would be for something she loved to do. Something she knew she could excel at but would also fill a need in the town.

"Building a business often requires money," her mother said.

"I know." Mary sighed and smoothed the top of Josie's hair. "What did you two do today?"

"We made bunches of baskets. I found a little squirrel and almost caught it." Josie beamed up at her and Mary grinned.

"Excuse me…" Lou's deep drawl interrupted them.

She looked up and felt that odd catch in her stomach again. His hair had grown too long since the shooting. It gave him a wild, untamed look. The scruff on his jaw only lent to the dangerous edge he exuded and deepened the blue of his eyes.

"Yes?" She tried to swallow the dryness from her throat. Nerves prickled.

He didn't look at her mother or Josie but focused his gaze upon her, increasing the flame of anxiety that flickered through her body. "Just wanted to verify you'll give me my shave and trim after supper."

No, she wanted to yell. Instead, she found herself stuck nodding a wordless yes.

Every ounce of her felt caught in that magnetic gaze of his.

Finally, he looked away, and she could breathe again.

"Josie, pack your things tonight. We leave at first light," he said.

"Where are we going?"

"Tomorrow we're taking you to your mother." A strange catch in his voice tripped Mary's attention.

Was that pain traveling across his face? The emotion passed too quickly and once again his features settled into a carefree smile.

"Oh." Josie quieted beneath Mary's hand, which still rested on her head.

He shouldn't have broken the news to her like this. Mary frowned and guided Josie to rest her head against her leg. She stroked the little girl's hair. "Don't you want to see your mother?"

"I guess...." Her voice trailed off. "I just don't want to see *him.*"

"We're gonna take you straight to your mother. Only her. And I'm going to make sure you're completely safe before I leave." Lou's eyes darted to Mary before he squatted in front of Josie. "Your mother missed you and thought you were visiting relatives."

"She sent me away," Josie said in a very small voice.

Something bitter and sharp pricked at Mary. She swallowed hard and tucked a hair behind Josie's ear. She felt her mother's gaze.

"I know, sweetheart." Empathy filled Lou's tone. "But she didn't want you to be gone forever, just to visit family. And now that we've found her and I'm better, Miss Mary and I are going to take you home so your mommy won't be sad anymore."

Josie turned her face into Mary's skirt and mumbled something.

"Sometimes a mother makes a very big mistake," Rose said quietly. "It takes a wise little girl to forgive and offer a second chance."

"I'm not gonna go." Josie pulled away, and Mary caught a glimpse of the stubborn glare she aimed toward Lou.

"Mary, please make sure she's packed for tomorrow," he said in a soft voice. He gave Josie a tender smile before looking to Mary. "I'll be ready after supper." He turned on his heel and strode away.

True to her word, Mary showed up after the dishes were done and Rose had taken Josie back to the house for sleep. He watched from the sitting room window as she came up the porch and paused before the front door. She adjusted her skirt and appeared to take a deep breath. Her face looked flushed and her eyes glimmered.

Was she nervous?

Her body language said so.

He stepped away from the window, rubbing the back of his neck. If there was another way to save her this discomfort, he would. Unfortunately, James was busy checking their route for tomorrow and making sure everything was in order while they were gone. He didn't have time to be a barber, too.

The idea of making Mary uncomfortable bothered him deeply, but after spending these weeks here, he realized he'd done wrong in keeping her so isolated. Seeing her with Josie, it had become obvious she loved children. Maybe even wanted a family of her own. Sometimes he worried he'd stolen that from her by keeping her so comfortable at the ranch that she rarely left.

Yes, she'd needed time to heal from her kidnapping, but that didn't seem reason enough now for her isolation. A deep compulsion drove him to do something more, make sure she was okay before he left Harney County for good. But what could he do?

The front door creaked and then there was the click of it closing. Mary appeared in the doorway, her hair neat and shining, her face devoid of emotion. He gestured to the chair near the window where he'd set the supplies. "Have you ever done this?"

"A long time ago."

Her voice wobbled, betraying what her face hid.

A fierce surge of protectiveness shot through him. And uncertainty, because something about him was making her nervous lately. Was she feeling what he was? That could be dangerous for both of them.

The thought soured his positive feelings and turned his voice curt. "Just don't cut me, then. Try to make things even in the back."

"I'll do my best."

He settled into the chair. At least he wouldn't have to see her face, look into her eyes. The deep calm of them had always pulled at him, drawn him in a way he'd hated. But as her fingers combed through his hair, wetting and straightening, he realized that being in this vulnerable position was infinitely worse. Silently groaning, he forced himself to ignore the warm strength of her fingers against his nape.

She worked in silence for several long, torturous minutes. The sound of the scissors snipping took the place of any words they might've shared.

"Have you packed?" he asked at last. Staying quiet seemed worthless when there was something to be said.

"Not yet." Her voice, a lyrical blend of sound, floated over him.

"You should do that. Make sure Josie is ready, too."

"I will." Now she sounded defensive. "She needs time to adjust. We should have given her that."

"She had to know she would go home eventually," he pointed out, despite the guilt twisting his gut.

His head tugged back a little more roughly than normal.

"For some reason, she doesn't want to return home. Don't you find that suspicious?"

"Yep."

"And yet you'll still send her?"

"I told you that I'll be arranging for her protection, but can we talk about this when you're not armed with scissors?" He tilted his head to meet her rather serious gaze. When he winked at her, the color in her face deepened. Yep, definitely not immune to him.

Despite the inconvenience of this unfortunate attraction, he settled back in the chair again with a satisfied feeling. He could handle things. Get Josie out of danger. Find the shooter. Settle James and Mary before he moved on.

Based on that telegram he'd picked up in town, he had a couple of options.

The clink of the knife against the washbowl drew him out of his thoughts. Mary, armed with a towel and shaving cream, hovered in front of him.

"Ready?" she asked.

He nodded and closed his eyes as she dabbed the cool cream across his skin. Then there was the rasp of the razor against his throat. She moved quietly and smoothly, making no conversation. Her scent hovered just beneath the scent of his shaving cream.

As she worked, the unease in his gut spread. Ever since that day he'd seen her in the valley with Josie… This wasn't good. Attractions were best left alone. Then again, sometimes all it took was a kiss to know the woman he'd been mooning over wasn't for him. There'd been a couple like that, women he'd thought might ease his loneliness, maybe help him forget Sarah and Abby.

They never did.

And Mary, well, he didn't even know if she'd ever been kissed. He cracked a lid. Her eyes were focused somewhere around his chin and her brows narrowed in concentration. His mouth twitched. Her attention shifted to him.

Her gaze lingered a little too long before darting away. He shut his eyes but couldn't temper the emotions ricocheting through him, nor the knowledge of what he'd just seen.

Mary felt drawn to him.

Something deeper and more elemental than mere attraction rushed through him. The emotion settled in his chest, patient and alert, waiting for expression.

He forced steady breaths and held perfectly still while Mary continued the shave. His biceps bunched when her skirt brushed against him. Mouth dry, he waited.

For what, he wasn't sure, but suddenly things changed. Moved to a different place. He opened his eyes again. Mary looked at him, soft lips pursed. What would it be like to kiss her? She, who seemed so unreachable?

"Can you turn your head just so?" Her palm cupped his chin.

He reached up and encircled her arm, resting his fingers against the warmth of her inner wrist. Her eyes widened. She began to pull away, but he stood and slid his hand down to hers, lacing his fingers within hers. With his other hand he reached for the towel and roughly brushed it against his lips.

He tossed it to the ground.

"Wh-what are you doing?"

Her stammer did nothing to ease the pulse hammering through him. No, those wide eyes only beckoned him closer. To know exactly what he was dealing with.

"Are you afraid of me?" he rasped.

Her eyes held his, so deep, so full of mystery. "No," she whispered.

His chest tightened and he reached for her, pulling her close to him, drawing her lips to his, searching yet careful, probing yet holding back.

Until he felt her resistance crumble.

When she responded, that band inside his chest snapped and he became voracious, longing, wishing for something that seemed so far beyond his reach. *Home.* The scent of flowers and sage swirled around him in a heady, pulsating rush.

He was the first to pull away. He forced himself to separate from her. Her cheeks were flushed, her eyes burned dark and fathomless.

That kiss had been exquisite. Incredible.

The absolute biggest mistake of his life.

Chapter Thirteen

Mary couldn't stop trembling.

Lou had pulled away and was busy toweling dry the rest of his face and neck. "How much is left to shave?" he asked.

"I completed the task." Her lips burned, but she didn't dare touch them in front of him. Would he see how she shook, how unsettled she felt? She stepped back and bumped against the window.

"Mary...I shouldn't have done that." He faced her and the look of chagrin on his features nearly crumpled her. Was it so bad to have kissed her, then? "We have too much going on to dabble in romantic affections. Why, this place could be sold in a week, and then we'll probably never see each other again." He kept talking, his words swirling through her mind with an odd energy. Each time his lips moved she felt something inside her grow more brittle and finally, when she could stand no more of his pointless ramblings, she stepped away from the window and fixed him a very pointed look.

"*You* kissed me," she said briskly, thankful her voice did not betray her shakiness. "Do not pull a 'we' into this."

"But you liked it."

At that, her cheeks caught fire. A boldness in his bright blue eyes made her think he wasn't as chagrined as she'd previously thought. "My feelings on the subject are not important."

"Oh, but they are. Tell me, Mary, *did* you like it?"

She wanted to be anywhere but here. If only she could escape, but with her back to the window, there was nowhere to go besides past Lou, and with that curious look on his face, there was no telling what he might do. She squirmed beneath his scrutiny.

"It was…" She paused and then settled on a word. "Enlightening."

His arms crossed his chest as he grinned. "How so?"

"Like s-stumbling on the right recipe for piecrust," she stuttered. The conceited man was still smirking, broad enough to give her a hankering to toss an egg at his face. She wanted to tell him so, but restraint held her lips closed. Instead, she settled for a dark scowl.

He busted into a loud laugh, the kind she hadn't heard from him in too long.

"I'm glad, Mary, real glad you liked it. It worried me a bit that you might be scared and all." Despite the smile, his gaze searched her.

Affronted, she felt her scowl deepening. "I am no longer the young woman brought to you on the threshold of collapse."

"Very true." His gaze dropped to her lips.

She felt that look to the marrow of her bones. Swallowing hard, she fixed her gaze on him. "As a matter of fact, I am looking into opportunities at this very moment. There are several available stores in Burns and I believe I can rent one and run a business."

"What kind of venture are you thinking of?" Lou tossed his towel to the chair. It slipped to the floor.

She bent to pick up at the towel the same time he did.

"I reckon she could do just 'bout anything" came a voice from the doorway.

Hurriedly, Lou straightened, the towel in his hand, and as he did, a folded paper fluttered to the floor. Perhaps from his shirt pocket? She plucked the note off the floor while Lou and James spoke of the trip tomorrow.

The paper between her fingers looked suspiciously official. Could there be more news on who'd shot Lou? Perhaps the perpetrator had been caught. Should she open it? Nibbling her lower lip, she peeked at the men.

They spoke in hushed voices, bodies facing away from her. She turned her back to them and pretended to organize the shaving utensils while an internal war ensued. Unlike Gracie, she didn't go around eavesdropping or telling people what she thought.

She was careful. Considerate… Her nose wrinkled. Boring.

Yes, Gracie was fun and alive and she, Mary, led a very careful, very structured life, with no room for surprises. Not until she'd brought Josie home.

The letter mocked her, its flap open just enough for her to see the typewritten note inside. Biting her lower lip, she cast the men one more look before positioning her body at an angle best designed to hide her sneakiness.

Her heart knocked about wildly in her chest. Quickly she unfolded the paper and scanned its contents. As she did, her pulse ratcheted until she could no longer quite contain her breathing.

How dare he? Throat tight and pained, she very neatly folded the paper, creasing the lines just so. Her fingers shook as she pressed on the paper.

"That right, Mary?"

Startled, she sucked in a lungful and pivoted, the letter

clutched in her right hand, which she dropped to her side. "I missed what you said."

"James says you should start a restaurant. I agree. Your baking is superb," said Lou. The rat. The coward.

Betrayer.

All those names, and more, hopscotched through her mind and stuck there. A pounding took up residence in her skull, along with the words of the letter. He'd known. This entire time, he'd known and not said one word. Speechless, she could only stand there as her skin set aflame with anger.

"Well, now—" James scratched his head "—I do believe she's angry."

"About what?" Lou scoffed.

"Iffn' I knew, I'd say so, but women get me all gandered up. I can't tell left from right."

Lou's cheeks bunched. "Nah, Mary only gets angry once a year."

Her eyes stung.

"Hoooeeee, I'm hightailin' it out of here." James gave her a once-over, then his mustache twitched. "Just came by to say things are all set for you leaving tomorrow. I'll take you to the train in the morning and the bureau is getting you some hotel rooms for one night only. Time enough to find Josie's mom and then skedaddle." He edged backward.

Mary fought tears, refusing to show her weakness. James disappeared from the doorway and Lou turned to her, forehead crinkled in a charmingly deceptive way.

"What's going on? A delayed reaction to the kiss?" He swiped the towel from where it hung around his neck and tossed it to the chair. "It's better to talk now than to hold things inside."

The letter lay in her palm. She could throw it at him in

some infantile display of temper. Demand he answer her. But she held back.

"Are you going to give me the silent treatment like you did the first year you were here? I tolerated it then, and even a few years ago when you got mad about your mama, but I certainly won't take it now." He advanced, dangerous intent sizzling in his expression.

Before he could completely crowd her against the wall, she squared her shoulders, summoned self-will and shoved the paper between them. He stopped. Glanced at it, then to her, his face shuttered.

"Where did you get that?"

"Does it matter?" she managed to squeeze out from beneath stiff lips.

"Sure it does." Faster than the pop of bacon in a pan, he snatched it from her fingers and opened the page. He looked at it briefly before returning it to his shirt pocket. His eyes found hers. The intensity of them disturbed her. "Did you read this before or after our kiss?"

She shook her head.

"Before or after?" he repeated.

"After."

"Good." He started to turn away.

"Good?" she said needlessly.

"Yep."

She reached for his shoulder but he kept going. Desperate with rage, she darted in front of him. The door waited behind her.

"How dare you," she said.

"Me?" He had the audacity to look surprised. "It's not against the law to apply for new employment."

"We rely on you. And this letter references your inquiry over two months ago." Suddenly words filled her mouth and she did not dare let them dry up like the desert outside, unsaid, unplanted. "Plans needed to be made, then. How much time do we have now? Have you any clue how long it takes to start a business? The money involved? The time and effort and ingenuity?"

His brows lowered. "I never planned for you to not be taken care of, Mary. And you bought Trevor's house, so I didn't see the problem in selling the ranch. I'm happy to give you whatever money you need."

"Yes, I'm sure you are. So that you may gallivant off to wherever you're going. Asia, correct? And what will you do there?" Her hand flung through the air, narrowly missing his chin. He stepped back, a bewildered expression on his face. She didn't care. "You must realize what sort of position you have put us in. It was unthinking and…and unfair." Her voice caught.

Oh, no, she was going to cry. Swallowing hard, she fought the angry tears.

"Mary, everything is going to be okay. You don't have to worry." He moved as if to hug her, but she put out a hand to stop him.

"I am not worried. I am angry. Very, very angry."

Shaking and not sure how much longer she could hold her inopportune tears, she turned and fled.

Lou's wound pulsed with pain. He pressed on the scarred area with his palm. With his other hand he shoved the letter farther into his pocket, wincing when the front door slammed shut.

Leaving that letter in his pocket hadn't been the smartest thing, but at least today's telegram hadn't fallen out. For a second he'd thought Mary was going to hit him.

Sweet, docile Mary.

Lately the woman acted as though something had been set on fire behind her. Anger and defiance marked everything she said. A natural occurrence as she grew more comfortable expressing herself, but still, it was uncomfortable for him.

Unbidden, the memory of her arms around him crept past his defenses. He blinked, willing the sensation away.

"James," he shouted.

No answer. Shrugging, he gathered up the shaving supplies and stomped out of the sitting room. The hallway gleamed in the darkening evening, thanks to Mary's cleaning skills. She kept up the house better than most.

Shining floors, delicious dinners. She'd make some man a fine wife. His mouth soured at the thought. He put the shaving supplies away, then called for James again.

Still no sound. Had the old man gone home? He lived in a little house down a ways on the property, near the bunkhouse where hands stayed when they'd been doing more ranching. Not anymore.

With the way people were clearing out in this county, the town of Burns might be lucky to survive. Logging seemed to be going well, however, especially with the railroads spreading across the country.

Mary should thank him for pushing her out of the nest, so to speak.

Yet, as he opened the front door and stepped into the approaching dusk, twinges of conscience pinged him. He closed the door and then clomped to the stairs. In the distance, two silhouettes stood against the horizon.

The shadows turned and he noticed the skirts. Mary and her mother? Another problem he wished he could solve for her. If Mary knew her mother had been the one who'd told Mendez where she lived twelve years ago, the one who'd made the kidnapping possible, then she wouldn't let Rose live here. He debated telling Mary about her mother's part but decided against it. What good could come of exposing such a thing? Only more hurt for Mary. Best to just keep an eye on Rose and make sure she didn't put Mary in harm's way.

He went down the porch steps.

Maybe the ladies had seen James. Besides, he needed a reason to look Mary in the eyes again, to reassure himself that her feelings weren't hurt by his dismissal of the kiss.

After all, he had plans. So did she. There was no room for fickle emotions. Heart thumping, he strode toward Mary and her mother. They began running to him. As they neared, his stomach plunged at the expression on their faces.

"What's wrong?" he asked quickly, noting the glazed appearance of Rose's eyes.

"It's Josie." Mary's features were drawn. "She's missing."

Chapter Fourteen

"Missing?" A dumbfounded expression slacked Lou's handsome features.

"Yes," Mary snapped. "Mother and I are going to mount up and look for her near the ranch house. She has a fondness for the cows."

"James and I will track her," he asserted, seeming to snap out of his daze.

"He is already looking for her footprints, though darkness will soon make that impossible. Please search the house." She refused to let her voice tremble. Time for that later. "Let's go, Mother."

"Wait." He stopped her with a palm to her shoulder. The intimacy of the touch only served to remind her of what had transpired during his shave. "You and I'll search the property. We know it better. Rose can search inside the house."

"A good plan," she reluctantly admitted, forcing her mind to the present, forcing her lips to stop remembering his kiss.

Lou's hand moved off her shoulder. He gave Rose a stern look. "I'll know if something goes missing."

Mary gasped. "That's a hateful thing to say."

"I am not offended." Rose nodded to him and set off to his house, her shoulders slumped despite her quick pace.

Angry and afraid, Mary whirled away from Lou and ran for the stables. His even breaths behind her told her he kept up easily. Feeling bitter and not liking the words in her heart, she ignored him and kept going.

"You know your mother can't be trusted," he said.

Her chest burned. She bit her lip as a stitch formed in her side. Forced to slow down, she refused to look at the man beside her. The employer who'd been hiding his secrets for two months. What else did he hide? "What does it matter to you? You are leaving, and I choose to keep my mother by my side."

"Regardless of what you may think, I do care for you. Mary—"

"Josie is missing." She whirled. "Until we find her, this conversation can wait."

"That's how it's going to be? Ignoring important things?"

Pulse racing, she glared at him. "Yes. Josie is more important than anything else right now."

A serious look crossed his face. "You're right, but don't think we won't talk." He strode ahead of her and reached the stables first.

Inside, the air was musky and warm. A few horses nickered at their approach. Harnesses jingled and hooves rustled against the straw-strewn floor. She didn't particularly like being in a stable with its overarching odors of hay, manure and mildew, preferring the outdoor air instead, but she'd been in here enough to know which horses she rode the best.

She found a spotted pinto she'd ridden in the past and led her out of the stall. After tying her up, she went to the tack room for her saddle, a smaller version of Lou's.

"Let me help you." His breath tickled her ear and did nothing to stop the nervous queasiness taking hold of her. Before she could pull the saddle down, he'd reached over and lifted it off its hook.

She followed him back to the pinto, hand pressed against her stomach. The sun's rays were already weak and disappearing. A few more minutes and then darkness. Where was Josie? Mary shuddered. Many dangers existed in the desert. How could a little girl protect herself?

Maybe she wasn't alone, though.

That possibility frightened her even more. She watched Lou saddling her horse, thankful for his calm thoroughness when her hands were shaking so badly. "Do you think..." She trailed off, stomach twisting.

"Think what?" Lou tightened the stirrups and faced her. Deepening light shadowed his face into planes and angles.

"Maybe someone took her. I—I thought someone might be following me this afternoon."

"And you're just now telling me?" His mouth arced downward.

"If that man has her...I need a weapon." She'd left her derringer at home. No more. From now on she'd carry it everywhere.

He studied her silently, then turned and disappeared into the tack room. He emerged moments later, a small sheath-covered knife nestled in his palm. "Take this. Use it if you need to.... In the eyes is where you should aim first, if possible." He paused. "You should have told me about being followed."

She slipped the blade from his hand, thumb smoothing over its fine ivory hilt. "There is a chance it was only imagination."

"Always tell me everything. I'll keep you safe." Sincerity rang in his voice. His eyes shone with it.

Swallowing back the boulder-size lump in her throat, Mary mounted the pinto. "That is a fine thing to say, Lou Riley, but the truth of the matter is that in months you will be gone and then I shall be in charge of protecting myself." She secured the knife in the pocket of her skirt and urged the horse around until she faced the entrance.

A gentle nudge and she soared past Lou and into the deepening twilight, where shadows canvassed the surroundings. Feeling desperate and a little angry, Mary headed toward the east section of the property.

How dare he say that he'd protect her? Fill her with hope and promises when he planned to leave. And to talk that way of her mother… She growled. It felt good, that primal vocal expression reverberating around her. Thankfully, the pinto didn't seem to notice.

Once they were a good ways from the stables, Mary slowed the horse and began scanning the shrubs and dips in the land. She wanted to call for Josie, but if the girl had been abducted, that might alert someone. On the other hand, if Josie was lost, she'd be frightened, and the sound of someone calling would be soothing.

Biting her cheek, she slid off the pinto and walked carefully, heart thudding in her chest. *Please, God, let us find her.*

If only she'd told Lou about the strange sensation of being followed sooner, but the truth was that she'd forgotten. Being near him, cutting his hair, shaving him, that breath-stealing kiss…and now someone might have their sweet little girl.

She fingered the blade and continued searching.

Lou grumbled as he readied his horse and then cantered to the west, worry over Josie riding his shoulders. He hated that Mary was right. Within a few months he might be gone, sent to Asia on special assignment. Possibly never to return. The thought of that foreign, exotic land of spice and music usually excited him, but at the moment, in the darkening night, searching for a lost little girl, he could only imagine a life without Mary to return to.

Her presence was ingrained in this place.

He slid off the saddle and cupped his hands around his mouth. "Josie!"

Insects and a stiff breeze answered. The unyielding line of mountains fuzzed on the horizon, shimmering with the setting sun.

"Josie," he yelled again.

If she had been kidnapped, his yell might rustle up the kidnappers into making a mistake, maybe some noise. Though, if they were on horses, which was likely, then they were probably long gone. His gut clenched at the thought.

Had someone actually followed Mary? She wasn't one to imagine things like that. Neither hysterical nor prone to fits. Jaw tightening, he strained to see the shrubs around him, looking for odd shapes or movement. His horse jingled beside him.

"Josie, answer if you can hear me." Feeling grim, he trudged ahead. His shoulders bent against the chilly breeze. Now that the sun was down, temperatures dropped quickly in the desert. Josie might be shivering somewhere, alone.

Memories rushed in on him and he bent over, gasping for breath. He wouldn't think of it, not now. Not when he had a different little girl to try to save. Straightening, he gulped deep breaths until he could breathe easier.

Then he continued walking, calling, searching the moonlit horizon. A few times the scurry of a small animal startled him into thinking he'd found the girl, only to watch the form materialize into something not human.

No giving up, he told himself. Hadn't he survived a

war and deaths? Perilous conditions that took the best of men? Ears pricked, he stopped and listened for any unnatural sounds.

The slightest wisp of something carried on the wind. Holding his breath, he smoothed his horse's neck as he listened.

There it was again. To the left. Leading the stallion around, Lou went in that direction and continued to call the girl. As he neared, the sound sharpened into staccato sniffles. A relief so profound it nearly buckled his knees rushed through him. Gripping the reins, he hurried to a shrub that looked irregular beneath the moon's iridescent glow.

"Josie." His feet swished through the grasses until he reached the child, who sat hunched over, head buried in her drawn-up knees.

The overwhelming urge to scoop her up and hold her near his heart almost did him in, but he refrained, choosing instead to kneel in front of her.

"We've been looking for you."

She didn't look up. In the silvery light from the moon, he could see her hair matted in places. Her cries cut into the night, unnatural and heartbreaking.

Clearing his throat, Lou tried again. "Josie, honey, it's time to go back. Miss Mary is real worried. She, Rose and Mr. James have been looking all over for you."

The girl mumbled something, then started sobbing as if her best friend had died. Should he just reach out and grab her? Pick her up and carry her?

Throat constricting, he put out a hand to pat her head. She scooted back, out of his reach, faster than he could blink.

Frustration welled up. Frowning, he sat back on his haunches. "Listen. You either come with me now or I'm going to leave you out here. It's getting cold. I bet you're hungry. Is that what you want? To be stuck out in the desert all night long…?"

He cringed as his words trailed off, hollow echoes broken by Josie's quieting cries. He could almost see Mary's disapproving look at his tactics.

He gentled his voice. "Come home, honey. We've got cookies and—"

"You're just trying to get rid of me." The pouty words made his lips twitch. Better than her sobs.

"So you ran away, huh?"

The look she gave him was far too old for a five-year-old, and angry, angrier than he'd anticipated.

"I'm not going back. Ever." She promptly stuck her forehead against her knees again.

Sighing, Lou moved closer. This time when he put his hand on her head, she didn't try to escape. "Your mama misses you. We went over this before."

"Why can't you bring her here, where we'll be safe?" An earnest expression crossed Josie's face.

"Safe from what?" Lou peered at her, instinct rearing. He was missing something. Something important.

Her voice dropped. "You know."

"Josie, you've gotta answer me on this." He turned her shoulders to face him, marveling at how small she was, how tiny. How much would he have given to see his Abby grow up. She'd be thirteen now. His breathing snagged. Almost a woman.

"What, Mister Lou?"

He focused on Josie's eyes, that rare purple the color of a mountain violet. "Who dropped you in the desert? Who left you there?"

Her face scrunched, dirt tear trails zigzagging down her cheeks. "I don't know. Mommy gave me tea and a kiss. Then I woke up all by myself…." She looked away. "I was all alone, and I was so thirsty. I was cold." Her face wrinkled up even more and hurriedly Lou rubbed the top of her head.

"Okay, sweetheart, okay." Someone wanted her dead. But who? Why? He'd get to the bottom of it somehow. "Let's go home."

He got to his feet, then bent and picked her up. She was light and didn't resist as he feared she would. Instead, he felt her cheek against his shoulder, her arms around his neck.

"I'm hungry, Mister Lou."

"That's what happens when you run away." But he patted her back to soften the words.

He walked carefully toward the stallion, who stood patiently for him. Holding her close, he took the reins and started in the direction of the ranch. They'd ride in a bit. The girl was tired, her body boneless in his arms.

"I talked to God," she said suddenly, her voice a mere whisper.

"You did?" His own voice cracked a bit.

"I asked Him to send someone and He did."

"Oh…well, that's good." Nice to know God answered some prayers.

"Do you talk to God ever?" She yawned against his neck.

"Once in a while."

"Miss Mary says He likes it. That He gets lonely and is always waiting to listen. She told me He'd help when I was in trouble. She was telling the truth, right, Mister Lou?"

Funny how a sleepy kid could jabber so much. Might be time to stick her on the horse. He lifted her away from his body and set her in the saddle. "Hold on," he said gruffly.

He mounted behind her, then situated her to be comfortable for the ride back, and safe.

"Was Miss Mary telling the truth?" Her voice drifted upward from where she lounged against him. "Does God hear me?"

Good question. One he couldn't answer honestly.

"Mister Lou. Does God hear us?"

"Uh—"

"Was Miss Mary telling the truth?"

He wished he knew. "Go to sleep, honey."

"But does God hear me?"

"I found you, didn't I?" he said, hoping that would do. Mary filled this child's head with nonsense, the kind of truths he used to hinge his faith on, but he knew better now.

Yet tonight…on all these acres of land, he'd found Josie. Scared but unharmed. What did that mean? And if God cared enough to save her not once, but twice, then where had He been when Lou's family was dying? Why hadn't He saved them?

Heart weighted with questions and arms heavy with a snoring bundle of warmth, he headed home.

Chapter Fifteen

"You're traveling *alone?*" Miss Alma readjusted her colorful feathered hat. "Are you sure that's wise, Mary?"

It was early morning. Lou waited in the wagon with Josie who, despite the bumpy ride into town, remained fast asleep. The poor girl was no doubt exhausted from last night's antics. James had needed to go to the post office before he took them to the train and she'd decided to stop in at the dry-goods store for thimbles. Mary encountered Miss Alma by the pincushions. There were only two, and the sweet lady appeared to be debating over them until she noticed Mary behind her.

It took only moments for her to discover Mary's plans and now she studied her with a suspicious look in her bright eyes.

"Not really alone," Mary amended. She scanned the shelves above the cushions for some durable thimbles. She'd forgotten hers at home. "Josie will be with us."

"And on your way home?"

Her cheeks heated. She avoided Miss Alma's gaze.

"Really, Mary." Miss Alma bustled closer and laid a gentle hand on Mary's arm. Her voice lowered. "You must be more careful with your reputation. I only say that out of concern."

Mary met her friend's gaze. "Thank you, but there really is no other way." She'd thought about asking her mother to chaperone but had decided against that. Especially after Lou had practically accused Rose of stealing. And James was needed at the ranch.

There was no one else.

She patted Miss Alma's hand. "Please don't worry. I hardly think my reputation could be more tarnished than it is."

"Oh, pishposh." Her elderly friend let out an unladylike snort. The hand that had been on Mary's shoulder flapped, dodging through the air, waving away Mary's comment as if a pesky fly. "People here love you. We appreciate your goods at our events, your gentle spirit and the herbs you bring to the store. I am simply thinking of your future good. I wasn't going to say anything but—" she leaned forward conspiratorially "—a certain young man has been asking for you."

Mary felt the blood drain from her face and gripped the shelf. "Does he…does he have strangely colored eyes?"

"Oh, my, no. Brown as a log." Miss Alma tittered. "I won't say who he is but he's well respected and a kind young man."

"I'm getting quite old. Rather on the shelf." Mary pulled a wry face, which made Miss Alma giggle.

"Now, don't you worry. Every man is young to me. He'd do well by you. Come to our summer picnic, my dear. Bring your goodies. Something chocolate."

Mary smiled. She adored chocolate, but it was expensive to buy. However, if chocolate made her merry and soft like Miss Alma, then perhaps she should experiment a wee bit with some new recipes.

"Miss Mary? Time to go." James's gruff voice broke her thoughts. He came around the dry goods and stopped suddenly. A look of horror crossed his face.

She stepped forward. "Are you okay?"

"James." A high-pitched note, more akin to a squeal, escaped Miss Alma's lips.

Surprised, Mary looked at her friend. A becoming blush colored her cheeks.

"I've been waiting for you to come by my house and repair my sink. I fixed a special pie for you just this morning." Miss Alma bustled between James and her. "Mary, darling, take care. I shall be praying fervently for you and that sweet little girl." Miss Alma hooked James by the elbow and led him toward the spooled thread.

Mary stood dumbfounded for a moment, and then she laughed. Well, she hadn't seen this coming, but Miss Alma looked perfect on James's arm. Or rather, he on her arm. Chuckling, she scooped up a thimble for herself and then searched until she found a child's size.

The trip would be long and arduous for Josie. Perhaps a stitched doily might turn Josie's attention and leave her with a keepsake. She palmed the thimbles and headed for the counter.

After picking out penny treats and paying for everything, she stepped into the early-morning sunshine. Wispy clouds drifted across the surface of the sky, rippling the sunbeams and providing snatches of cover from summer rays. A brisk wind picked up dirt and swirled it around her skirt. Covering her eyes, she spied Lou's wagon across the road. Lou lounged in the front, hat pulled over his face, most likely sleeping.

Once at the train station, they'd board the Union Pacific short line. It had been years since she'd ridden on a train. Prickles bumped across her skin. She did not relish the close quarters she would share with strangers.

Returning Josie was a necessity, though. Her heart quailed at the thought and the thimbles dug into her palms. Not only must she part with the sweet girl who'd become entrenched in her heart, but she must suffer riding with Lou.

The ride to town had proved easy enough. Lou and James discussed matters of all sorts, from selling the ranch to the government's plans regarding prohibition. As they spoke, Mary kept finding herself torn between staring at Josie, memorizing her sleep-peaceful features, to watching Lou and the movements of his mouth.... Had he really kissed her?

Her fingers moved to her lips.

It hadn't been her first kiss, but it had been the only one she'd enjoyed. Sleep had eluded her last night, for memories had risen unbidden to the surface of her subconscious. They'd invaded her sleep, dreams from long ago. From childhood. And then nightmares.

She should have expected those. After all, the only kisses she'd ever experienced had been forced upon her by rough and ungodly men. Though they had not assaulted her, for it would have diminished her worth, they'd nevertheless taken liberties no man should take with a woman. One week of terror when she'd been kidnapped.... It had ruined her image of men for life. Or so she'd thought.

The past years had been healing, but not until yesterday, when Lou had kissed her, had she realized that maybe she could move on from what had happened so long ago. Perhaps the evils Mendez and his cohorts had perpetrated upon her no longer had the power to bind her spirit.

For that knowledge alone, she should thank Lou. And yet she felt as though he'd betrayed her somehow. As if he'd offered the most delectable dessert, waved it beneath her nose, then snatched it back.

Her throat closed and she glanced away from Lou's wagon, down the street, watching as the town awoke. Mrs. Hartley swept the walk outside her fabric store. Others drove or rode past, on their way to various employments.

This was her home.

No matter what happened with the ranch, this place remained hers. God had brought her to this town, and it had been here where she'd found healing. Inhaling deeply, she relished the scents of the restaurant next door and the sage always present in her beloved desert.

"Let's git on with it." James burst out of the store, Miss Alma on his heels.

"But won't you come pick up your pie, at least?"

"I don't want nothin' to do with it." He spun around, right in the middle of the road, and pointed a finger at Miss Alma. Right at her nose actually, effectively stopping her in her tracks. "You leave me alone...you...you confounded woman." He threw his hands up in the air and stomped off toward the wagon.

Lou leaned forward, elbows on his knees, and squinted at them. Mary looked both ways and then hustled to the center of the road, where Miss Alma still stood.

Gently she laid a hand on Miss Alma's shoulder. "Are you okay?"

"Oh, me?" She turned and patted Mary's hand. "Don't worry, my dear. He'll come around." Her hand went to her heart, and she let out what could only be described as a lovelorn sigh. "He's a handsome fellow."

Mary tried not to gape.

"Well, then." Miss Alma patted Mary's hand again and then removed it from her shoulder, where it had lingered, paralyzed by Miss Alma's frightening proclamation. She dropped her arm, trying to assess this odd situation that had seemingly appeared out of nowhere.

"He will come around, no doubt," repeated Miss Alma with brisk optimism. "You take care and don't let that Lou Riley ruin your reputation."

With a swish of her skirts, she left Mary in the middle of the road and bustled back to the walkway.

The trip to Portland was torturous. Worse than the time Lou had been captured during the Great War and thrown into a dank dungeon for weeks. He'd chosen to travel by train because he hadn't wanted to run his tin lizzie over the highways. His Model T was relatively close to the ground and it was too easy for rocks and other debris to lodge up underneath it. That was why he'd insisted they take the UP's short line. He didn't normally mind riding the railroad. He knew all the switches they'd need to make, and at which towns, but traveling with a little girl and a woman proved disastrous for his peace of mind.

For one, Josie didn't stop talking. And she wanted to sit by the window. Being it was the last time he'd see her, he obliged, but that forced him next to Mary. Somehow she managed to still smell like flowers and sage, despite the cramped quarters and dusty stops. She wouldn't look him in the eye and every time he thought about making conversation, he changed his mind.

He was planning on leaving. Mary deserved better, someone who could offer the home she wanted, the love she needed. Sometimes he thought she felt something for him, maybe even love. But he wasn't sure and not knowing could take a man down perilous mental routes.

He hid his uncomfortable, traitorous feelings by doing paperwork. Mary stayed busy sewing all sorts of things.

He'd see her fingers flying and find himself intrigued by the motion.

There was a grace to her movements, a slender fragility in her hands that belied the briskness of her stitches. She urged Josie to sew, even offering a fancy little doodad for her finger, but the little girl alternated between sleeping, yapping and sitting in stony silence.

Finally, after the uncomfortable sleeping arrangements and smells and noises, they arrived at Portland's Union Station.

"*Ewww,* what's that smell?" Josie wrinkled her nose.

Lou hooked a finger into the collar of her dress to keep her close by. "You should be used to it."

"The odor is strong," Mary remarked, moving closer as passengers jostled around her. She clutched her luggage to her chest.

"Here, let me take that." Before she could protest, he hefted her suitcase from her arms and tilted Josie toward her. "You hold the boy's hand."

Josie giggled. "I'm a girl."

"You are?" He waggled his brows at her, enjoying the mood of the city with all its quick pace and noise. Various smells permeated the air.

Musky river odors dominated the brisk breeze, padded with other scents that weren't altogether unpleasant. Sounds reverberated all around, talking, clanging from streetcars, horns from automobiles…the city at last. Smiling, Lou gestured to a spot on the sidewalk near the Romanesque clock tower, the depot's glory piece.

"We'll go over there to talk," he yelled. Ushering them ahead of him, he guided them through the crowd to a quiet spot against the wall of the building.

Mary's eyes were wary. "It's changed."

"How long since you've been here?"

"Since I was a wee girl. Perhaps twenty years?" Her brow furrowed.

"Back then, the roads used to turn to mud from all the rain. They had to build wooden sidewalks to get out of the mess. Now look at it." He waved at the busyness around them. "Electric streetcars are the way to travel now."

"I like the red ones," Josie chimed in, beaming a smile at him.

He couldn't resist smiling back, though there was the slightest pain to it. In a very short time, this charming sprite would leave them for good. He knelt down in front of her. "Did you take a lot of red cars?"

"My mommy likes them, when she feels good. We went up really, really high." She leaned toward him, eyes wide and bright. "I wanted to touch the sky."

She obviously meant the Council Crest streetcar. It was a popular attraction, taking people from Portland into the highest parts of the hills around them. He knew the feeling of wanting to reach too high. And the rip of the spiral downward.

Throat tight, he touched her face briefly. Then he stood and scanned the station and the roads leading out of it.

"What next?" Mary asked.

He noted her knuckles white on the handle of her luggage. "We've got to get Josie home. That's first on the list. Then I have a meeting with the head agent on my case this evening at the Portland Hotel. The bureau has reserved rooms for us. Did you bring a dress?"

"N-no," she sputtered. "I did not realize—" she cast a look at Josie "—that we'd be staying the night."

"You'll go home in the morning."

"You're staying?"

"I've got to keep an eye on Josie and her mama." He shifted on the heels of his feet, not liking the look on her face. "I've been out of commission for weeks. There's paperwork, unsolved cases, interrogations, not to mention catching the sap who shot me."

Was it his imagination or did something spark in that dark gaze of hers?

"Do I have to go back?" Josie interrupted them and for once, Lou was glad for it.

He avoided Mary's frown, turning to Josie instead. "Your mommy needs you, but I'm going to personally make sure that no one hurts you again, okay?"

Her bottom lip quivered and suddenly Lou's good mood deserted him. Two upset females was more than any sane man could handle. He fixed them both with a stern look despite the pain in his heart. "Look here, girls, I've got work to finish up and don't have time to cart you around Portland."

Josie burst into tears. Lou tripped trying to back up, but righted himself against the wall of the station. Horrified, he watched as the girl sobbed as though her heart were breaking.

And maybe it was.

An unwelcome spear of conscience poked him. Even though he'd arranged for bureau protection, that wouldn't start until tomorrow. For today, what was he returning her to? He'd asked a junior agent to poke around in the girl's mother's background, but his agent found nothing problematic. The family came from money, the father was deceased and they lived in a good part of town.

If he could, he'd never take the girl back, but the threat of a lawsuit was a very real problem he couldn't ignore.

But why did Josie insist on staying with Mary and him? A nagging pressure in his chest distracted him. He rubbed his heart, watching as Mary scooped Josie close, cradling her. Much as he had when he carried Josie to the ranch on his horse.

Frowning, he rubbed harder, but the ache refused to lessen. More and more, Abby came to memory. Her chubby smile. The scent of her skin, soft as a foundling's feathers. How he'd felt when he watched Sarah hold her... Something pricked his eyes and he blinked hard.

Enough of this.

Setting his jaw, he strode forward and snatched up their luggage. "Let's go, ladies."

He felt the fume in Mary's glare but chose to ignore it. Tension filled the space between them all the way to the neighborhood where Josie's mother resided. He glanced at the telegram in his hand, then flicked a look at Mary.

Her face was stone. Several people had given her curious looks. Some more disdainful than curious. Oregon's population was mostly Caucasian, and racial barriers rose high and impenetrable. The usual victims of the whites' prejudice were the Asian immigrants who worked in the lumber mills for next to nothing in pay.

But Mary, with her exotic features and dark eyes, qualified for being too different and thus drew attention. Lou knew the feeling, having visited China and being the only blue-eyed man in a sea of dark-eyed faces.

Their streetcar shuddered to a stop. People rose to exit and Lou looked over at Mary. "This is it."

Eyes blank, she handed him the luggage and took Josie's hand. He was determined not to look at the little girl anymore, for her tear-stained face was starting to give him heartburn.

It seemed he couldn't win no matter what he wanted. Mary refused to show her emotions, and Josie was all feeling. Setting his jaw, he led them out of the streetcar, and as a resolute trio, they found the address listed on his telegram.

Josie's mother. Mrs. Lauren Silver. He unlatched the gate and ushered Mary and Josie ahead of him. The house loomed before them, tall and freshly painted. The fumes permeated the humid summer air. A set of steps led to an ornate door. Baskets and pots of flowers surrounded the porch, and their floral scents became more apparent as they neared the front door.

"I don't like this house," Josie muttered, her little legs lifting high to manage the stairs.

"You live here a long time?" Lou inquired carefully. Everything inside roared for him to snatch the ladies and run. He couldn't do it, though. That was a sure ticket to jail, and then how would he protect them?

"Nope. I liked my other house better. It was by the ocean."

Interesting. She'd recently moved and then somehow ended up in the desert where Rose had found her. While finding his shooter, he'd also figure out why someone had done that to Josie.

In fact, he might question the mother a bit. He rubbed at his chin, thinking.

Mary was first to the door. He saw her back rigid, her shoulders set as she stepped to the side to allow him to knock. Josie huddled next to her, forehead furrowed and fingers twisting in her skirt.

He cleared his throat, set the luggage down and rapped on the door.

It swung open, revealing an ancient-looking man whose shock of white hair hung precariously over a furry set of eyebrows. "May I help you?" he croaked.

"We're here to see Mrs. Silver. Very special delivery." He winked at Josie, but the little girl didn't smile. He held his own smile in place, even though it felt broken. Could he do this to Josie? God knew, he didn't want to. God knew, if it was in his power, he'd keep Josie safe with Mary. But the situation was out of his hands. He could only do now what he'd been ordered to do, or risk more danger to the little girl by being completely cut out of her life if he resisted the law.

"Mrs. Silver isn't here." The man sniffed, then peered at Josie. He lifted rheumatic eyes to Lou. "I see you brought the troublemaker. You can keep her."

The door slammed in their faces.

Chapter Sixteen

"That ol' Baggs." Josie sniffed. "I never liked him."

"Josie," Mary gasped while fighting a smile. "That's not a nice thing to say."

"It's his name," Josie replied pertly, "and I always tell him he looks older than a bag of bones. He should trim his nose hairs."

Mary's jaw dropped. Had no one taught the girl manners, or did she say whatever she felt, regardless of consequences? It must be pleasant to be so unencumbered by niceties.

"That's enough," Lou said firmly. "We'll wait here until your mother returns."

"Fine." Josie trudged to a swing set in the far corner of the porch. Looking glum and very pouty, the she sat and rocked, using her toes to push herself.

Poor darling. Mary sighed deeply and tried to ignore the pressure at the base of her skull that could quickly turn into a headache. What a stressful situation, only to be compounded by a mother who obviously didn't care about seeing her daughter. "Where do you think Mrs. Silver is?" she asked Lou, careful to keep her voice low.

He shrugged. "I sent a telegram saying we'd arrive

today, but there wasn't a time given. Could be she's at the doctor's or something."

"Maybe we should ask…Mr. Baggs…if he knows her whereabouts. Surely he could direct us to her."

Lou's brow rose. "Could try that, I suppose. If he answers."

A low hum interrupted their conversation. They looked in Josie's direction. She'd gotten to her knees, facing outward to a mass of flowers that peeked over the porch rail. Her voice quivered as she sang. Her fingers gently stroked flower petals and sun spilled over her head, a dumped bucket of gold that washed her in light.

Mary's breath caught, suspended as a slow knot formed in her belly. She didn't want to leave this precious child here, alone with a sickly mother and odd circumstances. She glanced at Lou, prepared to beg, or to at least see what options they might have, but his gaze remained fastened on Josie. His eyes looked shadowed in the dimness of the porch, pained, even.

She traced the shape of his face with her glance, giving herself free rein to stare while he was so occupied. His strong nose and jaw, the wild hair she'd kept a tad too long yet remaining fashionable.

In this moment, she realized how dear he was to her. How safe and kind. Sure, now, he had frustrating qualities. Stubborn, flippant, never anchoring anywhere for long… yet somehow she'd become attached to him.

Uneasy, she forced herself to look away, to the road where a fancy, newer-model Ford chugged to a stop in front of the house. A man emerged from the passenger door, tipping his hat to them before moving to the rear door.

Lou moved beside Mary. She caught a whiff of Wrigley's and felt the warmth of his arm near hers. Focusing on the people in front of her, she watched as the man scooped a lady from the rear seat of the automobile.

The man carried the woman up the steps, his face young and unlined. Brown eyes met hers in passing, then traveled behind her, to where Josie still hummed on the swing. Lou rushed to the front door, opening it without knocking first.

The man nodded his thanks and disappeared inside.

"Come on." Lou slid into the house.

He expected her to follow, but she hung back, startling when a hand slipped into hers. She looked down into Josie's wide eyes.

"I don't want to stay," Josie whispered.

Mary tried to ask why but her throat was closing up. This was it. After weeks of caring for Josie, she must say goodbye. She could feel her heart cracking apart inside, sending pulsating waves of emotional pain through her body. Blinking quickly, she knelt to face the girl.

"Do you know how much I love you?" She smoothed a curl from Josie's eyes. "You are special and a joy. Never forget that."

"But I don't want you to leave." Her lip trembled and those beautiful eyes turned shiny.

"Friends are forever, sweet girl." Mary pulled her into a hug, inhaling her scent, enveloping her in her arms and trying to memorize every moment to hold on to.

"You said God heard me. I told Him I wanted to stay with you and Mister Lou…." The girl's voice was as trembly as her lips.

"He heard you, honey."

"Then why am I here? My mommy can go with us. I don't want to be here, never, ever. I never wanted to come back."

That knot in Mary's stomach grew. Drawing in a deep breath, she pulled back and looked Josie in the eye. "Mister Lou is going to make sure you're safe because your mommy needs you here with her. Do you still have that thimble?"

Josie nodded.

"Whenever you're lonely or scared, hold the thimble and remember that I'm always praying for you. And that God is looking out for you and loves you dearly."

Josie sniffled and a lonely tear seeped from the corner of her eye. It rolled down her cheek unchecked. Mary swallowed hard, gave her one last hug and then, hands held, they went into the house.

Mary barely remembered the trip back to the hotel. Leaving Josie had been horrendous. The girl had sobbed, and Baggs had held her tightly when Lou and Mary exited the house. The sound had tormented Mary on the streetcar. She couldn't speak.

When Lou stopped at his office to drop off paperwork and make arrangements for who knew what, she sat on a bench outside. Clouds drifted over the sun, and before long it started raining, but she hadn't even noticed until Lou reappeared, picking up her luggage and leading her to a waiting streetcar.

They arrived at the Seward Hotel in the afternoon, dodging through the rain to the entrance. The massive building loomed before her. Elegant. Expensive.

Blinking back raindrops, she tried not to gape as she followed Lou inside.

She discovered the lobby was gapeworthy, however. A bell motif rounded the interior. Sparkling and clean, people of obvious wealth studded its landscape. Fur stoles, shining shoes... She huddled in a corner of the lobby while Lou checked them in, feeling out of place and wanting to disappear. A shiver coursed through her, and belatedly she realized her clothes were sopping wet.

What was Josie doing right now? Her mother was barely capable of speaking, she was so sick. She'd seemed kind, though, her eyes a paler shade of Josie's, her smile soft yet weak. Tuberculosis was what was killing her, she'd said, speaking past her face mask. A rare strain, the doctors told her. One they had trouble treating. It seemed the Great War, coupled with the disastrous influenza pandemic, had increased tuberculosis cases. Or perhaps made them worse.

Either way, what would happen to Josie when her mother passed away? Who would care for her? The worry nibbled at Mary incessantly. She clutched her luggage closer as another shiver vibrated through her.

Lou stalked toward her, his lips still and serious. "Ready to go up?"

She nodded and followed him to an elaborate staircase. Its surface shone and she wondered how long it had taken the staff to make it look that way. How often must they clean it? She gingerly stepped up.

Lou turned to her. "Let me help you with your bags."

"I can handle them."

"I want to help you. Please." His voice was sober, so she relented. "Now, our rooms are side by side. We have a dinner to attend this evening and I've left you something in your room. A fellow agent picked it out, in case you don't have anything to wear."

"I'm supposed to dress up?" She frowned.

Lou shrugged and slipped her a quick look. "You don't have to, but we'll be eating in the hotel's dining area. It's exquisite, I've heard. There's music, candles…" He trailed off and looked straight ahead.

"Why such a fancy dinner?" They reached the top of the stairs and Mary followed him to the right.

"It's been a hard day. A soothing dinner will be relaxing, don't you think?" He shot her a half smile that faded when he saw her face. "I thought you would like it."

Mary shook her head. "Why? Why would you think that?" Her voice sounded high-pitched, even to her ears. "This is too much…too much noise, and people. A restaurant will be filled with those who stare." She swallowed and made her voice calmer. "I can't help thinking of what Josie is doing right now, if she's still crying. What will happen when her mother dies? What if that man looking for her is really her father? Or some relative who wants to hurt her?"

Lou stopped in front of a door. His jaw was clenched. She saw a muscle work in his neck. "There's already an undercover agent that has been hired on in the house. He'll be there tomorrow. I'm doing the best I can, Mary. Leave it be."

"I can't," she insisted.

He turned slowly toward her, the key dangling from his finger. "It's out of our hands. Your mother found a little girl and didn't report it to the authorities. Josie's mama has been frantic with worry and was ready to take legal steps." A sheen crept into his eyes before he blinked it away. "Take a nap, get ready for dinner, and tonight I'll outline how I plan to protect them."

Hope fluttered for a moment, then spiraled to a crash. "I'm never going to see Josie again, am I?"

His gaze closed. He held out the key to her. She took it. He set her suitcase near the door. His hand came up, near her face, and she almost flinched. Some instincts couldn't be undone.

But he moved softly and the next thing she knew, his hand was cupping her chin. Warm. Gentle. His eyes were tender.

"If it were possible, I'd make sure Josie could stay with you forever."

Her breath caught, suspended by the unfolding of rare and beautiful feelings inside. It was as though a thousand butterflies had taken flight within her rib cage, fluttering, no, pounding to be let out. This man who'd protected her, who looked at her with such *seeing*... Her pulse thrummed with strange and heady emotions.

Lips dry, she wet them with the tip of her tongue.

Lou blinked and the moment ended. His hand dropped to his side. "I'll meet you in the dining room at seven." With that, he pivoted and left her alone at her door, the imprint of his touch still sizzling against her cheek.

It took her a moment to recover, but when she did, she let herself into her room. The spacious interior welcomed her with warmth. A package lay on the bed, but rather than opening it, she flopped onto her back and stared at the ceiling.

So many feelings ricocheted through her that catching her breath, let alone resting, proved impossible. Thoughts of Josie intermingled with memories of The Kiss. Both tangled her nerves. After an hour of futile search for sleep, she sat up and opened her traveling case. Taking out her brush, she went to the private bath, washed her face and then combed her hair. The snarls made her wince, but she persisted until her locks fell in waves against her back.

She glanced at the package, a simple white box, which remained unopened.

"Oh, Lord, I don't know what to do," she whispered. Life's even road had just become twisty and uneven. To find her footing required a wisdom she wasn't sure she possessed. Inhaling deeply, she went to the box and lifted the lid.

She gasped. With careful fingers, she lifted out a dress

more lovely than she'd ever touched. She'd seen beautiful fabrics. French silks, velvets and chiffons. But this… The fabric fell through her fingers, a wispy garment the color of a desert sunset.

She nibbled her bottom lip and surveyed the tiny glass beads across the hem, the swirls of deep reds that dashed across the bodice.

She couldn't wear this.

She couldn't.

And yet the simple dress she'd traveled in hardly qualified for a refined dinner.

But this dress was audacious. Every head would turn. Stare. She shuddered and dropped the silky thing to the bed. Why would Lou do this to her?

He didn't pick it out, she reminded herself. Taking steadying breaths, she paced the length of her room. A rose sachet sat upon the dresser, but she missed the scent of her sagebrush land. She glanced at the clock on the wall.

Six o'clock.

There was time to spend praying or reading the Bible. Perhaps the Proverbs. They'd always been her comfort in times of need or stress.

When she finished chapter one, she moved to chapter two and kept going until six-thirty. Feeling more calm and as though her fears were minuscule, she put her Bible to the side and changed into the dress.

How the agent knew her size, she'd never guess. She wasn't a tall woman, smaller than most, actually, but the dress fit perfectly. The seams stitched even and small at the hem. The narrow shoulder straps exposed more skin than Mary thought she'd ever shown in her life.

Thank goodness she'd brought her black shawl.

Now for her hair. She twisted and pinned and when a knock sounded at her door, she was ready.

She snagged her shawl and opened the door. Lou faced the opposite way, his head bent as though reading something. She closed the door behind her, hearing a subtle click.

Lou rotated toward her and his face went slack.

"What?" She touched the collar of the dress. "Did I wear the wrong thing?" She patted her hair, but everything felt tidy.

"You are..." He trailed off. Was his face turning splotchy? She stepped closer.

"Are you all right?" She'd never seen him look so...so flustered. At a loss for words. Despite the riotous emotions of the day, an overwhelming urge to laugh bubbled through her.

She covered her mouth as Lou's jaw worked but no sound emerged.

"Resplendent," he finally said. He stuffed the paper he held into the breast pocket of his sleek jacket and advanced toward her. Yes, his face colored pinker than normal, but his charming grin was firmly in place.

The giggle bubbled out, perhaps exacerbated by nerves and exhaustion. His smile stretched to show a hint of teeth. "May I have your arm?"

"You may." Nerves quivering, she offered it to him.

His grasp filled her with warmth. He pressed her arm firmly to his side, effectively encasing her in his cologne and security. They matched steps. Down the stairs. Through the lobby. Into another area that served as the restaurant.

She felt eyes on her, the way they followed and perused, but the tingly apprehension she so often suffered failed to materialize. Hardly daring to breathe, let alone talk, she allowed Lou to lead her to a table.

Dinner passed in an odd mixture of unexplained excitement and lingering sadness over Josie's absence. She'd gotten used to the girl's energy and uncontained words. And yet the candlelight on the table, the sound of violins and clinking forks led her back to a reality in which her employer sat across from her, handsome, alive and very, very interested.

At least it felt that way.

Self-conscious, she smoothed her dress, watching as his eyes traced her movements. Heat crept through her. "Thank you for the meal, Lou."

"It's nice to see you enjoying yourself."

"Good food is worth celebrating," she returned, feeling a tug at the corners of her mouth.

"Indeed. I agree." He lifted his glass. "And so is good company."

Feeling flushed, she nodded. They finished their food and before she knew it, they were ready to leave. His eyes sparkled beneath the glow of the chandeliers.

"Care for an evening stroll?"

Why not? She might never visit this place again, and would she even see him after this? She pulled her shawl more snugly around her shoulders and smiled at him. "I'd love one."

They meandered out of the hotel, away from the perfumes and into a different type of atmosphere. She clutched her shawl closer as a chilly breeze brushed by. She glanced at Lou. He looked completely relaxed, the planes of his face smooth. He'd gotten a shave somewhere, and the shadowed line of his jaw was strong beneath the street lamps. He walked as though he knew this place well.

Which, of course, he must, having the bureau's field office here.

"It's odd being alone together, don't you think?" she asked.

He gave her a funny look. "Not odd to me. It's…nice," he finished. "Do you miss Harney County?"

"This place is so different, so many people. But what I miss more is my kitchen. My hands itch to bake."

"Really? A literal itching?"

She smiled at him, lifting her hands. "Do you not see the rash?"

He peered at them.

She giggled and dropped her hands. "I'm teasing you, Lou."

"Oh." Then he cracked a smile that split through her defenses. "Mary the jokester. I like it. And what did you think of your meal tonight? You know, your cooking is tastier." At her doubtful look, he held up a hand. "No, really. I've been around the world, Mary O'Roarke, and your meals rival any fine-dining experience."

What did a girl say to that? They kept walking, and then Lou cleared his throat. Never a good sign. "I don't know how else to say this, but tonight I was brought a telegram. We've got an offer on the ranch."

Chapter Seventeen

"**D**id you hear me?" Lou paused beneath a streetlamp.

Mary nodded, though her heart felt as though it had lodged painfully in her sternum.

"Well, say something," he said, his tone strained.

But she couldn't speak. The words remained bottled inside, not yet fully formed. What could she say? It was his ranch. She'd been blessed to stay there. She blinked to ward off any unwelcome tears.

"I wish you'd say something. Tell me how you feel." He swiped a hand through his hair. It hung in lopsided angles, tangled by his regret. "This wasn't how I planned things to happen. The sale was expected to take months. Then, if you didn't want to stay on with the new owners, you'd have time to get a new job and place. Independence is within your grasp."

She swallowed hard. "I *should* want such a thing."

"What?"

"Independence. I am thirty years old. Unmarried. I should want to have my own home, shouldn't I?" What was wrong with her that she didn't? No, she wanted things to continue as they had. Peaceful. Secure.

Lou looked away. "Everyone wants different things, Mary. I'm sorry for uprooting you, but it needs to be done."

She exhaled a shaky breath. "Why? For what reasons must you sell?"

He looked at her then and his eyes pierced her. "It's never been my home. Ever. It's been a place to sleep and a place to eat. That's it."

His answer cut her to the core. "Never? All those times we ate and laughed?" There'd been many times she sewed by the fire while he shared an adventure he'd just been on. It had been cozy. Familial, even. "You never felt…home?"

He sighed heavily. "Home is not something I expect to ever feel again. That's just the way of it, and I don't want to talk about it anymore."

"Perhaps I do not own the ranch and am nothing more than an employee, one you've conveniently cast aside for new employment, but I have feelings. You don't want to talk about it, but the longer I stand here, the angrier I get." There, she'd told him. There had been a knot of anger growing in her belly, maybe ever since she'd found that letter after his kiss. "And furthermore, how dare you kiss me knowing you have no intention of returning?"

Yes, anger was coursing through her now, heating her blood and pouring rash words into her mouth.

"Now, Mary, hold on a minute. That kiss was completely unexpected."

"Was it?" she challenged, and was surprised to see a furrow appear at the ridge of his brow.

"I just needed to…"

"To what?" The wind picked up, whipping hair around his face. The lamplight surrounded him and she felt as though she must be standing in darkness. Could he see her anger? How he'd hurt her with his indifference?

Shivering, she glared at him.

He nudged his coat from his shoulders and draped it over her before sighing deeply, heavily. "I don't know, Mary, and I'm sorry for that. I got carried away with emotion and it wasn't the right thing to do."

His apology irked her, though wasn't it what she wanted? The scent of his jacket surrounded her, filled her senses and warmed her.

"Someday," he continued, "a fine man in town will take to courting you. All this will be in the past."

"Do you mean forgettable? The way you've conveniently forgotten Josie? You handed her off like a package to be delivered." Her voice broke.

"Don't bring her into this. She doesn't belong to you or me." Lou's voice lifted, causing passersby to glance their way. "And our kiss wasn't forgettable. If you don't understand my meaning, I can show you right now."

To her surprise he moved nearer, out of the circle of light and into the shadows between them. Energy sizzled through the air, tension emanated from his body, and a quiver unrelated to cold shuddered through her.

"I think not," she said coolly, and moved opposite him so that she now stood closer to the lamppost. Her pulse hammered. "I have had enough of your kisses to last a lifetime."

"You didn't complain about them before," he said tightly.

Confident, carefree Lou was gone. Where he went, she didn't know, but before her stood the real man. Edgy. Determined. And for some odd reason, angry. All because she'd brought up Josie. Again she thought of secrets. He possessed them, and in abundance.

She nodded at him slowly. "You are a practiced kisser. It was a fine experience."

"A fine experience," he mimicked, then let out a bark of laughter empty of joy.

"It was also disruptive," she said gently. She must tread softly, for mentioning God in the past had often upset him. "Kissing did nothing but stir up a mess for both of us." In truth, she hadn't stopped remembering that kiss and doubted she ever would.

"Perhaps it was something that needed stirring." His confident voice conflicted with the turmoil she saw in his eyes.

Unsettled, she shook her head. "That is unlikely. Romance is not what will make me happy, Lou. I don't need a man's kisses or even his love. God has given me so much—" She stopped because his brows lowered and, in the darkness, it almost seemed as though his eyes flashed.

"So no marriage in your future? You think you can live without baking for anyone ever again?"

"If I open a restaurant, I shall bake for many," she inserted, trying to follow the train of his thoughts, why he'd jumped to marriage.

"And do you deny the way you felt caring for—for Josie?"

"No," she whispered.

"Well, you need a husband to have a family."

She whipped back as though he'd slapped her. "Perhaps I'd have someone to take care of if you'd looked into Josie's family a little more. You *know* something is wrong. Someone in that family is dangerous. Don't you care?" A surprising boldness took hold of her and she stepped right up to him, nose to chest due to her shortness, but it would have to do. He'd see her eyes and realize she wanted answers.

"Tell me, why do you avoid children? Why do you run from the ranch as often as you can?" A thought occurred to her as the realization of a pattern emerged. "And your stays at the ranch... You've always cut them short after we spent time together in the evenings. What are you afraid of?"

His glare deepened and he took her arms in his hands, pulling her closer than she'd ever been to him, save for that kiss.

"You don't know what you're saying, woman."

"I know exactly what I'm saying. You're afraid—"

"No," he hissed. His grip tightened. "That's enough. No more."

"Then tell me," she pleaded. When he tried to look away, she cupped his face and forced him to look down at her. "Help me understand why you dropped Josie with her mother like a hot ember in your hand. Does it hurt so much?"

She saw it now, the pain that tightened his mouth and crowded his eyes.

His throat moved, and then his head was resting in the crook of her neck. He groaned, and the sound caused hairs to stand on her skin. He let her go. She stumbled back, rubbing at her arms where his hands had clenched her.

"It doesn't hurt," he said at last. His gaze lifted. She stifled her gasp at the rawness of his expression. "It burns. It's a searing ache that never leaves."

Yes, she knew that kind of pain. "It can heal, if you let it."

"How, with God?" That broken laugh of his echoed off the sidewalk. "Don't you see? *God* did this to me. He killed my wife and Abby."

Lou shoved his hands through his hair again, wishing he could wipe away the pain as easily. Mary's eyes were shiny and he couldn't tell if tears glistened or if the lamplight played tricks. He wanted to say something, but his throat hurt with the strain of containing his emotions.

Groaning, he pivoted and started back for the hotel. She walked quietly beside him. Every so often a hint of her perfume teased him. He could feel the questions burning in her. She expected an explanation. *Who is Abby? You were married?*

As though his thoughts had been spoken, she said, "You do not have to explain anything to me, but if you ever feel the need to speak of this again, I will be here."

"Thank you," he managed to say. At least his vocal cords had shrugged off their temporary paralysis. He held the door to the hotel for her and she glided inside.

Near the stairs, she stopped. "Thank you for dinner."

He inclined his head, glad the rush of pain had drained away. "You're welcome."

"Are there specific plans for tomorrow?"

"Yeah, about that." He tapped the railing of the stairs. "An agent will pick you up at your room at nine o'clock and escort you back to Burns."

"I see."

"Don't give me that look, Mary."

"What look?" But the obstinate disapproval on her face didn't change. Or was it hurt?

He couldn't tell, and the gut-spilling earlier had exhausted him. "Just be ready. Your breakfast and room will be taken care of."

Her gaze lifted and she searched his face. "Will I ever see you again?"

"Sure. I've got to come back and handle this sale. I want to see you and James safely settled and—"

Her lips made a funny movement, as though she was holding back a smile.

"What?" he asked.

"I was just remembering how Miss Alma chased him out of the store. If she has her way, I believe James shall be quite all right." Her smile lit up her face and unexpectedly, Lou felt the strangest wish that Mary would chase him into the road, too.

He shook his head. Focus. She wasn't in the plans. Not even close. "James doesn't know what hit him," he said lightly. "I don't think he's ever settled down with a woman, and she seems pretty determined to snag him."

He grunted. This conversation opened old wounds and he didn't plan to let it continue. "Like I was saying, I've got to get things settled. I'll be back."

She bit her lip, studying him intently. Then her gaze skittered away.

He touched her arm. "Until next time, then?"

"Yes," she said, backing away. The dress she wore glittered with her movements, and the attraction he tried to hold at bay surged again.

"Goodbye," he said.

"Goodbye," she answered.

And then she was gone, moving through the late-night guests, up the stairs and disappearing around the corner. Sighing, he settled at the side of the wall and waited.

He had work to do. All this internal caterwauling over the past, Josie, that kiss… It made a man's head spin. He remembered Trevor getting all worked up over Gracie. They'd lived at the ranch as a married couple before traipsing off to California for fun, and Trevor seemed happier than Lou had ever seen him. Now that they'd been married a bit, Trevor seemed better.

Marriage wasn't for Lou, though. No way, no how.

He scanned the guests, looking for one in particular. Mary might accuse him of not caring, but it wasn't the truth. No matter his past, he didn't stand by and watch children get hurt. Women, either. Josie's mama might be dying and frail, but some low-down, evil one had handled her roughly. He'd seen the faint purple smudges on her wrists when she'd hugged Josie.

It only took a call to find out Mrs. Silver was a widow, but she had a brother who happened to have been busy traveling recently. Who happened to be staying in this very hotel tonight. And his last name happened to be Langdon. It was pretty obvious this fellow was the same guy who'd been lurking in Burns.

Why the man hadn't stayed with his sister, he didn't know, but he aimed to find out. So he waited, checking his watch every few minutes. The brother had been described as tall, brown-haired, strange blue eyes that bordered on purple. He matched the description of the man who'd come to the ranch.

And the man who'd recently been accused of murder in Burns.

He needed to know what this man did for a living, but above all, he needed to make sure Josie and Mary were safe from him.

"Sir?" A young man addressed him from his right.

"Yes?"

"I'm Special Agent Smith."

Smith. The name clicked. "You'll be escorting Miss O'Roarke tomorrow?"

"Reporting in. We'll be leaving at nine o'clock and our expected arrival time is—"

"Have you ever done this before, Agent Smith?" Lou cut him off. He looked far too young to be protecting Mary.

"I served in the war effort." Agent Smith gave him a level look. "Appearances can be deceiving. I'm well equipped to take care of your lady."

"She's not my lady," he said by rote, breaking their visual standoff to scan the lobby again.

"I beg your pardon, sir, but I saw you at dinner."

He cocked a brow, meeting Smith's look square on, hiding his surprise. "And what did you see?"

The agent shrugged. "It wasn't business, that's all."

Lou grimaced. No, their dinner hadn't been. This one might do after all. He hadn't noticed him once, and that ability to blend would aid in keeping Mary safe, should the need arise. Lou gave him a curt nod. "Very well. Telephone headquarters when she's safely home."

"Will do." A quick nod and Smith left.

Lou pulled out a stick of Wrigley's and continued his surveillance. Chewing thoughtfully, he crossed his ankles and waited several more hours. Langdon never showed up.

Or he'd missed him, just as he'd missed Agent Smith at dinner.

Heading upstairs to bed, tiredness riding his back, the realization that he'd lost his mark plagued him. He was too caught up in emotions. Could only see Mary.

His attention had been on her—not a good thing, but he didn't know how to stop it. And then she'd had the nerve to bring up God.

He turned the corner and entered the corridor. *God.*

Did he really blame God for losing Sarah and Abby? In the haze of anger and pain, yes. But then he thought of Mary, a woman who hadn't known Jesus growing up. Who'd been abducted and mistreated, deeply so, and yet somehow still managed to find peace in the way he no longer traveled. How was that possible?

Yep. This job was messing with his head and causing him to lose focus. The sooner he sold the ranch, the better he could work and forget all this malarkey.

He ticked off his goals in his head as he walked.

Tomorrow he'd find Langdon at breakfast, have a little word with the upstart, then he'd finish up his work at headquarters. Track down the shooter, cuff him, maybe get some more information from him before heading home. Sell the ranch. Start a new job, far away.

The list was supposed to reassure, but as he let himself into his empty hotel room, he didn't feel anything at all.

Chapter Eighteen

Mary woke before the sun. She enjoyed the silence of morning, nothing but the birds and their early songs. Normally she felt refreshed, but today, the morning she'd be heading back to the ranch, unease beset her.

Lou had been *married*. And begotten a child. How could she not have known? He'd kept this secret from everyone. Were Trevor and James aware of this? Was she the only one in the dark? No wonder he didn't care to hear of God. No wonder the sight of Josie pained him.

Feeling a tad sick to her stomach, she swung her legs out of bed. Quickly she packed her meager belongings, made her bed, took care of toiletries and then glanced at the clock. Still too early. She had many hours until the agent arrived at her door.

And what then? Go home and search for a new job? Try to get that loan at the bank so she'd have the capital to open a business with? She could stay at the ranch with the new owners, but was that what she really wanted?

Gripping the handle of her suitcase, she opened her door and slipped into the hall. Perhaps they'd be serving breakfast. She could do with a strong pot of coffee.

The lobby was empty when she entered it, though the

heady scent of maple syrup permeated the air. Her mouth watered at the thought of pancakes.

Josie loved them.

What would Josie eat this morning? And with whom? Alone perhaps, since her mother was ill. She paused as an idea so beguiling, so dangerous she could hardly believe it, flirted with her thoughts. Her suitcase grew heavy as she stood and pondered the burgeoning plan.

Lou would be furious with her and yet…he had no charge over her decisions any longer. Swallowing hard, a disconcerting excitement building, she marched through the lobby, left a note for Lou and then burst outside, just in time to catch the streetcar.

Odd looks followed her, but she ignored them and focused on remembering the way back to the Silvers'. By the time she stood at Josie's gate, the sun peeked a sleepy eye over the horizon.

She gnawed her cheek, staring at the wrought iron. Yesterday felt far away. Was she really ready to do this? She thought of the note she left to be delivered to Lou first thing. If he tried to stop her, well, that would be too much. Too invasive.

Perhaps he'd shared a dark and sad past, and perhaps he'd opened his home to her, but he did not control her and any claim he made to her time must end with his sale of the ranch.

A vehicle cranked up behind her, startling her and urging her to open the gate. It groaned but gave way. She started up the walk, up the stairs, but before she could knock on the door, it opened.

Baggs glowered at her. His eyebrows were just as furry today as they'd been yesterday. Mary remembered Josie's comment and a reluctant smile tugged at her lips.

"You again?" he muttered.

"Yes, it is Miss O'Roarke. May I speak with Mrs. Silver?"

"She has not risen yet."

"Oh." She blinked. "I can come back later."

"You may wait. She'll be about soon." The butler, or whoever he was, swung the door open in a reluctant fashion, but Mary was too determined and set in her path to care.

She stepped into the ornate home. A hint of perfume reached her. Baggs led her into the same room they'd met Mrs. Silver in yesterday. She took a seat on the brocade couch.

"Anything to drink? Tea, perhaps?"

"That is kind of you to offer, Mr. Baggs. I would very much like tea."

He shuffled out of the room, closing the door behind him. She studied the great portraits about the room. Studious and elegant, they dominated the walls and lent the room a somber air. Soon Josie's painting would rest with those of her ancestors, if she was related to these people. No doubt she was related somehow to the man looking for her.

Langdon, the sheriff had called him.

She did not wish to remember how it felt for him to be standing in her home, her sanctuary.... Stifling the remembrance, she felt through her bag until she found her knitting needles and newest project. A wedding gift for Miss Alma, who no doubt would find James by her side very soon.

The door opened, and Baggs brought in a platter with steaming tea. He situated it, and Mary thanked him, preferring to pour her own. "Do you not have a maid?" she asked in a gentle tone.

"Left us last week," he grumbled.

When he left, she sipped the strong brew and worked on Miss Alma's gift. The wait felt interminable. She kept straining to hear Josie's happy voice. The patter of footsteps even, but nothing broke the muted silence.

After almost an hour, the door opened again. Baggs wheeled Mrs. Silver in. She did not wear a face mask today. The faded state of her eyes and pallor of her skin sent prickles across Mary's body. She tucked her knitting back into her bag. An air of death cloaked Mrs. Silver. It hovered over her and as she neared, the odor of it filled the room.

Mary blanched and then schooled her features to blankness, though inside, her heart pounded against her chest. What would happen to Josie when her mother passed? Surely she wouldn't be left with that horrid Mr. Langdon.

"You wish to see me?" Mrs. Silver's voice did not pass a whisper.

Mary nodded, putting her hands in her lap. "I thought perhaps you might..." *Courage, don't fail me now.* She wet her lips and tried again. "With your illness, I hoped you might be in need of a nanny for Josie."

Mrs. Silver's lids fluttered.

"Your daughter is spirited and bright and I have grown quite fond of her. I can provide schooling in many areas—"

"She will attend a private school," Mrs. Silver murmured. She studied Mary, though it seemed to drain the energy from her features.

"I see." Hope seeped away, but she did not allow herself to slump. "Perhaps you might be looking for a housekeeper? Or a parlor maid?"

"You are so desperate to see my Josephine?"

"Not desperate, but I am in search of employment and I care deeply for your daughter. I would like to help."

Mrs. Silver's fingers tapped the arms of her wheelchair.

"It fills my heart with gladness to see your love for my daughter, but I must refuse."

Mary's fingers tightened on her satchel.

"You see, her uncle shall be in charge of any plans for Josie. She is at the age where she would benefit from the structure of such a pla—" A harsh cough ripped the rest of the words from her. She hunched over, body racked with the cough of tuberculosis. She pressed a hankie against her pale lips.

Mary watched sadly, knowing she should return to the hotel now. This had been a shallow hope with little chance of success, but she'd needed to try.

"I apologize," Mrs. Silver said when the fit passed. Baggs handed her a glass of water and she sipped it gratefully.

"There is no need for apologies." Mary rose. "Thank you for taking the time to meet with me. I would love to see Josie but do not want to unduly upset her. Please, may I leave my address with you? I've included the hotel I'm staying at, though I won't be there after today." She handed Mrs. Silver the paper she'd scribbled on earlier. "If you or Josie are ever in need of anything, write to me and I shall come."

"Thank you…what is your name?"

"Mary O'Roarke, and you're quite welcome." She gestured to the door, the bag heavier than ever. "I shall let myself out."

Mrs. Silver inclined her head and Mary headed to the doorway, eager to escape before her burning cheeks gave away her angst. She reached the door frame.

A shadow passed in front of the opening. Mr. Langdon appeared before her, his disturbing eyes fixed on her face.

She skidded to a stop, bumping a fragile table near the wall. The vase on it shuddered and she reached over to steady it. She breathed shallowly and tried to slow her quick breaths before she panicked.

An evil-looking smile lifted the corners of his lips. He appraised her and she hauled her bag in front of her.

"We have a visitor?" he asked.

Mrs. Silver's wheelchair appeared beside Mary. "Yes, this is Mary. She brought our Josie back last night. She was just leaving." Another cough seized Mrs. Silver, but Mary did not dare look away from Mr. Langdon.

No, she could not for fear of what might happen. Mrs. Silver and Baggs were no match for him. He frowned at his sister, then turned that unblinking gaze on Mary.

"You're leaving so soon? Might we have a word?"

Before she could react, he caught her arm in a painful grip and propelled her out the door and into the hallway.

"Brother," Mrs. Silver gasped, but he yanked the door behind them. It pounded shut and then they were alone in the hallway.

His gaze bore into her, as deep and painful as his grip on her arm. The look on his face was menacing in its lack of emotion. "Forgive me, but I overheard your conversation. You must know my sister is very ill. Dying."

He said this last word as though he relished the thought.

Mary's skin prickled all over.

"Therefore, as custodian of her estate, and of my niece, I feel it's in Josie's best interest to be at home during the last days of her mother's life. I will personally pay for you to stay on and teach Josie for one year. When my sister passes, I will relinquish the guardianship of Josie to you."

It sounded too good to be true. That alone made her pause. Be employed by this man to take care of Josie and eventually become her legal guardian? Both elation and terror filled Mary, two opposite emotions that tangled her senses. She blinked. Swallowed. "And if I do not accept?"

Now he smiled, if the baring of his teeth could be called such a thing. "Her mother will think she's been sent off to school. That won't be the case. There are plenty of orphanages for girls like her...or other places."

A sick feeling rushed through Mary so quickly her vision wavered. She knew what he was suggesting, knew his plans for Josie, should she decline his offer, were evil, but this? No, it could not happen.

Still, one thing she'd learned from Lou and Trevor was caution in bargaining with wicked men. Forcing a calm look to her face, refusing to let him see that his threat had already won him what he wanted, she met his gaze.

"I will consider your proposal."

Lou woke in a surly mood. Everything got worse when he found the note on the floor outside his door.

> Dear Lou,
> As I am not sure how I'd like to be employed in the future, I have gone to see about another opportunity. I appreciate the agent you're sending to escort me home but am unable to pass up the job I have in mind. Please give the agent my regards and I do apologize if I have complicated the situation. I shall be fine on my own. Thank you for all you have done.
> Mary

Where could she have gone? Groaning, he passed his palms over his face. Stubble grazed his skin. There wasn't time to track down a stubborn woman today, let alone shave. He had a ten o'clock meeting and before that he was determined to find Langdon. He also wanted to meet the undercover agent assigned to protect Mrs. Silver and

Josie. If he could see the guy for himself, his gut would let him know whether Josie would be safe or not in his care.

Lou snatched the note, folded it, and then slid it into a pocket. After tossing on blue jeans and a respectable shirt, he stalked out of the hotel room. He grabbed a slice of banana bread on the way out of the hotel.

The ride to the Silvers' seemed to take forever. He scanned the case files he'd been handed yesterday, a few reports, but his brain insisted on taking him back to how Mary looked last night. What he'd told her... His chest pinched.

Worst of all, he'd exposed something he hadn't meant to—the root of his anger at God and everything religion represented. He felt like a fool. He pressed his head against the wall of the streetcar, glad no one tried to make conversation with him.

He was lousy at that type of thing.

Mary would be better off without him. An attraction didn't guarantee a good marriage. Let alone their differing religious beliefs. He cringed at what had sneaked into his thoughts.

Marriage.

Rolling his eyes, he straightened and began pressing the paperwork back into his satchel, listening as it crumpled into place.

Marriage.

He'd been so young with Sarah. Naive and in love. He thought he knew all the answers. He worked a job with the military that required long hours. Applied for a place in the new unit known as the Bureau of Investigation. He left Sarah at home and worked hard. She waited. He visited.

They had Abby. A tic tugged at his eyelid. He blinked. So many mistakes he could never take back, and now his thoughts had wandered to marriage. Absolutely unthinkable. He couldn't even blame the detour on a single kiss, because he'd kissed others and never had he felt what he did when he embraced Mary. It was a cruel realization that over the course of twelve years, Mary and her quiet presence had worked itself into his soul beneath the guise of friendship.

His only recourse remained backing off. Leaving town and letting the figurative dust settle. If Mary opened a store, she'd surely meet a nice fellow to create a home with.

The tic pulled his eyelid again. He blinked and held on as the streetcar slowed to its next stop. The Silver place loomed across the street. Lou got off with a few others and separated from them.

Time to don his "agent" hat and get to work. Worrying about where Mary might be could wait for later. But as he made his way up the walk, opening the gate, and taking the stairs two at a time, his stomach clenched.

"Focus," he muttered, then rapped quick and hard on the front door.

Almost immediately it swung open. A man with eyes bordering on purple faced him. His hair was slicked in the fashion of the day. He wore a neatly pressed suit and his face was clean-shaven.

Lou disliked him immediately.

"Langdon, I presume?"

Langdon's brows rose, but he quickly recovered and stepped outside, closing the door behind him. "What can I do for you?"

He flipped his badge open. "Special Agent Lou Riley with the Bureau of Investigation." He put the badge away. "Would you mind going to my office to answer a few questions?" His tone brooked no argument.

Langdon bared his teeth. "I've business to attend to."

"We can talk here." Lou gave him a look designed to get his point across.

"I really must go, but here is my card. You may call me." The man's voice was slicker than a politician's on election day.

Lou scowled and closed the gap between them. They stood head-to-head. His instincts roared that something was wrong. "What were you doing in Burns?"

"Business." Langdon's cheeks bunched in a mocking manner. "I stopped by your place."

"I heard." This guy didn't get to own the conversation. "Also heard you murdered someone."

Langdon's eyes flickered. "Really? How odd." He moved back and bumped the front door. "Isn't that business for the police, though? I thought the bureau dealt with other, more important, things?"

"You saying you did it?"

"I'm saying the sheriff has himself the murderer. Go talk to him." Langdon pulled out a pocket watch and made a point of looking at it before stuffing it back into his over-pressed suit. "I really must say goodbye."

"Don't think so." Lou cocked him a smile that froze most men. He propped a hand against the door and leaned forward. "You see, Langdon, I'm here unofficially. Your trail… Let's just say it's putting off an odor." He narrowed his eyes. "I'm going to fix that. You might think you're slick, but I'm onto you. With the murder and with your niece. You won't get away with anything."

Langdon inclined his head, a smirk plastered to his lips. He casually brushed off his right shoulder, as if Lou's words had landed there and stuck. "Since you're here unofficially, I believe I might have something that belongs to you."

"That a fact?" Unease skittered up his spine.

Langdon turned and opened the front door. "Someone's here for you. Come, come, don't be frightened." He cast Lou a smile that chilled him to the core. "I'm afraid I might have been a little too…harsh with her."

Confused, Lou's gaze darted to the entryway. Movement, and then Mary emerged, eyes wide and lips pale.

Lou snarled and yanked Langdon up by the sleeve. The man's cologne reeked. "What did you do to her?"

Chapter Nineteen

Langdon tried to shrug out of Lou's grasp, but he tightened his grip and jerked him against the wall of the house. Mary gasped, but Lou ignored her. His pulse hammered through him, and his fingers moved to the scoundrel's collar.

Langdon made a choking sound but didn't try again to get out of Lou's hold. Rather, his lips tilted. "You should take better care of your property."

Lou released him abruptly and turned to Mary, who edged through the doorway in a pained way. A sound like a train filled his ears and his vision blurred. Whirling, he pushed Langdon up against the door.

"You better talk, and fast," he said.

"Release me or I'll have the police arrest you for assault."

Lou's jaw hurt. He ground his teeth and forced his fingers to unlock from Langdon's arms. "You're done for. Don't forget it."

Langdon sniffed and readjusted his shirt. "Have a pleasant life, Special Agent Riley." He turned and pushed into the house. Silence ensued.

Mary gazed off the porch, her face unreadable. A bird

twittered. Streetcars rumbled past, casting long shadows against the street. He stalked to Mary.

"Are you okay?" he asked.

She nodded but didn't look at him. He couldn't help himself. He touched her shoulders, gently moving his hands down her arms, looking for any bruising or indication that Langdon had physically mistreated her.

She didn't flinch.

"Are you sure you're okay? Absolutely sure?" He grasped her shoulders, searching her eyes for something, anything, to take away the worry that was cleaving into him.

"I'm sure." Her smile was calm as she backed out of his grip.

Clearing his throat, shoving his hands into his pockets, he asked, "Do you want to walk back to the hotel?"

"That's quite the walk," she murmured.

"I have an appointment at ten." He glanced at his watch. "That's in forty-five minutes. We can be to the office by then and you can wait. The agent in charge of escorting you has been reassigned, so it looks like—"

"I don't need an escort, Lou." She looked at him, her eyes earnest. "I'm a grown woman, quite capable of traveling home."

"I wish that was true, but times are troubled." He thought of the papers in his briefcase.

"They seem fine to me. Prohibition has things a bit topsy-turvy, but the war is over, our economy is recovering... What do you find to be the problem?"

"Let's walk," he suggested as he debated how much to tell her. She held her head high beside him, and if she noticed the stares of those they passed, she didn't let on. He rubbed the back of his neck for a moment and then gave in to his gut. "Our office has received some disturbing information. The Ku Klux Klan is reorganizing. Strategizing. We're expecting to see some integration of their policies and beliefs in the coming year, we're just not sure where or how much they'll be able to infiltrate the public psyche."

Mary's stride didn't slow. "I haven't heard such a thing."

"But you feel the stares, don't you? People look at you and see someone different than them. There's distrust here in Oregon of foreigners. Our office found disturbing evidence that the Klan will prey on people's fears. Especially with the influx of Chinese migrant workers."

"This is nothing new to me, Lou."

"It could influence laws," he said gravely.

"That may be so, but I believe they've already been influenced since the beginning of the country. You're a white man, Lou. Blond hair, blue eyes." She stopped walking and turned to pin him with those bottomless eyes of hers. "For you, life in America has been fair. It has not been so for others." She held up her arm, darker than his, and Lou found his gaze traveling the length of her bone structure, up to her shoulder, then across her dress, which he just now realized fit her perfectly.

He couldn't recall seeing her in this outfit before and abruptly noticed how the dress tapered off at her knees, exposing her legs and ankles. Heat rose to his neck. He yanked his eyes back up to meet hers.

Her mouth was parted, and suddenly he was filled with remembrance of the kiss they'd shared. He blinked, jerked the direction of his gaze to the road and began walking. "Every day we're making strides, though. The Klan is a dangerous group of people and the worst thing is, people in positions of authority are involved. I don't want you traveling alone. Not just because of your heritage, but because you're a beautiful woman."

There, he'd said it. A lump clogged his windpipe. He

peeked at Mary. A sober expression rested on her features. The wind stirred up her dark hair, and again he thought of their kiss.

"Many have called me beautiful," she said quietly and without pride.

"You don't like it?"

"Beauty brings challenges…." She trailed off.

"Life brings challenges to everyone." He took her arm and they crossed to the other side of the road. "We're almost to my office. After I deliver these papers, we'll figure out what to do with you."

"Excuse me?" She popped out of his grasp. "I have my ticket. Your twelve years of baby watching has finished."

He halted, gaping, while she strode ahead. "Wait…"

Her hand fluttered up, waving through the air as if dismissing him. He set his jaw and forged ahead.

"Now, stop just a moment," he said, grabbing her shoulders and stopping her. She felt fragile beneath his fingers and he loosened his hold. "You've been caring for us, Mary, not the other way around."

Her gaze flickered. "Either way, that time has passed. We're moving in different directions now."

True, and yet the knowledge pained him. He studied her, taking in the faint flush in her cheeks and her dewy eyes. A stray hair fluttered across her cheek. Using the tip of his finger, he drew it back over her ear. She released a soft breath that brought him full circle, right back to their kiss.

"Please don't look at me like that," she whispered.

"Like what?"

"Like you plan to kiss me again."

He couldn't help the smile tugging his lips. "And if I do?"

"This can't work. You know that. Do you plan to quit

your job? Stop traveling to foreign places and saving lives?"

He shook his head.

"I didn't think so," she said. "Quit worrying about me and live your life. I'm thankful for the shelter you provided, but that season is over."

"We're here." He gestured to the building in front of them with his briefcase, glad to stop this conversation in its endless tracks. "Come in and let's work this out. Then we're going to have an early supper and you can tell me what Langdon said to you in that hallway."

A few hours later, Mary chewed her bottom lip, watching as Lou spoke with the waiter at the hotel's restaurant. They'd returned to check out. A cramp tried to work its way through her toes, which she'd stuck into heels to try to look nice for Mrs. Silver.

And maybe for Lou.

It was the last day she'd see him after all. She fiddled with a button on her dress, wondering how he'd remember her. What would supper bring? More arguing? Surely so, if she told him what Langdon had said to her. He was to call her at the hotel, she'd told him, and she'd give him an answer.

There was only one answer to give.

Shuddering, she turned away from Lou's direction. While she'd waited at his work, she debated her possible courses of action. She could tell him the truth at supper and see if he'd help her or offer a different solution. Or she could go home, ignore Langdon's plan and look into getting a loan and opening a business.

"We're ready." Lou appeared beside her, his arm on her elbow and his breath minty. He brought her to the table. After they were given glasses of water, Lou gestured to the menu. "Order anything you want. My treat." His eyes sparkled.

She'd been drawn in by those eyes for too long. Could she forget how he'd sold the ranch beneath her feet? Even though he'd arranged for her to stay, his action had felt like a betrayal of sorts. No, she could not trust that sparkle as much as she longed to.

It was a longing she must deny herself.

Ordering was brief. The waiter took their menus, and then quiet followed. Lou folded a napkin across his lap and leaned back in his seat, hands lightly clasped on the starched tablecloth.

"I finished some work at the office today," he finally said.

She sipped her water. "Have they caught the man who shot you?"

"No, but we will. I'm on his trail. After supper today, I'm going to drop you at the train station, where a special agent will meet you and escort you home." At her look, he grinned. "You really think I'm going to let you traipse off all by yourself? I wouldn't let any woman do that."

"The point is that you're not in charge."

"Once you're safe," he continued without missing a breath, "I'm hunting this fellow down. I didn't see his face, but there was another man I caught a good look at. Talked to, even. A few visits to some unsavory places, and I'm thinking I'll find my shooter and maybe even a crime to tie him to."

"Besides shooting you?" Mary asked drily.

"Exactly." Lou gave her a slow wink, obviously pleased with all his plans.

The cad. He both infuriated her and made her smile. This back-and-forth was exhausting, though.

"Tell me," she said, aligning her knife with the edge of

her napkin. "What will you do when I'm not at the ranch when you return?"

His ego appeared to trip along with his grin. "Why wouldn't you be there?"

"I can think of a few reasons."

"I'm not gone yet. The buyers have agreed to keep you on as housekeeper. This sale... It's an offer, but that doesn't mean it's final. I wired Trevor the information yesterday, and he and Gracie are going to talk things through. He never needed the home he sold you, but Gracie's partial to the ranch. In fact, they'll be meeting me here tomorrow or the day after to talk things through."

The fact that he was trying to look out for her should have comforted her, but it didn't.

She let out an exasperated breath. "Do you not hear yourself? Why are you selling if Gracie and Trevor don't want to? Why bother? Can you not travel as you've always done? And things may remain the same."

The grin slid from his face. He leaned forward and pulled her hands toward him in a heated grip. His grasp was decidedly larger than hers, and she had to tear her eyes from their entwined palms to focus on his next words.

"Is that really what you want? To live out your days on secluded property?" His gaze probed her. The way his hands enveloped hers felt so right.... Her tongue tied within her mouth, and she could only look at him.

"I know you want more. You're made for more, Mary." He hesitated and then said quietly, "God has given you talents. Don't hide them on a ranch. Don't waste them on people who aren't around to appreciate what you have to offer."

He spoke of God. She blinked and pulled her hands free from his.

"I have never considered myself wasting away there. The meals I made, the clothes I darned and ironed, the prayers I prayed... It was healing. Not one second of my time there has been a waste." She had to work hard to keep her voice from shaking. "I am sorry your perspective is so very different than mine."

He started to speak and she held up a hand.

"Either way, what I do with my life is not up to you. Your plans for tomorrow are all well and good, but you have given no consideration to what I want. Did you plan to ask? Or do you plan to do whatever you want and then expect me to be there?"

His eyes widened. "I'm sorry—"

"Excuse me, miss. There's a telephone call for you." The waiter pointed to the lobby's desk, visible through the restaurant's entrance.

Lou's gaze narrowed. Mary ignored him, though a trembling had taken up residence in her stomach. "Thank you. I shall be there in a moment."

"Is there something you need to tell me?" Lou stood and walked around the table to her. "What did Langdon say to you?"

Sitting left her at a disadvantage and so she also stood, though it did little good with her small stature. Nevertheless, it must do for now. Lou and his authoritative ways must stop. She placed a hand on his chest and gave him a little nudge.

"This is a telephone call for me."

"Mary." His voice sharpened. "You're playing with a criminal. If there's something you need to say, say so now, because I'm not having my employee involved with the likes of him."

"Don't you think I know what he is?" She nudged him harder, but he refused to move. Well, she'd just go around him, then. But as she stepped to the side, he mirrored her. She hissed and glared up at him.

"Kindly move."

"Not until you tell me what's going on." His eyes were blue steel.

Very well. A surprising burst of anger popped through her. She threw her head up and gave him the sternest look she could muster.

"I know criminals, Lou Riley. You forget, I spent a week with them. It might've been twelve years ago, but I haven't lost my senses. My mind works just fine and I know exactly what I'm doing." Maybe not *exactly,* but at this moment she thought things were quite clear. "Move yourself before I make a scene."

The threat sent hotness to the back of her neck. She prayed he did not force her to do such a dreadful thing. His jaw worked, and his hands went to his narrow hips. He studied her, and she was torn between the irresistible urge to allow him to kiss her again or to scurry past and pick up the telephone.

He seemed to come to some internal decision. His jaw hardened. "Nope. No employee of mine is carousing with criminal types. I've said my piece. Now sit back down."

"Why you…you overbearing oaf." An unbelievable heat swept through her body and pooled in her belly. Her hands clenched. She ignored his raised eyebrows and sputtered, "F-fine, then. If you choose to be this way. Then. I. Quit."

His hands slid off his hips. She took advantage of his slack jaw to skirt around him, hustling to the telephone as fast as she could and hoping he didn't beat her to it.

This was the moment her life would change forever.

Chapter Twenty

Mary couldn't quit.

Lou was tempted to follow her, but her last words had punched a hole in his steady breathing. He opted to keep his distance and reassess the situation when she returned. Moments passed, filled with the sounds of conversation around him, clinking silverware, the aromas of food, and then she turned from the counter.

Her head was tilted down. Shoulders slumped. He frowned. Thoughts ricocheted through him, knotting his gut. He tapped his knuckles against the table.

The indecision twisting through him was unexpected. He didn't like the feeling, but stopping it was another matter.

She'd actually had the audacity to quit.

That wasn't like her. Did she mean her words? The look on her face… He'd never seen it there before. He'd wanted her to be independent, to be okay so he could leave this place for good, but now that she'd flung her independence in his face, well, what could a man make of that?

He rapped the table again, thinking. Plans were going well. Exactly how he'd thought he wanted months ago when he'd set things in motion. Even with the unforeseen shooting. It hadn't changed his plans, but it had affected him personally. Somehow getting shot and being stuck at the ranch with Josie and Mary had changed him, but he wasn't sure how, and even if he figured it out, he was pretty certain he wouldn't like what he found.

His own father had been trapped at home raising two sons alone after his mother died. And his brother, Gracie's dad, was held beneath the sway of his wife. He'd even cut off contact with Lou for almost twenty years because his wife disapproved of Lou's career choices.

No, he'd seen what a man leashed by hearth and home became. When he was young, he hadn't worried too much on it, but losing Sarah and Abby had reinforced his instincts and for twelve years he'd been just fine, footloose and fancy-free.

Until now.

Mary's independence threatened his own. That much he was sure about. After so long looking out for her, did he really want her gone from his life? *No.* But being hogtied to one place gave him the urge to draw his gun and target practice.

At least he might get to do that soon. This morning a junior agent had shared some fascinating intelligence. He and another agent had linked Lou's shooter to an international ring that was smuggling alcohol from Canada by way of Oregon ports. Given international waters were involved, the smuggling became a federal crime and he'd been given free rein to bring his shooter in. If he could just find a name…

Mary neared, cutting off his thoughts. A flush stained her cheekbones. He put his hands on his hips and battled the urge to apologize. And for what? Trying to protect her? It was an illogical, insensible reaction.

Scowling, he sat in his chair. She followed suit, sitting

across from him and fiddling with her silverware again. Busy fingers meant nervousness. He eyed her, but she wouldn't meet his gaze.

"Your food, sir." The waiter set their plates down.

"Thank you." He ate, but the food was tasteless. Mary picked at her potatoes. "You might as well tell me what that call was about. I'm going to find out eventually."

"I know. And that is what upsets me." She lifted her eyes.

"So let the cat out of the bag." He shrugged, though he felt anything but nonchalant. After all this time, it was as though she didn't trust him. The thought rubbed him wrong.

"I've been offered a deal of sorts. Employment in exchange for something." Her eyes dropped.

Lou's throat clenched and for the second time that day, a red haze crept into his vision. Fingers curling into fists, he took deep, even breaths. When he thought he could speak without yelling, or worse, scaring her, he said, "What's the exchange?"

She shook her head. "It's between us. Regardless, I'm in need of employment, and though I'd like to open my own shop someday, I think this will work better for now. It is a good thing for me to quit now rather than later. My future is secure, and you need not worry about me or my mother."

He scoffed, if only to let out the tension tightening every muscle in his body. "I'm not worried about her."

Mary frowned. "Despite how you feel, my mother will be in my life. I suppose it's also good you plan to leave."

Fighting words. He should be alarmed, but they eased his tension a little. Whatever plan she'd agreed to couldn't be permanent or she wouldn't be talking about keeping her ma in her life.

"A good thing, huh?" He flashed a little teeth and leaned forward.

"Don't try to charm me, Lou Riley. Your distaste for my mother is upsetting." She pushed her dish to the side. "I wish you would try to see her side of things. Forgive her, even."

"Sorry, but I have a hard time forgiving anyone who hurt you the way she did. That's just the fact of the matter."

"I see."

"I don't think you do."

She glanced to the right, where a clock perched against the wall. "It is time for me to leave."

Panic knotted the base of his neck. He had to fix things, and quick. "Look, I'm sorry for bossing you around earlier. What say you stay and give me the lowdown on the situation? Maybe I can help with this trade you're doing?" He kept his smile in place.

She shook her head. "I'm the only one who can fulfill the terms of the agreement."

"That so?" he drawled. His chest burned with the effort of staying calm.

"I'll be back to the house in a year or so. We shall meet again, I'm sure. Are you okay? You look…red."

He felt it. Drawing a heavy breath, he said, "This agreement isn't illicit, is it? Tell me it's not, Mary. Tell me you haven't sold yourself to protect that little girl."

She gasped. Then her face darkened as she shot up from her seat. "How could you think such a thing?" Her mouth worked.

He stood, too, but she was already reaching for her luggage. She rushed past him, leaving the restaurant in a flurry of movement. He groaned and tossed money on the table to cover the food. He'd really bungled this.

Maybe she wasn't planning a liaison, but he'd seen

Langdon look at her. He'd seen her paleness. Didn't take a genius to put two and two together. She might not plan to give in to Langdon's advances, but Lou had met his type before.

If someone didn't step in, Langdon would try to force himself on Mary, and she would never be the same.

Lou spun on his heel and stalked out of the restaurant. Yes, he had a shooter to catch and a ranch to sell and a new employment opportunity, but Mary meant more to him than material things. And so did Josie.

This so-called deal put them in danger, and he would do whatever it took to stop it.

The nerve of that man!

Mary strode the streets, brushing past people as she worked to clear the steam from her head. How could he think such a thing of her? Did he really believe she'd ever put herself in that position? Perhaps this plan could use some finessing and it might require a bit of dodging, but she hoped for the optimum.

To raise Josie as her own.

A breeze rustled up against her and waltzed with her skirt. She should have brought a sweater of some sort. Oregon's personality was moody, and chill bumps rose on her arms in reaction to the cool wind.

Or maybe it was the thought of having a family. Though her heart ached for Josie, knowing the child's mother might pass soon, Mr. Langdon had assured her that there were no living relatives, no one to claim Josie. Without him, she would be put into an orphanage. Mary couldn't abide such a thought. Perhaps her own childhood had been unstable. Constantly moving, a father who was in and out of her life physically, a mother who was emotionally in and out, but there'd been many times of love. There'd been food and clean clothes.

She'd seen orphanages, but worse, she'd heard tales of them. Many of the prostitutes her mother worked with came from these places. Many had been more girl than woman.

A shudder swept through her.

No. Mr. Langdon and the orphanages wouldn't get her sweet girl. His plans for Josie were vile enough to let her know that when Josie's mother died, the girl would be in harm's way. Mr. Langdon's wicked plan *had* to be an answer to prayer. God could use evil and turn it to good. Perhaps that was His plan for her.

She stopped at the corner and waited for the coming streetcar. She wrapped her arms firmly around her ribs. A year or less. If she could make it through that, then both she and Josie would be okay.

She'd agreed to show up in the morning for the job, which meant she should find somewhere to sleep this evening.

"Mary!"

She whirled to see Lou sprinting toward her. His broad frame filled her with a restless longing, an unfair yearning. She closed her eyes, pressing them to block out his image.

He reached her, his breaths short and shallow. Perhaps his scar still ached.

"You shouldn't be running," she said, opening her eyes.

"I'm fine. Look—" he swiped a hand through his hair "—I really am sorry. I've got no business telling you what to do. The past few weeks have been crazy for me. Getting shot, seeing Josie, which brings back all sorts of memories… Let's just say I'm trying to make things right and I feel like I'm failing." The words sounded strained as he said them.

A streetcar rumbled to a stop in front of them. She stepped onto it, and Lou followed. They held the railings as it picked up speed. What could she answer him? Seconds turned into minutes. He let her think, for which she was grateful.

Finally, she turned to him. He still wore that pained, uncomfortable expression. It pulled at the creases of his eyes and made him quite attractive. Stifling a smile, she said softly, "I suppose you're not used to apologies."

His lips tilted. "I'm used to being in charge. Giving orders and having people obey."

"Perhaps there was a time for that in my life, but being by myself so much at the ranch has taught me to make my own way." She hesitated, then reached out and touched one of his hands. His skin was tanned and scarred, rough beneath her fingers. "Your desire to protect me is noble, but I must be free to make my own choices. To control someone is not loving."

His throat worked. His eyes were such a clear blue, penetrating and serious. "The last thing I want is to hurt you or treat you less than what you deserve. I'm going to try to trust your judgment, but I need you to trust me, too."

"When it comes to my life, I reserve trust for myself."

"What about God?" he countered.

The jab stung a bit. "Perhaps my trust in Him is not perfect, but I'm working on it."

"I guess that's the most anyone can do." The streetcar jolted to a stop. They shifted closer to allow a woman laden with bags to squeeze past. Lou's cologne and minty scent enveloped Mary. She was so close she could feel the warmth of his breath on her hair.

As soon as the woman passed, she shifted away, ignoring every impulse to stay near him. The car started up again.

"So…truce?" Lou asked.

She faced him, taking in his sober look. "I suppose so."

"Great. Let me help you, then. What's the plan? What can I do? I have resources you can only dream of." He gave her a lopsided grin.

She reciprocated, thankful the tension between them had ebbed. "For now I must find a hotel to stay at. Tomorrow I will begin my new job."

"Your ma know yet?"

"I'll send a telegram once I'm settled."

"You don't think she'll worry?"

Mary quirked a brow. "Do you?"

"A little." He rubbed at the light stubble at his chin. "Truth is, she's a hard one to pin down, but I can usually see when someone is up to no good. She's about spent all her no-goodness, I think."

"I'm not sure whether you just complimented her or if that was an insult."

"Call it the truth." He winked at her, then his face went stiff. His eyes narrowed. "Don't move," he said softly.

"What?" She turned to look where his gaze had fastened, but he was already shifting, putting his body between hers and whatever he saw. She swallowed. Holding still this way made her more aware of the rapid pump of her pulse and the dryness of her mouth.

"There's a hotel at the next corner. Small but nice. You mind staying there?" He swung her a quick glance, questioning.

"No, no, that's fine." She swallowed hard. "Is everything okay?"

He hesitated.

Suddenly the need to know overwhelmed her. The need for him to share with her more than the curious oddities or the amazing inventions he'd seen on his travels. She wanted to share in his struggles and perhaps even his adventures. An unfamiliar prickle crawled across her skin.

"Please tell me," she said quietly.

He looked around and then bent his head forward, blocking her view of everything but him. "The man behind me sought me out to parlay information right before I was shot. I believe he followed me onto this streetcar, or maybe it's just chance, but I've got to talk to him."

"But first you need to see me settled?"

"Yes." His eyes searched hers.

"That's not necessary. I can do it myself."

He was already shaking his head. "No. Not in this city, not at night."

The streetcar shuddered to another stop.

"Really, I'll be fine. Surely a reputable hotel like you've suggested will be a safe place."

"Maybe so, but it's a risk I'm not willing to take."

And there it was again, that urge to wrap herself in his arms and to never let go. The feeling struck her with such force that she couldn't speak, could only lose herself in the intensity of the moment.

Movement grabbed her attention. Bowler Hat disappeared out the door. She pointed.

Lou blinked, spun around. He grabbed her wrist. "Will you come with me? It's dark, dangerous… I'll try to keep you safe, but you'll need to trust me."

Indecision rooted her feet and each second passed in agonizing slowness. The engine's gears ground, propelling her into action.

She moved forward. Slipped her hand into his and let him lead her into the night, after the mysterious man.

Chapter Twenty-One

Their breathing melded with the sounds of evening as they dropped from the streetcar to the cobbled road. Lou's hand tightened around Mary's smaller one. He couldn't believe she'd come with him, that he was actually going to bring her with while he interrogated this guy.

Her hand was warm in his as they stepped near a brick building. The light was waning, turning into a smoky dusk. He searched for the bowler hat. People still lingered outside, some going to work, others leaving after a hard day.

Businesses lined this street. Women clicked down the sidewalk in heels. Men in suits and eyeglasses who'd stayed longer than expected locked their offices for the night. Still no hat. The man reached medium height. He'd blend in well.

Lou groaned. Mary's fingers flexed in his.

"He went that way," she whispered. Her chin nudged to the right.

He followed the direction of her gaze and spotted a dark alley ahead, hidden between two narrow buildings. He strode forward, releasing her hand. When they reached the crevice, he turned to her.

"Stay here."

"I should go with you." Her eyes shone black in the encroaching night.

"Nothing can happen to you." That knowledge resounded through him. No matter what, she had to stay safe. "You can keep an eye out. Stay here, in the shadows." He moved her inside the alley, up against the wall. "No one will see you, but you'll see them."

Gut tight, he left her there, clutching her dress and looking nervous. It couldn't be helped, though. The man waiting at the end of the alley had something to impart. He wouldn't have followed Lou otherwise.

He edged against the wall, reaching for his revolver. Nothing stirred in the alley. The light from the street only reached so far. A dank, putrid smell pervaded his senses. He blocked it, focusing on the barely discernible shadow at the end of the alley.

Flattening his back, he peeked at Mary. He could barely see her. That was good. He whipped his gaze the other way.

"You wanted to talk," he asked, keeping his voice low, letting the natural echoes carry his words to the other party.

A clatter punctuated the stillness. Then rustling. Finally, Lou's eyes adjusted and he could see the outline of a hat as the man moved near. He adjusted his gun, keeping it low at his hip and aimed lower. His trigger finger flexed against the revolver's hilt.

"Took you long enough." The Irish lilt in Bowler Hat's words confirmed Lou's thoughts on his identity. The guy sidled up, hands in the air. "I'm not armed, so you can lower your weapon. I just need to talk."

Lou kept his revolver aimed. "Come closer."

"I'm coming, mister." Scuffling ensued, and then the man stood opposite him. The odor of fish guts clung to him. Dusk had settled long ago, marking the way for darkness to creep in. Lou wanted to see his face, but the crescent moon left a lot to be desired for light.

"That your woman over there?" the man asked.

"Who wants to know?" Lou countered.

"No sirree, I'm not stupid enough to give my name. I just wanted to pass on some information and I've heard you're to be trusted. You don't take bribes."

"Go on." Things were getting interesting, and not in a good way.

"There's been talk about shady characters in the bureau. It's been a few weeks, but I didn't have anyone else to give my information to."

"Why me? Besides all your jabber and flattery, you've got no need to pass this on." Besides, Lou had one use for the guy. "Tell me who shot me, and you can go your way."

The man let out a short laugh. "If I knew that, I wouldn't say. I've my reasons for singling you out, and they don't include a shooter. When I tried talking to you last month—"

"You got me shot," Lou interrupted, feeling his patience grow thin. "If you've something important to say, then let's go down to the station and write it down legal-like."

"I told you, mister, there're eyes. This is for you and only you." The man scuffled again and then moved to the center of the alley. "Wasn't my fault what happened last time. I'm telling you the truth. This time I was careful, though. Followed you and made sure we wouldn't be interrupted." He took a step toward Lou. "I'm handing you the correspondence, and you can decide what to do with it. As for me, I'm leaving town and don't want you searching me out."

Lou swallowed his scoff. As if he'd really let this bootlegger slide through his fingers.

The man swept the bowler off his head, closed the distance between them and handed it to Lou. "The information is in the seam. Before I go, I need to know this lady friend of yours isn't going to be in the way. Distractions get a man killed real easy. Even when it's just the messenger."

Lou grabbed the hat, his blood thundering through him at the guy's proximity to Mary. Messenger or not, he didn't know who this man was or what he was capable of. His number-one priority right now was to protect Mary. He placed the hat on his head and stepped into the light.

"Whoa, mister…" The man backed up, hands in surrender.

"The lady means nothing to me." He jerked his head to the alley opening. "Make sure whoever sent you knows I'll take care of the situation. No distractions." He waved his gun. "Now, scram."

"What a disappointment," Lou muttered.

Mary flinched when he took her by the arm. The mysterious man had faded out of the alley and disappeared onto the street, but her limbs still felt paralyzed both by the situation and the words exchanged. Somehow she set into motion next to Lou, her lips like cotton and her heart pattering an uneven rhythm.

They found a streetcar still operating and settled in a corner. The people around her looked tired and bedraggled, no doubt from a long day's work. They would never guess the drama that had just transpired.

Bribes in high places. Strange stalkers. Unknown assailants. She almost wished she hadn't followed Lou off the streetcar, and yet the experience had given her a different perspective of her former employer. That carefree smile he wore masked so very much. In the alley he'd sounded completely in control, powerful. Not lighthearted in the least.

How many times had he faced such danger? She

chanced a glance at him and the hat upon his head, which supposedly contained the secret missive.

Gracie would find this all very exciting, but Mary was only conscious of exhaustion. She longed to be home, kneading bread, breathing in the delicious aroma of yeast and flour and milk. She wished to listen to Josie's chatter and to feel the sage-scented breeze upon her brow, not to ride a loud streetcar filled with odors and stares. Adventure wasn't for her.

Home and hearth. Family. Those filled her heart.

"Are you okay?" Lou's brow crinkled, and Mary flushed. He'd caught her daydreaming while still looking at him. Did he think she'd been ogling? The thought quivered through her.

"I am fine," she said.

"You look shaken," he persisted.

"Really, all is well. I am simply tired." And heart worn. Not only had the experience been exhausting, but Lou's words still echoed in her head. *The lady means nothing to me.*

"We'll get you to the hotel, then. Are you sure you want to go through with tomorrow? I don't trust Langdon."

The one thing she felt for certain was that she didn't feel like arguing. Tiredness weighted her very bones. "You shouldn't spend time worrying about him when it sounds as though you have something wrong with your Bureau of Investigation."

He snorted. "I doubt that."

"Why so certain? The government has a long history of deceit and underhanded methods." She'd heard the stories of her maternal grandmother and grandfather. How they'd been forced to march. Offered land only to have it rescinded. And more tales of blood and lies. No, Lou might do much good, but that didn't mean all men in government were like him.

"You're right about that, but in this case, I have a different feeling."

"Feelings are not a solid guidepost for life." She crossed her arms.

"Right again, but the gut never lies."

She grimaced, and he laughed.

"Instinct and feelings are two different animals," he continued. "One to be trusted, the other to be wary of."

"At last we agree." She felt the corners of her lips lift unexpectedly.

They arrived at the hotel too soon. After situating her in a room, Lou said an unnervingly brisk good-night, and she shut her door.

Alone at last.

The room smelled a little of mildew, but she trusted the bed to be clean. The space looked sparse, filled with only a dresser, a bed and one nightstand. A lone lamp stood in a corner. She set her bag beside the bed, and then went to check the tub. The hotel had running water, thank goodness.

She cleaned up and even rinsed her dress, hoping it would dry by morning. Sending it down to be laundered seemed a waste of money when she must leave in the morning. As she worked, Lou's words revolved in her head.

The lady means nothing to me.

Deep down, she knew she meant something to him. Something more than a friend. But to hear him so casually dismiss their relationship to the bowler-hat man sent apprehension through her. The words had left his mouth without effort. Whatever he felt for her, it wouldn't impede his job or change his life.

And did she want it to? The memory of his kiss tingled her lips. She rubbed at them and climbed into bed.

No, she had never wanted a husband. Kisses were one thing, but everything after could only stir memories she'd long healed from. Or at least suppressed. The thought nagged at her. She pulled the blankets up and rolled to her side, staring at the wall.

Hadn't Miss Alma helped her? Years ago she'd told the kind lady everything that had transpired when Trevor's mother had arranged for her to be kidnapped by a gang of evil men. They'd planned to sell her, and though there'd been rough talk, handling that still gave her chills, and countless leers, no one had assaulted her.

The emotional impact had still been traumatic.

Memories traipsed through her mind, rolling silently like one of those new films they showed in theaters lately. Only her memories were in both color and sound, and she couldn't turn them off with a flick of the reel.

Restless, she rolled to the other side and plumped her pillow. Things that had happened so long ago shouldn't keep hurting, but they did. Granted, the fear had subsided and now she felt only an uncomfortable knot of tension.

Why was she thinking of marriage in conjunction with Lou, and what would he do about the attraction between them? And if he did do something, how would she respond?

Marriage might bring it all back, stir up too many issues. Despite Miss Alma's assurances, the thought of being trapped, powerless, in a permanent contract with a man, closed her throat in a panic.

Even if the contract was with Lou.

His kiss, his many kindnesses throughout the years, shouldn't drag her thoughts in this direction. Why had being with him these past weeks make her think of marriage? Perhaps Miss Alma's hint in the store about a young man sparking for her was what had sent her mind down the path. Or it could've been the way Lou interacted with Josie. In so many ways he reminded her of her own departed father. When he'd been in the beginning stages of drink, he'd been quite affectionate and loving. Though his mood had often turned to moroseness followed by oblivion, she'd treasured the first hour of attention he gave her. Children needed that. Lou didn't drink, but he had that same playfulness when dealing with Josie.

And that was why future thoughts of Lou must halt, because any path they took together could only lead to a dead end.

Besides, there was no way she'd leave Josie. Mr. Langdon had made quite clear what he *thought* might happen to the girl when her mother passed away, and though Mary longed to turn him in for the evil he'd suggested, she doubted any official would take her word against a wealthy businessman like Mr. Langdon. She couldn't prove his words, and he'd done nothing illegal that she knew of.

One year. She'd give one year or less, just until Mrs. Silver passed away, and then Langdon had promised to give her guardianship of Josie. She would press to adopt the girl, though she had little to bargain with.

She probably should have told Lou what Langdon had threatened.

She squeezed her eyes closed, longing for sleep to take these burdens away. Her eyelids burned with exhaustion, but worry kept her awake.

If she hadn't accepted Langdon's employment, Josie would be in harm's way. There had been no other choice, she tried to reassure herself.

Yet she kept thinking of the way he stared at her. The

predatory quality to his look. She couldn't escape the feeling that she was walking into a trap.

She shifted again in the bed before rolling out and digging through her luggage until she felt the small Bible Miss Alma had given her years ago. After clicking on the lamp, she leafed through it until she found Psalms.

Her finger followed chapter 69, to verse 16.

Hear me, O Lord, for Your lovingkindness is good; turn to me according to the multitude of Your tender mercies. And do not hide Your face from Your servant. For I am in trouble…

Prickles scattered across her skin at the words.

Hear me speedily. Draw near to my soul and redeem it; deliver me because of my enemies.

She read to the last verse and into the next chapter. She read until her soul felt settled and her thoughts calm. No matter what occurred in the next year, she could trust God to be near, to be her help in time of need. She closed the book, laid it beside her pillow and crawled back beneath the sheets.

The sound of a door closing nearby made the walls shake.

Was Lou leaving? For a second, the preposterous urge to follow him swept through her, but then logic intervened. Traipsing all over Portland because of curiosity wasn't something she could afford to do. She must be rested and feeling well for tomorrow.

The last thing she wanted was for Mr. Langdon to change his mind.

With thoughts of Josie and Lou crowding her mind, images of them playing at the picnic, riding on the train, she finally slept.

Chapter Twenty-Two

It wasn't hard to find his mark, even in a city the size of Portland. The bloke's eyes and coloring, combined with his accent and odor, brought Lou to the Willamette River's docks. He'd left the hotel long before sunrise to get a head start on the dockworkers.

He wanted to see who showed up. The man claimed to be leaving town, but experience had taught him that people usually stayed with the familiar, even at their own risk. Unless he was in immediate peril, Lou doubted the man would just give up his job and leave the state.

Water lapped at the dock, dank and noisy. A heavy mist coated the air and made him glad he'd worn his coat. He watched the sun slowly start its trek upward. A hazy orange that brought new hope to some, new despair to others.

He shook the maudlin thoughts away. He was a man of action, seeking out criminals, pursuing justice, not pondering the mistakes he might've made. Or the people he'd hurt.

He hadn't missed that look on Mary's face last night when they'd exited the alley. There'd been a fraction of a second where her calm facade slipped and he'd seen hurt... but from what? Maybe he'd misinterpreted things. Still, when he'd dropped her at the hotel door, guilt had turned him into a brusque person, and he'd skedaddled before she could stir his emotions up any more.

Things had been better when she'd kept house while he'd traveled. Whenever he went home and life started feeling too cozy, he headed out. She'd been right about that unconscious pattern.

Frowning, he watched as mist dissipated simultaneously with the arrival of men. Heavy boots clomped down the docks. English was the primary language spoken, but every so often he'd hear some Mandarin or Gaelic.

Such diversity. As a young man, he'd thought God was incredible and brilliant. One of the things that had attracted him to Sarah was her artwork. His wife had used wild colors in her paintings, scattering them across the canvas, her thick brushstrokes laying claim to the proof of God's beauty with her talent.

He'd loved her so much.

She'd been a vibrant fire, and their Abby was just like her. Alive and beautiful.

And then snuffed out before their lives had barely begun.

He blinked hard and studied the men. Most were small framed and sinewy like the man he'd met, but no one shared his towheadedness. Of course, the guy could've gotten a new hat to cover his blondness, but Lou doubted that. This kind of work was too physical. A hat might fall in the water and waste someone's hard-earned money.

These men worked long hours. He worked hard, too, but in a different way. Sarah had appreciated him, but she'd wanted him to come home. To be always home for her.

Just like Mary.

And yet they were different. Sarah had been a flame, hot and exciting with a quick temper and ready tongue. She'd challenged him defiantly…and he'd loved it.

Mary wasn't like that. She reminded him of a steady warmth, careful and secure, but no less exciting. Her flame was like that deep blue kind, the color beneath the bright oranges, the kind you needed to keep a stove cooking.

He grimaced at the mental analogy and decided to keep his focus on scoping out dockworkers, not beguiling beauties who had no trust for men and no taste for travel.

Forty minutes later he located his quarry.

Clamping his jaw, he strode toward him. Raucous laughs filled the air; grunts and the sounds of things hitting various spots filled the previous silence.

Lou dodged people and continued stalking his man. A foot away, the guy spotted him and took off at a run.

Just great.

Uttering a groan, he sprinted after him. His feet pounded against the uneven wood of the dock. Faces blurred as he raced past. He managed to jump an outstretched foot and couldn't resist whipping a grin at the offender. He paid for that, though, when his right foot connected with a bucket. It flew forward, landing to his right.

"Hey," the guy next to it sputtered. Lou ignored him and kept going, hopping over a pile of salmon, never taking his sights off the man in front of him. The docks shuddered under his gait, but his breath stayed easy. Good news for the old wound.

Sucking in another lungful of fish-scented air, he rounded a corner in time to see the bootlegger duck into an old brick building. The place looked unsteady, but Lou followed. At the door, he drew his gun and edged in.

"I'm not going to hurt you, I just have a few questions," he called out.

A clatter echoed through the room in front of him. Filthy windows allowed little sun to cut through the dimness of the place. It appeared to be a dilapidated warehouse, no longer used. Sliding forward, he moved behind a metallic-looking contraption and then peered around it.

Shafts of light hit the wooden floor, highlighting dust motes that danced in lazy abandon. Undisturbed. He couldn't see the floor well enough to track prints. He'd just have to convince the guy of his intentions.

"I'm going to step into the light," he said. His words carried well. Unless the man had slipped out, he had to hear him. "My gun is in the holster. I just have some questions about that hat I bought from you."

Sweat tickled the back of his neck and his scar burned. It was step out in faith or do nothing. But faith in what?

Banishing the thought, he forced his limbs into motion. Slowly and carefully, he inched onto the floor while holstering his weapon. His ears strained for the slightest indication that someone aimed to shoot him. Planning to dodge a bullet put an ache in a man's gut, that was for sure.

He made it out in the middle just fine, though. He exhaled a long breath. And waited.

The guy didn't make him wait long. A shuffle and a stirring of air, then the man who'd given him the bowler hat appeared in his peripherals, hands up.

Lou's neck relaxed a tad, but he kept his hands at the ready. He turned slowly. "We need to talk." Carefully, he gestured at the empty space surrounding them. "This place safe?"

"Yeah." The man appeared conflicted, edgy. His gaze shot around before his posture shifted to a more relaxed shape. He walked forward and held out his hand. "The name's O'Leary. I've been undercover, working the smugglers, trying to get a lead on which boats are bringing the hooch into Oregon. A few weeks ago I heard some blokes talking about a hit. It was put out you were going to die."

"Almost," Lou muttered.

"So I started digging because I recognized your name from a few years back. You helped take down that kidnapper, Mendez. It was a real coup. I've been in the bureau for a while now and I remember how he kept giving us the slip."

Lou gave O'Leary a look and his throat bobbed.

"Anyway," he hurried, "I tried to meet up with you, give you a tip, but I was there at the wrong time, too late."

"You risked your cover to keep me from dying? That's a dangerous move."

"Not quite. I'd had a hunch the smuggler in charge of this operation was nearby. I wanted to get a look at those arrested. I saw you by chance and recognized your likeness from a bureau photograph. I felt like God was prompting me to give you a heads-up."

"God?"

"Yeah, you know the Big Guy who loves us?"

"Don't tell me you're religious."

"Me and the Big Guy, we talk a bit. So I went to find you, but I guess someone was tailing me, or maybe lying in wait for you...." O'Leary's mouth twisted. "These bootleggers, they're talking about big money getting dished out. Well, people around here with big money include politicians and smugglers. I listened closer and found out you bumped off someone's cousin, and that someone has had a contract out on you for over a year."

"That long?"

O'Leary grinned, his teeth flashing in the muted light. "Your reputation doesn't do you justice. You're like a shadow, which is why it took me so long to get to you. People know you have a hideout, but no one knows where it is. If the higher-ups have any idea, they're not saying."

"Why didn't you take this information to them?" Lou

reached in his pocket and drew out the paper that had been hidden in the bowler.

Fear flashed across O'Leary's face. He backed up. "Why'd you bring that?" His glance swiveled across the room.

"Relax." He tucked the hat away. "I figured it would be safer on me than in any hiding place." Lou studied O'Leary. "Are you sure the information in it is correct?"

"Pretty sure. I jotted things down as I heard them.... Your lady... I don't know her name, but you should keep a watch on her. Keep her near. They have spies everywhere."

"Who? I need names. More than what you gave me."

"Look, I've done more than I should. If anyone hears, I'm a goner."

Probably true. Lou rubbed the back of his neck. Mary was by herself right now at the hotel. No one knew where they were, but maybe he should have brought her with him.

No. The docks were no place for a lady.

"I appreciate this, O'Leary, but I have to ask again. Why didn't you take it to my supervisor? He could have safely relayed the information to me."

"I didn't even know you were still alive until I saw you by chance at that hotel restaurant. And then...well, I told you, sir, ears and eyes, everywhere." O'Leary blinked, looked around, then held out his hand again. "It's an honor to meet you."

Lou gave a curt nod and shook his hand. "And you. Thank you for your service to our country. You're a real credit to the bureau."

O'Leary acknowledged the compliment with a flush and tilt of his chin, then he swiveled and melded back into the shadows. Lou backed up, too, until he knew he was no longer discernible.

The paper burned against his thigh. O'Leary had given

him the name of the smuggler he thought wanted him dead. It wouldn't take much to find out if he was related to Mendez.

His gut told him if he found the smuggler, he'd find his shooter.

The man had messed him up good, not just laying him up for weeks, but putting him through a bunch of emotional weirdness he wanted no part of. He had his plans, and they didn't include a beautiful woman, a sweet kid or a God he'd stopped trusting long ago.

Mary's head throbbed when she woke up.

The lady means nothing to me.

Perfect. Now Lou's words were following her into the morning. There really was no reason for them to still be in her head. Of course he hadn't meant them. She rolled out of bed, went to the water room and splashed her face clean. A clean towel at the side of the sink felt like bliss against the headache pounding her skull.

If only she were home, baking. Sinking her knuckles into floured dough, creating nutritious perfection. Inhaling the warm aroma of cinnamon and yeast. And when she took this job, she might be given the opportunity to work in the kitchen.

Drawing in a deep, cleansing breath, she prayed for wisdom and set about getting ready for the day. She left the hotel, head slightly clearer and walk brisk. Morning fog hugged the streets. Her luggage felt heavy without Lou to help her.

But he hadn't been in his room. Not in the lobby. And she was through relying on him. Through being the poor girl who'd been kidnapped. Sleep and reading the Bible had refreshed her spirit. She no longer wished to be taken care of but to step out and take care of others.

Determined, she asked someone for directions to a post office. After sending a telegram to her mother explaining the situation, she hopped aboard a streetcar and began her journey to Mrs. Silver's.

Closing her eyes, she leaned against her seat and thought of Josie's smile and endless chatter. Such a stubborn, sweet little girl. Her arms ached to hold her. Then Lou's smile invaded her thoughts. Her eyes shot open. The car shuddered to a stop and she realized she was near Mrs. Silver's home.

By the time she walked to the house, the mist had receded, but clouds rolling overhead warned of coming rain. The heavy scent of it filled the air. She let herself into the gate and moments later, faced a sour-looking Mr. Baggs.

"I'm here for employment," she said, the words wobbling out of her. She'd never applied for a job before. She forced her shoulders back. "Mr. Langdon told me to come this morning."

Mr. Baggs's eyebrows lowered. "Servants go to the back." He shut the door in her face.

Oh. She frowned. Perhaps she should have known that. She hefted her luggage and found her way to the back. Mr. Baggs opened the door as she neared. He must have been watching for her.

Lord, give me strength.

Her nerves thrummed a frantic tune as he let her in. The walls closed in on her. She followed him down a narrow, gray hallway. An odd smell permeated the place, and it was so very quiet.

Finally, they climbed stairs and then passed through a door that opened into a spacious room with pleasing blue wallpaper and regal furniture, and at last she felt she could breathe.

"Mr. Langdon will be right with you. Have a seat." Mr. Baggs gave her an odd look, his brows crinkling together like fuzzy caterpillars. The unexpected image caused her to smile, which prompted a disapproving grunt from the butler.

"Wait here." The door closed behind him with a grim finality.

Mary clutched her luggage to her chest. Was she doing the right thing? The enormity of this choice settled on her shoulders like extra weight. She sank onto a couch someone had positioned against the wall.

Pain in her knuckles caught her attention. She looked at her hands. White and strained. Her breaths quickened. This would be different, so different than anything she'd known. Her eyes prickled and she blinked rapidly.

She'd agree to work for Mr. Langdon, but wanted nothing to do with the man except for him to fulfill his part of the bargain. He'd promised to pull up a contract. Perhaps she should have involved Lou after all.

But what could he do? This was employment. Yes, Mr. Langdon scared her, but that did not mean he'd breach the contract or try anything inappropriate. Especially in his sister's house.

"Miss O'Roarke." The subject of her thoughts sailed into the room and held out his hand.

Out of habit, Mary stood, leaving her luggage on the floor, but she did not offer her own hand in return.

His features remained placid even as his hand lowered, but his eyes… She repressed a shudder. "Good morning, Mr. Langdon. Have you brought the contract?"

"Ah, yes, the contract." His lips stretched into an alarming half circle. "Unfortunately, circumstances have changed, and we will need to renegotiate terms."

Mary froze and a trembling started in her stomach, working through her body until her knees ached.

"You see—" his brows quirked up and he tapped his

finger against his chin "—this morning I experienced a most unsettling and inconvenient loss. Quite unexpectedly my sister decided to die, thus ruining my plans for…" He flashed his teeth at her. "Well…for you, my dear."

Mary couldn't breathe. A paralysis had hold of her.

"I see you're afraid. Very good." His eyes slit. He moved toward her and his fingers pressed roughly against her neck. "Your pulse is jumping. Rather like a little rabbit leaping away. That's quite exciting…. May I call you Mary?"

She couldn't move. Fright had rooted her to the floor and every muscle in her body locked into place. This had been a colossal mistake. What had she done? "Where's Josie?" she managed to say through lips that felt heavy and numb.

"Josie is the least of your worries," he whispered, bringing his face close to hers. His eyes glowed with an unnatural fervor. "Mmm, your vein is pulsing."

His fingers dug into her neck and his thumb crept to the other side. He squeezed. Mary wanted to gag, to shut her eyes, to melt through the floor and disappear.

He released her and backed away. She sucked in air, too much, and her vision wavered.

"Don't faint, my dear girl. That wouldn't do. Terror is good for you. It speeds blood flow, increases awareness… Shall we talk a bit?" The door behind him opened and he turned to Baggs. "Send someone in with tea, would you? The news of my sister's demise has greatly upset our newest employee."

The door shut and Mr. Langdon turned back to her. "Have a seat. Rest your legs and take some steady breaths. I have a new proposition for you."

Chapter Twenty-Three

"Since my sister has passed away, my proposal of yesterday has become void. Furthermore, my needs have changed. I'm aware of your mother's reputation. Have you ever considered following in her footsteps? That's what I'm offering you now." A smug smile stretched his lips, as though he believed he'd already won. "A steady job at my side, seeing to my needs, in exchange for Josie. You'll have the full care of her, should you accept this offer."

Mary felt even more faint. His gaze burrowed into her, intrusive and cold.

She sank onto the couch, wishing to disappear within its confines. Never would she accept what he offered.

Never.

Could she bolt for the servants' hallway? What would happen if he followed? Her derringer was in her luggage, but dare she use it? She cut her eyes in his direction. He studied her as though she was a trifle to be bought in a store.

Her mind whirled. Mrs. Silver…dead. What about Josie? Was she safe? If she didn't accept this plan, who would protect Josie? She desperately wanted to be brave and stand up to Mr. Langdon, but the present seemed to be colliding with the past. She looked at him and saw Mendez.

She blinked. His features did resemble her late captor's, though his complexion was much lighter.

"Yes, you're putting it together, aren't you?" The smile on his lips chilled her. "Do you really think I stumbled onto that ranch house by accident? It's nestled in a valley and blends so well that none of my men have been able to find the place. It took me, the one with brains, to follow my cousin's directions accurately."

Her breath caught. It couldn't be…could it?

"Getting Josie to you was a small feat. You see, I've had plans for a long time now, and they've been foiled by ignorant men. Success took a woman's help, whether she realized it or not." He walked forward and sat beside her. The couch sank and she pulled back, away.

His breath, rank and sour, puffed over her. "I don't mean to bore you with the details, only to let you know you're rather stuck. You see, my plans have been in place since my cousin was ruthlessly murdered by that employer of yours."

He thought Lou killed Mendez? She met Mr. Langdon's crazy eyes and finally felt as if she could breathe. The adrenaline rush was fading, leaving a tiredness she must shake off if she was to survive this.

"Lou didn't kill Mendez," she told him shakily.

"Oh, he surely did."

"Mendez was poisoned. I saw him myself."

"Do you think I care how it happened or who caused it? My cousin was assigned a simple job. Find Striker and bring you back to me. I couldn't allow his obsession for Striker to stand in the way of what I wanted . He died trying to fulfill his duty. Don't you think I know who was in charge at that hideaway? You must understand, Mendez was my favorite cousin. We shared certain…qualities."

"I—I don't understand.... Why did you want me?"

"You don't remember?" His brows pulled together and his lips tightened. "My father visited your mother often. He brought me when I was twelve, and that's when I first saw you."

A rush of sickness rose in her stomach. She remembered him now. A young boy who had stared so much she felt uncomfortable and never met his gaze. She couldn't recall his eye color, perhaps because she'd avoided him so much. Months later, she and her mother left in search of her father, and then her mother had dropped her off at Trevor's.

"How did you find me?"

"By chance, as it were. I saw your mother on a business trip when I was a young man. She was frantic, searching for your father, and I realized we could help each other."

"You bribed her."

"It didn't take much. Women are emotional creatures, and your mother's loyalty is commendable. Too bad your father died before she could reach him."

Mary pressed her fingertips against her forehead, willing the ache to recede. All this time she'd blamed Trevor's mother for selling her, but it had been her mother who'd led the villains straight to her door.

Lord, help me. The prayer rose in her heart and crossed her lips.

Mr. Langdon uttered a harsh noise that masqueraded as a laugh. "God isn't anywhere near you. In fact, I'm quite certain He abandoned you long ago, right about the time your father left."

She flinched.

"That's right. I know all about him. Your mother, too. Like I said, she's quite loyal for a woman. Back to my proposition. In a moment, Baggs will be bringing your tea and some special paperwork regarding my newest offer. Don't look so disgusted. You worked at Julia's brothel, did you not? The one your mother left you at to chase down her foolish husband, the place where I found you."

"I was a seamstress, nothing more." The words sounded weak, even to her ears. She kept thinking of Lou's *the lady means nothing to me,* and now Mr. Langdon's assertion God was nowhere near. Had God left her again? Would He allow a repeat of the past? She could not bear such a thing, and yet it seemed certain to occur.

"You could have been more than—" his hand fluttered toward her "—this. You *are* more." He placed his hand on her knee and squeezed painfully. "Stay here, with me. You'll have your Josie then."

A knock sounded on the door.

"Come in." Mr. Langdon slithered to the other side of the couch.

Mary swallowed hard. She could make it to the door, but how would she escape this house?

Silverware clinked as Mr. Baggs shuffled into the room. Pattering steps followed Baggs and then Josie burst into the room, her eyes pink and tear-stained.

"Miss Mary," she cried and launched herself at the couch.

Mary caught her, pulled her close and buried her face in Josie's hair. *My little girl.* The thought didn't startle her, but rather strengthened her. She would do almost anything to save Josie. She'd wait for the opportunity and then be gone from this place.

And Josie would go with her.

That's kidnapping, prodded a voice from inside.

But what other option did she have?

"How did she get out?" Langdon's voice bit into the room. He grabbed Josie's arm, but Mary smacked his hand and he withdrew, brows narrowing into angry arrows. "You will pay for that."

"I apologize, sir, but there's a gentleman at the door for you. It won't wait. You might want to see him out quickly." Mr. Baggs inclined his head and whatever that meant, it propelled Mr. Langdon to his feet.

"Do you want me to take the girl?" asked Mr. Baggs.

Josie's uncle looked at them, a calculating gleam in his eye. "No, let her stay. She shall encourage Miss O'Roarke in her decision, no doubt. Just keep an eye on them, Baggs."

Mr. Langdon swished out of the room. Josie pulled away from Mary, tears spilling over her cheeks. "My mommy is dead."

"I know, sweetheart." She smoothed an errant strand out of Josie's eyes as her thoughts raced. This was their one opportunity, but could she do it? Could she get them out? She glanced at Baggs. Her only option was to overpower him somehow, but the thought rattled her. Hitting an old man did not seem the right thing to do.

Mr. Baggs cleared his throat. He blinked and held out a hand to Josie. "I might miss your chatter. That's all I have to say."

"Why, Baggs, I shall miss you, too!" Josie didn't take his hand but instead moved out of Mary's embrace. As she beckoned Baggs closer, Mary stood and reached for the teapot.

Josie leaned up and planted a little kiss on the man's weathered cheek. His eyes met Mary's as she raised the pitcher. Her stomach churned.

"Do it," he said, "or it's my life on the line. There's a door there." He pointed.

"That's my hideaway." Josie hopped over and tugged open the door Mr. Baggs had brought Mary through earlier.

"Wait for me in the hallway," said Mary, but Josie had

already disappeared behind the door. She swallowed hard. "I am truly sorry, Mr. Baggs, and hope I do not hurt you."

He gave her a curt nod. Drawing a deep breath, she brought the pitcher down upon his head. He groaned and crumpled to the floor. A line of blood appeared on the right side of his forehead.

Mary held in her sob and set the pitcher down. She dug in her luggage, retrieved her derringer and bullets and slid them in the pocket of her skirt. There was no Lou or Trevor here today. The onus rested upon her, and she'd do whatever necessary to save Josie. She raced to the door, spotted Josie near the stairs and ran toward their escape.

Lou paced the library, twirling his hat in his hands, as he waited for Mrs. Silver to appear. After his meeting this morning with O'Leary, he'd gone straight to the hotel to fetch Mary, only to find her room empty. While staring at the neatly made bed, he couldn't remember the last time he'd felt fear. True, bloodcurdling fear.

Despite its paralyzing hold, he forced himself to go to his office and make a telephone call to the director himself. After relaying the smuggler's name and the suspected boat carrying Canadian whiskey, Lou hightailed it out of there and headed to the Silvers'.

Where he'd found nothing of Mary.

Something was wrong.

She should have been here by now. Where else could she have gone? He perused the hangings on the walls, impatiently tapping his hat against his thigh. Dusty antiques. Family photographs. Langdon looked supremely arrogant in his still shot.

"Mr. Riley. To what do I owe this visit?" Langdon appeared in the doorway, a smirk marring his even features. Smart man kept his distance, though.

"I'm here to speak with Mrs. Silver."

"Ah." His smirk grew. "She has unfortunately passed on, negating your need to see her. I shall show you to the door."

Lou's fingers clenched the brim of his hat. "Where's Josie?"

"That's none of your business, officer of the law or no. She's my ward. Now, if you'll excuse me, I have funeral arrangements to attend to."

He took a deep breath and settled into the kind of calm that gave a man an edge over his opponent. And Langdon was worse than an opponent. He stalked toward him. The man faltered for a moment but didn't budge.

"I smell...something." Lou sniffed. If this guy was a bootlegger, and based on O'Leary's notes, Lou felt certain he was, there should be a kind of hint somewhere.

"Perfume from the arrangements. My sister's favorite."

"Indeed." He took another breath and realized it was true, he did smell something floral, and not the prohibited whiskey he'd been ready to accuse Langdon of importing. "Funeral flowers aren't a pleasant smell on you, but I suppose it works well to mask the odor from your day job.... You know I work for the Bureau of Investigation, right?"

"You flashed your badge in my face."

"You're a smart man. Maybe coming into money soon?" Lou gestured around him, watching Langdon's face closely.

His lids flickered. "The terms of the will have yet to be disclosed."

"Maybe you've got your own money?"

"Maybe it's time for you to leave, Special Agent."

"Yeah, because your heart is real broken by your sister's death." Lou moved closer still, frowning when he whiffed that scent again. Something unforgettable... Mary.

His jaw clamped. Deliberately he loosened his jaw and

bestowed a predatory smile on Langdon. "Heard you're a rich man. In fact, I have a source who tells me your income is swimmingly large. You own a boat, right?"

"Are you trying to accuse me of something? You're in my house, on my property—"

"You mean your sister's?"

Langdon's face settled into stubborn lines. "Get out of this house."

Lou held up his hands. "Relax. I'm just here to pick up Mary."

"Who?" But Langdon's eyes flickered with recognition.

"Your new employee," he said smoothly. "She asked me to meet her here."

"Oh, yes, the nanny. She left moments before you arrived."

"Really?" He leaned forward, anger a frigid weight in his chest. "I smell her."

Langdon chuckled. "She's very, how shall I put it? Friendly."

Lou's gaze snapped up to meet Langdon's hard eyes. He had to play this smart. "Which way did she go?"

"The same way her type always goes. Now kindly leave this house or I'll have you escorted out."

"Thanks for your…help." Lou flashed his teeth. "I'll be back, though, and next time you might want to be more convincing."

He spun and headed toward the door. He felt Langdon behind him and his rage grew. Fine way God took care of Mary. Bringing her to this place, putting her right into the hands of danger. They stepped into the hall and that was when Lou heard what had been covered by the carpeted study.

An uneven tap behind him. A sound that resonated in his memory. He stopped abruptly and faced Langdon. His gaze dropped to Langdon's boots. Shiny, definitely expensive and outfitted with spurs. A vision of a dark alley crept through him. Moonlight. A gunshot and pain...

"Problem?"

Lou tucked his thoughts away and forced a grim smile. "Nope. Just admiring your shoes."

"Some say vanity is an evil thing, but it's served me well. I call these my lucky spurs. When I wear them, great things happen." Langdon's eyes flashed, belying his amused tone.

"Looks like I need a pair of those." Lou pulled on his hat, tipped it and scooted out of the house. Once down the porch, he walked the block, turned a corner and hurried across the street. Sliding into the shadows of a different house, he removed his hat, untucked his shirt, slicked his hair back and stuck a piece of gum in his mouth.

The disguise would have to do for now. He bent the rim of his hat upward on the sides. It would ruin the fit and the leather, but circumstances called for it. He could always buy a new one. Adjusting his gait, he meandered down the sidewalk until he passed the Silvers' place. One house down, he found a hiding spot near a newer home's expansive porch.

No gate and the perfect spot to blend in.

From here he could see everyone entering and leaving the front of the Silvers'. The servants' quarters looked to be on the side of the house, and he thought he could see a gate exit near the backyard. This was the optimum vantage point.

He settled into the corner where the stairs met the house and waited. Heavy clouds warned of impending rain. There was a definite bite to the air. He hoped Mary was safe.

She might be in the house, but without a warrant, he couldn't force his way in there. She should have stayed at the hotel and never taken this deal. Trusted him to take care of Josie. He chewed his gum, hoping for inspiration to kick in.

He could leave and get some men to follow Langdon. Now that he knew who his shooter was, it made more sense to personally follow him, but who'd take care of Mary? She couldn't wander Portland for long by herself. She didn't have any money that he knew of for a ticket home.

And he was sure she wouldn't leave Josie.

He couldn't, either. For all he knew, the will stipulated Josie be sent to relatives, but if it called for her to be left with Langdon... He mashed his gum. Not good.

This was the problem in getting involved with people. He liked his job of catching criminals. Investigating crimes. He didn't like getting close because it worried him, and a worried man couldn't accomplish anything.

Look at his past.

He'd held Sarah in his arms after Abby died. Instead of running for the doctor, he'd worried and fretted. Rocked her tenderly, but she'd lost the will to live and, letting the pneumonia have its way, slipped away quietly the same night.

O'Leary thought God had led him to Lou, but after losing his family that way, Lou had trouble believing God cared.

Yet Josie believed God had used him to find her in the desert. He swallowed hard now, feeling the rough wood of the house against his bare arm. It was solid and real.

Why couldn't he feel God that way? Had he ever?

Watching the Silver place for movement, he let his mind stew on the thought. Maybe he hadn't felt God the same way he felt this house at his side, but he sure felt some kind of presence when he'd gone to that church picnic with Mary.

Years ago, Sarah and he used to pray together, and there'd been a certainty inside that the God he talked to was real and cared about him. Thoughts jumbling, he blinked at the emotion encircling his chest. How could he have been so wrong then if things had felt so right?

And did that mean he was wrong now, despite how he felt?

He glanced at the sky for an answer. Swollen clouds greeted him. Back in the desert the air would be dry, ripe with the scents of rock and sage. He missed that. Selling the ranch had seemed like a good idea months ago, but suddenly it felt like the wrong move.

He scoffed at himself.

Dwelling on feelings changed nothing. They shifted like the clouds above, always at the whim of change. Just as he'd moved on…away from God, from faith.

The thought hit him square on.

He'd left God. Said goodbye and refused to let Him near.

An automobile moved into his line of vision. Classy high-end car. Black. He noted the rims and distinctive chug of the engine as it drew to a stop outside the Silvers' gate. Arrogant Langdon was on the move, but how was he supposed to follow him?

Hissing between his teeth, he rose from his position and sauntered onto the sidewalk. He couldn't follow, but he could intimidate. Langdon rushed out the front door. Lou stuck two fingers in his mouth and let out a piercing whistle.

Langdon jutted to a stop and, despite the distance, Lou saw anger in his movements. He waved, throwing his hand up and letting it flow casually above him.

"See you at the docks," he called out.

Chapter Twenty-Four

Escapes surely put a cramp in Mary's stomach. She bent against the neighbor's manicured, thorny bushes, Josie at her side.

"See you at the docks" a voice called out. Lou? She peeked through the leaves and saw a man waving at a fancy automobile as it sped past. Then the man put a quick pace to his steps and started up the sidewalk. Definitely Lou. She'd know that swagger anywhere.

"It's Mister Lou," Josie whispered excitedly. "Let's go get him."

"No." Mary shushed her, thoughts racing. She could do this. She could rescue herself and Josie without a man's help.

The lady means nothing to me.

Her mouth tightened. He'd proved that and more. Selling the ranch out from beneath everyone. Always following his job wherever it took him. She had no right to be miffed, and she really didn't want to be, but at the same time, thinking about his actions gave clearer insight to his character.

He didn't want chains. He didn't want commitment.

But now she knew she did, and that changed everything.

Chin up, she beckoned Josie to stand. "Let's go. Your uncle left in that vehicle, so we should be safe for a while."

"Where are we going?"

They stepped onto the sidewalk, Josie's hand fitting snugly within hers. She wanted to smile and reassure her, but her lips refused to relax. "I'm not sure, sweetheart."

She could go to the police, but what would she tell them? *Please help me save this little girl. Her uncle is a rich ogre who has had an obsession with me.* Or perhaps they could disappear and she could find work elsewhere?

A solid plan, but could she break the law that way? Maybe Langdon had lied to her about Josie's family. What if she had loving relatives who wished to take her in? The idea stabbed Mary's heart, but she must face the fact that she wasn't the only one who wanted Josie.

She might as well admit the only one who could help her now was on his way to the ports. Her best recourse was to follow him. Josie couldn't go with her, though. Maybe waiting at the hotel might prove a better solution.

Yes.

She'd do that.

Feeling more secure in her decision, she smiled at Josie and hummed a little ditty she'd learned as a child. Josie picked it up and together they walked to where she knew a streetcar passed. The money she'd brought from home helped immensely. She might even have enough to bring both herself and Josie back to the ranch…although that presented a new set of problems. Namely, kidnapping charges.

Right now she could defend her actions as a rescue. Possibly. She frowned. Things were altogether confusing.

"Excuse me, ma'am?" An automobile pulled up beside them. A man leaned out the passenger door. His scruffy features sent a frisson of apprehension through her, prickling the skin of her palms.

She stopped reluctantly, placing Josie behind her. A fat droplet of rain splashed against the shiny hood. "Yes?"

"Thought you might need a lift. You and that young'un."

"No, thank you, we're quite fine."

"Well, now, we weren't asking."

The flurries in her stomach took flight and Mary pivoted forward, causing Josie to emit a squeak as she strode away from the vehicle. The bushes beside her seemed too thick to dodge across and the next house sported a forbidding wrought iron fence.

From behind, a hand clamped on her arm and spun her around, jerking her toward the car. "You'll be coming with us, Miss Mary."

"Let the girl go," she gasped, her arm aching beneath the force of the man's grip.

"Nah, we'll be taking her, too. Langdon has plans, and I'm not fool enough to interrupt them."

The driver opened the back door, and her captor shoved her in. Josie came next, Mary's body breaking her momentum and cushioning her against the side of the vehicle. She hugged the girl close, pulling her onto her lap. Josie buried her face in Mary's shoulder, and she felt the trembles rippling through her.

Fright filled her, too. She tightened her hold on Josie.

The scruffy man hopped into the front of the vehicle. "Let's go," he told the driver. "Looks like it's about to rain, and I don't fancy getting wet."

The ride took forever, a confusing maze of twists and turns. She kept eyeing the latch on the door, but the way the driver sped through the streets disabused her of the notion to jump out. She'd never forgive herself if Josie was hurt.

But they had to get away somehow.

"Excuse me," she shouted above the noise of the engine and whip of the wind. This type of automobile had a roof that only covered the backseat. She hoped it rained on her captors. Served them right.

The men in front ignored her. Worrying her bottom lip, she peeked out her side. Vehicles swerved around her, proving a jump out that side would be foolish. She shifted and glanced toward the passenger side. The sidewalk had disappeared when they'd left the residential neighborhood.

The air felt thicker, laden with the odors of water and fish. Would anyone at the docks help her? Knowing the rough elements as she did, possibly. Many men working in these conditions were honest and didn't care to see a child come to harm. Then again, many drank too much and had allowed their morality to emulate the tide, coming and going as it pleased.

The driver finally swerved to a stop on a street hugged by ramshackle warehouses. The man in the passenger seat jumped out to open their door. "Slowly now," he warned. "I've no patience for uppity women."

Despite the fear curdling her stomach, she stifled a snort and the tart reply she wished to give him. Josie refused to move off her lap, so she scooted across to the passenger door. "Tell the girl to get down," the man ordered.

"I shall hold her," she said, daring to meet his eyes.

He shrugged, a leer on his lips. "Your choice. I'm just the deliveryman."

As she moved over, the driver made an odd sound. She whipped him a glance. He'd removed his cap and she had to swallow her surprise. His blue eyes were familiar. The bowler-hat man from the alley? He met her look and winked so quickly she almost missed it. "All will be well, miss," he said with his familiar brogue. "Follow directions, okay?"

She nodded and continued out of the automobile, trying to keep her balance on the broken sidewalk. Josie clung to

her but she managed to hold her steady enough. Bowler-
hat man pulled the automobile away, and she was left with
the scruffy man.

Her first instinct prompted her to run, even with Josie
in her arms. Her captor must have seen the impulse on her
face because he grabbed her arm and propelled her toward
a large, nondescript building. The road steeply declined
toward the Willamette, whose muddy waters lapped lazily
against the docks. Dockworkers rushed from boat to boat,
making her dizzy.

Or maybe it was panic at this man's manhandling. He
stopped at a building only feet from the river and thrust
her through a narrow doorway. It took several seconds
for her eyes to adjust. The sound of the port dulled in this
place, replaced with a muffled stillness that swathed the
shadows. No movement. If she could reach her pocket, then
things would be solved quite neatly. She'd have to put Josie
down, though, and make her move quickly.

"Come on," the man growled behind her. His grip dug
into her arm as he plowed ahead. If she was going to run,
she must do so now. She yanked her arm back, causing
the man to let out a startled oath. "What're you playing
at? Let's get moving."

"We are not going with you." She yanked again, and
he was so shocked by her words that her arm slid from his
fingertips, albeit painfully.

"I'll not be having any of this," he snarled. He reached
for her, but she dodged his hand and backed up.

"We must run," she whispered into Josie's ear. The little girl's head moved imperceptibly in a nod before she
wiggled out of Mary's grasp.

The man reached for her again, but she whirled away,
dragging Josie with her. The door behind them had shut
and so she opted for scuttling near the wall. Darkness

closed around them as they moved farther into the shadows of a corner.

The man's heavy breathing filled the space, combining with the dank odors of mold and rotted wood. As far as she could tell, he wasn't following them. And how could he? The lack of light served her well. She ran her fingers down Josie's cheek before grabbing her hand again.

"I'm going to find you," their captor said suddenly, his voice grating in the silence. "And when I do, it won't be pretty."

They crouched in the darkness, every breath seeming a siren to her, but still, no movement to be heard. After an interminable wait, a scraping to her right made her catch her breath. One hand gripping Josie's, she used her other to slide the derringer out of her skirt pocket.

The metal fit coolly into her palm, comfortably. Just imagine he's a target, she told herself. A wooden target, like the kind she and James practiced with. Drawing a steady breath, she willed her heartbeat to slow.

She'd just achieved a sort of eerie calm when something flew into the room, startling her. Her captor as well, for he made a noise, followed by the loud pop of his weapon. The sound echoed through the room, filling her ears. And then out of the shadows, he lunged toward them. All she saw was his shape before instinct took over and pulled the trigger.

Lou arrived at the docks minutes after Langdon. He'd been fortunate in that Portland traffic's heaviness slowed the man's automobile enough for him to hop a streetcar headed in the same direction. If Langdon saw him, he gave no indication.

Now he stalked to the port, weapon at the ready. He spotted O'Leary pulling away from the curb near an old, broken-down building. Careful to be inconspicuous, he gave O'Leary quick eye contact, only to be surprised by the undercover agent's swift chin jerk toward the building before speeding away.

Hmm. Lou tapped the pockets of his blue jeans. He probably should have stopped in at the office and set up some sort of operation. For now he would just observe. Hopefully, he'd see enough to get a warrant later. Plan in place, he edged up against the building. Filth covered the panes of glass.

He peered in anyway, but saw nothing. Moving forward, he kept his back to the building and his eye on the docks. Only feet away, workers bustled and moved. No sign of Langdon, but the name of his vessel should be obvious soon enough.

The rough wood of the building behind him scraped at his shirt. A man pushing a wheelbarrow toward him gave him a wary look. Stifling a groan, he jammed his hat more firmly in place. People in these places had no use for authorities.

Looking like a policeman closed more mouths than if he waltzed in with his badge flashing. Maybe he should lose the hat. At the least.

He took it off his head and inched toward the door to the building. He pressed it open and poked his head in. Met nothing but stink. Perfect. He whipped his hat into the dark room and then stiffened when a muffled *oomph* issued from the depths.

Before he could draw his weapon, a volley of gunfire blasted out. He dropped to his stomach, revolver at the ready.

The noise ended abruptly.

He drew his knees up under his stomach and held still, listening. Someone groaned from inside.

"Bureau of Investigation. Hold your fire," he shouted into the room. A crowd was gathering across the street, but he ignored them.

The sound came again, and then a scuffling sound...or was it sniffling? Crying? He rose to his feet slowly. "Come out, weapons down, by order of Lou Riley, special agent to the Bureau of Investigation."

"Lou?"

It felt as if his gut dropped to his feet when he heard Mary's voice. She appeared in the doorway, Josie in her arms and a small Remington derringer clutched in her fingers. She blinked as she came out of the dark.

The sound of police drawing near scattered the crowd, most of them having no desire to be seen in this vicinity.

Lou couldn't take his eyes off Mary.

Her eyes were huge, shocked. Filmy spiderwebs clung to the mussed strands of her hair. Josie was nestled in her arms, her shoulders shaking with the force of her fear. He swallowed, his throat tight and dry. Carefully, he reached for Mary's hand, prying the pistol from her cold fingers.

Her eyes met his. "I shot him," she whispered.

Local police pulled up behind him. Taking his gaze from her, he flashed his badge, introduced himself and gave them the details. He put his arm around her shoulders and steered her and Josie to the side, away from the open door and closer to the end of the building.

She felt tiny and frail beneath his hands. What had happened in there? How had she come into possession of a pistol? He had a million questions, but seeing the look on her face stilled them all.

No tears. Just a blank heaviness.

He knew exactly what that felt like.

He tucked his fingers beneath Josie's ribs, but she wouldn't let go of Mary.

"I'm okay," Mary said, her voice quiet and flat. "You should check that man...." Her voice trailed off and her gaze dropped.

Lou pulled her to him, pressing her hair against his chest, dropping his lips to her and Josie's heads, cradling them and warming them. This shouldn't have happened. Just like before. Just like Sarah and Abby. He'd been too busy working.

He should have been here for them.

And where had God been?

Absent, as usual.

A hot anger started in his stomach and spread through his chest. He tightened his grip on them as a vow worked through his blood. Langdon would pay.

No matter what.

He would pay.

Chapter Twenty-Five

Mary had killed a man.

Feeling numb, she watched Lou pace a few feet away, engaged in discussion with a man in a wrinkled suit, maybe his superior. The crowded, busy office of the bureau wasn't what she'd expected. The rooms bustled with business. Telephones rang and rang, adding to the flow of conversation and creating an atmosphere of bare walls and cacophony.

She and Josie waited on a hard bench while Lou tried to straighten out their situation. Beside her, Josie sipped hot chocolate a kind man had brought for them a few minutes ago. Her legs swung in a pendulum rhythm and she didn't smile.

Mary gripped her own cup of chocolate, an immense pressure compressing her heart. This was her fault. If only she hadn't taken Josie from that house. She should never have tried to do things her way. If only she'd prayed for wisdom this afternoon instead of going with her instincts…

Because of her foolishness, someone lay dead. Not only that, but Langdon was missing and a little girl had been through far too much. The blame for Josie's fright rested solely on her shoulders, and that knowledge crept through her like a slow poison. She swirled her hot chocolate, watching the curves in the liquid disappear and then reappear.

If onlys never changed anything. She wished they could.

Movement at the corner of her vision drew her attention from the cup to the center of the room. Lou threw his hands in the air and stalked away from the man he spoke to. His agitation shook Mary even more. She blinked hard, her lids burning and gritty. How had this happened?

But she knew exactly how.

Thinking she should manage things on her own. Leaving no room for help, not even from her Savior.

Where could she go from here? How could she escape this disgrace? This guilt? For it tore at her, shredding her tattered confidence, leaving her protected by nothing but a rag not worth stitching back together.

"Mary." Lou stood before her, drawn and unsmiling. "Can I talk to you alone?"

She cast a look at Josie, who blew bubbles in her hot chocolate.

"An agent friend's wife will be here in a moment to sit with her," he said softly.

She touched Josie's shoulders. An unforced smile came to her lips when the little girl glanced up, her mouth rimmed in chocolate. "I'm going with Mister Lou for a moment, but I'll be right back."

"You're not gonna leave me, right?" Josie's voice quivered, and Mary's stomach clenched.

"No, sweetheart. I'll be right over there." She pointed outward, not really sure where Lou planned to take her.

"In that room there," said Lou. He dropped in front of Josie and pulled a peppermint stick from his pocket.

"These are good for stirring. By the time this is gone, we'll be back. A nice lady will come and sit with you, okay?"

She nodded and reached for the stick. "It's going to be gone fast," she told him gravely.

A grin cracked his tired features, and a surge of emotion vaulted through Mary at his smile. "We'll hurry then, my sweet girl. Stay here." He patted her knee.

Mary followed him to a door that opened into a tiny room.

"Interrogations," he explained, noticing her look. "Were you okay with yours?"

"Yes." It had been terribly exhausting to explain how she'd ended up in the warehouse. Then the hardest part had come, describing the *oomph* of noise into the dim room, which she'd later found out was Lou's hat, and then the lunge as her captor appeared right in front of her, his pistol at her nose.

She'd shot him without thinking. An immediate reaction. He hadn't expected that she'd have a weapon. He'd dropped his gun, falling backward, clutching his belly. Gut shot. That's what the detective told her it was called. Most often fatal.

"Hey. Come back to me."

A feather brushed her cheek. No, Lou's finger. He was touching her, close, his eyes so very blue and serious. "It's going to be okay, I promise. There was nothing you could do."

"I had to protect us." She faltered, her voice abandoning her.

"You did good. None of this is your fault."

"Have you found Langdon?" she asked.

"Not yet. Let's talk privately." He applied a soft pressure to her shoulder, moving her farther into the room. Lou tucked his hands in his pockets and studied her. "We have a situation with Langdon and Josie regarding custody. I've a man bringing in the family attorney right now to figure out where Josie needs to go."

"And me?"

"You're not being charged with anything. The shooting was clearly self-defense and we have a witness who saw him force you and Josie into the automobile." He cocked his head. "How'd you get a pistol anyway? Let alone know how to shoot it."

"James taught me years ago. I bought the derringer one year after a scare with wolves."

"Where was I?"

"Working."

An odd grimace crossed his face. Did it bother him that he hadn't been there? Surely not...and yet a hard little knot began to grow in her stomach.

"What about the driver...the man?" She stumbled over the words, her tongue feeling thick and unwieldy. "The one who gave you the hat?"

"Don't worry about him. I'm taking care of things."

Exhaustion weighted every limb. "Where do I go from here?"

"Gracie and Trevor are on their way. They're going to take you back to the ranch." He paused. "I've decided not to sell it— Look at me, Mary." He tipped her chin, his fingers warm against her skin, and she met his eyes. "I'm *not* going to sell the ranch. Our place is rich in history. I don't want to lose that. While here in Portland, I realized it's home to me in a way other places can never be."

She blinked at his words, an onslaught of emotions rushing through her. Fear, happiness, everything coalesced into a giant wave of feeling that engulfed her and left her speechless. She touched his cheek. His unshaved skin scraped against her fingers as she cupped his jaw and held his gaze.

"I'm happy you're keeping the ranch. You have been my hero in so many ways," she began. "And yet I feel as though my hand is still being held." He started to shake his head, but she stopped him with a bit of pressure from her fingers.

A rueful smile crept across his lips.

She smiled back, her riotous emotions blending together, harmonizing into a single feeling that spread through her in rich pulses of energy. "I am not going to be your housekeeper anymore. I am going to open a business and thrive."

He reached for her hand, removed it and laced his fingers through hers. So gentle. He drew their entwined fingers against his chest.

"You are free to be whomever you want. To choose your way. I only want you happy." His fervent words touched a place deep inside her, bringing to life a longing she finally felt free to embrace.

Without hesitating, she placed her free hand on his back, pushed upward on her toes and kissed him. Their lips met in a union of warmth that blazed into a blistering heat, burning away any reservations she may have held. His mouth slanted against hers, minty and firm. He pressed her against the wall, and she melted beneath his love.

For that was what she felt. Love radiating from him. Care. Her own blood lit with a passionate joy she hadn't expected to ever experience.

And then everything ended. He pulled away, his breath ragged, his head hanging so she couldn't see his face.

But that was okay. She smiled despite her own uneven breathing and the rapid pounding of her heart. She stroked the top of his head, relishing the strands beneath her fingers. It had taken twelve years, but her heart had finally healed enough for her to accept the truth.

"I love you," she said. The words came out clear. Grinning, she said it again. "I love you, Lou Riley."

"I know," he groaned.

She stopped stroking his hair, her fingers lingering in a painful pause. *He knew?* And then it came to her that she had been foolish. Laying out her affections, thinking he returned them. Her heart strangled beneath her breastbone. She chose not to speak. She dropped her hands to her sides and waited.

He lifted his head, his eyes piercing. "I haven't done you right, Mary. I don't deserve your love."

She shook her head, surprised at his words. "But of course you do—"

"No." He gripped her shoulders. "I should have been there for you. Protected you."

"But you did." She touched his cheek again, amazed by the contrast of masculinity and vulnerability on his face. "God led you to us."

He shook his head, but she stopped him from speaking by holding up a palm. "I doubted God, you know. Words can do that, dig deep holes that are not easily filled. God seemed to forsake me. Now, when I needed Him with Langdon, and so long ago, when Mendez came for me. But then you showed up. Both times, you have been there. If you hadn't tossed your hat into that building, you may have continued past. I may have huddled with Josie in a corner until that man found us. I can't deny how God has used you to protect me."

"I don't know if I can believe that." A grimace passed across his face. "He wasn't there with Sarah and Abby. He could have spared them, but He didn't."

She tried to hide her flinch. "I am truly sorry for your loss."

Perhaps he saw something in her face that she hadn't successfully hidden, for his features softened. "I'm not saying I'm not glad you were spared. I am, more than you can believe. You and Josie are... You're special. I guess I'm just struggling with why God helps some but not others."

She had no answer for him and perhaps it would be unwise to speak anyway, because her emotions tangled within and skewed her perspective. She'd confessed her love, and he'd ignored that, even bringing up his wife and daughter. She'd thought what stood between them was his job, but too late she saw she'd been wrong.

It was so much more. What she'd felt in his kiss hadn't been love, it had been a normal, physical attraction. Her face burned at her naïveté.

He released her shoulders and took a step back. His face shuttered. "You deserve more than a washed-up agent who can't get over the fact God gets to make all the rules. If God cares, He'll give you someone wonderful to love."

He already has, but the man is too stubborn to realize it. She swallowed her reply. "Will you still be going to Asia?"

"In two weeks."

"And Langdon?"

"I'll track him before then."

So he planned to find Langdon after all. Frustration welled. "Shouldn't you let objective agents look for him?"

"No, this is too important." He cast a fervent look to the door, then leaned close to her. "The man put out a contract on me. He wants me dead, and I don't aim to give him that pleasure. I haven't worked out why yet, but that's not important."

"He and Mendez were cousins." She watched as shock etched slackness across his features.

"Who told you that?"

"He took pride in sharing that information with me, but I also noticed a resemblance in their bone structure." It was hard to speak over the pain of Lou's rejection, but she forced a calm facade. "From what I can piece together, Langdon was behind Mendez's obsession with me. The man worked for him and carried out his orders."

"Did he tell you anything else?"

"A little more." Only that because of her mother's part in this drama, she'd been kidnapped for one week and the course of her life had been forever altered. "Langdon met me when I was a child. I remember him as a boy who stared too much. I suppose I had reason to be wary of him."

"He discovered you lived with Trevor's mother and sought you out."

She nodded slowly. "Yes."

"That…" Lou sucked in a deep breath, his eyes angry and bright. "Go home and rest peacefully, knowing he'll pay for what he did to you."

"Please don't take revenge," she said quietly.

"I don't get revenge, sweetheart. I get justice."

Two hours passed before the lawyer arrived. Trevor and Gracie followed close behind.

"Mary! Lou telephoned our hotel. I'm so sorry." Gracie rushed forward, arms enveloping her in a gentle embrace that brought tears to her eyes. It had been too long since she'd seen her exuberant friend. Gracie had cut her hair short in a stylish bob, and her beaded dress swirled around her knees.

Mary's smile wobbled as she extricated herself from Gracie's grasp.

Trevor hugged her next, and she felt the support from her childhood friend in the firm pressure of his hands. He stepped back and put his arm around his wife's shoulders. They fit well together, and his face held a peacefulness that hadn't been there when he and Mary were growing up.

Warmth at her side brought her attention to Josie.

"This is Josie," she told them, patting the little girl's shoulder. She'd been too quiet today.

"A pleasure to meet you," Gracie said in her bubbly way.

Mary glanced at the lawyer behind Trevor, a lean man with a tired air to his sunken features. A chill rippled through her—this might be the last time she saw Josie.

Lou stalked toward them. She averted her gaze. She could not bear to look at him, not after their disastrous conversation.

"Are you okay?" Gracie peered at her, eyes wide, and Mary realized she'd missed something.

"I'm sorry. Just thinking."

"No, I shouldn't be chatting your ear off. They're going in for the meeting, though. I will wait out here for you. Shall I watch Josie?"

"Are you okay with that?" she asked the girl at her side. Josie's head moved slightly and though it pained her to leave Josie again, she took her hand and brought it to Gracie's.

"We're going to have great fun. I know a wonderful game…." Gracie's voice faded as Mary swiveled and headed toward the same interrogation room where Lou had kissed her. Her lips burned with the memory. Her heart ached.

He'd shot down her profession of love so easily…. Had she misread him this entire time? But surely he did not feel only brotherly things for her. No, he was a man in flux and there was nothing she could do about that. Feeling grim, she squeezed into the room.

The lawyer hadn't bothered sitting at the little table with

its scrawny chairs. Instead, the men crowded into the small space, filling it with the scent of cologne and rustling suits. Lou's blue jeans were out of place and yet he still managed to look more comfortable than everyone else.

Even Trevor waited near the wall, his eyes sympathetic. She flashed him a weak smile and took a spot in the corner. Another man stood near Lou, perhaps a fellow agent? She huddled against the wall, feeling its bareness at her back.

The lawyer cleared his throat. "This is a highly unusual situation. Unforeseen, actually. The will is binding and unchangeable." His eyes skittered to Mary. Did he feel her fear? She blinked and looked away.

She found Lou staring at her. His face was unreadable, his thumbs hooked into the pockets of his jeans, and yet she thought she detected regret on his face. Or maybe she imagined it. With difficulty she pulled her attention from him and focused on the lawyer who held the rest of her dreams in his hands.

Mentally she shook herself. No. God held her dreams. She must trust Him because she had nothing left, no one left, to turn to.

The lawyer held up the packet, which looked cumbersome to her. "Are all parties ready for the reading of the will?" he asked.

Chapter Twenty-Six

God worked amazing wonders.

Mary watched passengers board the train in front of her. People milled around her, their voices melding with the sound of brakes and steam. Dirt and perfume mingled in the air, stirred by the excitement of those whose lives would change with a train ride, if only temporarily.

"When do we get to go on?" Josie tugged the hem of Mary's dress, her eagerness palpable.

Mary grinned at her and pulled her close. "As soon as Trevor returns."

They'd stayed in Portland a few days longer, going to the funeral and making arrangements for Josie's home, which Josie had inherited in the will. It had become obvious why Mr. Langdon wanted Josie out of the picture. She was a wealthy little girl now, but if she died, the money went to Mr. Langdon as next of kin. The lawyer had pronounced Mary, of all people, to be Josie's legal guardian. Apparently Mrs. Silver had changed her will at the last moment. Not only was Mary the named guardian, but she was also in charge of funds for the child's care.

They spent the nights at the hotel, and Josie slept in Mary's room with her. Though joy filled her at the thought of taking care of her precious girl, at being a mother, she hadn't been able to sleep well.

Her thoughts always returned to Lou.

Beside her, Gracie bobbed up and down on antsy feet. "It's been so long since I was home. Has anything changed?"

"Not quite. I had planned to paint the sitting room but someone spilled the bucket." Mary winked at Josie, whose smile widened in the burgeoning dawn light. "Maybe we can try again."

"Ooh, I'd love to help paint," Gracie gushed. "A passionate purple. Or maybe a subdued pear. It will be just the thing, except... Well, I must be careful of the fumes."

Fumes? Mary looked at her friend and saw the secret smile playing about her lips. Gracie's fingers splayed across her belly and knowledge sunk in. "You must be very careful, indeed. No ladders, either," she said.

They smiled at each other, the moment bonded by friendship.

"Can I get on the ladder? I won't fall," Josie added, a determined look in her sparkling eyes.

"We'll see," Mary said.

"That means no." A pout curved Josie's lips.

"Let's go." Trevor pushed through the crowd and beckoned them.

Josie's hand in hers, Mary followed Gracie and Trevor to the edge of the train. She was just about to board when a hand on her shoulder stopped her.

She turned to see Lou, mouth tight, eyes shadowed, his hat lying at a crooked angle on his head.

"Can we talk?" he asked.

"Now?"

The train whistled, signaling a warning. Mary looked up. Gracie gave her a thumbs-up and put her hand on

Josie's shoulder, who was looking everywhere and hopping on one foot. Biting her lip, Mary moved away from the train, Lou right behind her.

He had filled her every waking moment. His smile. His kiss. The way she could talk to him, or even yell at him, and he didn't hurt for it. He didn't reject her.

Until she'd offered love.

"What do you need?" she asked now, more curt than necessary.

He studied her, gaze serious. "I need to know we're still friends."

Friends? She wanted to slap him at that moment. It was a shocking urge, so surprising that she clasped her fingers to keep from acting on it. Was it his fault that he still loved his wife? Could she fault a man for such loyalty? No, and yet her heart was splintering within her chest.

The lady means nothing to me.

He'd meant it more than she'd realized.

"Mary, I'm serious. I value your friendship and the way you've served our makeshift family. I know that lately I've been bossy. Demanding. But I did it for your own good." He doffed his hat and placed it against his chest. "I know I was wrong, though. That you're an adult capable of taking care of not only herself, but a little girl. She's something, isn't she?" A wistful look crossed his face, so at odds with the jut of his strong jawline and determined eyes.

Mary swallowed. "She is. And you and I are friends, always." Much as it hurt to say, she could never deny him that.

"You've always had such loyalty. I envy it. My own family refused to speak to me for years because of my work with the bureau, and it's tough for me to forgive them. But I look at how you treat your ma, I see the love of God in your actions...." He trailed off before saying, "The way you live encourages me to live better."

She shifted, uncomfortable with his praise. With the entire situation, really. If he only knew. She looked at him and saw how he gazed at her, his eyes like sapphires in the sun. She wanted to remember this moment forever. Wanted to memorize the lines of his face, to touch them and carve them into the tips of her fingers, to hold on to always.

"I'm not perfect," she blurted. "Langdon said my mother led him to me. All she cared about was finding my father. If not for her, I would have never been kidnapped. I might be married, with a family. Emotionally whole." Her voice caught and she couldn't continue.

Her throat felt tight and raw. She waited for Lou's shock, but it didn't come. Instead, he winced. The minuscule movement stunned her. It was a physical blow. She staggered back, the pulse of her blood surging and then slowing, her lungs constricting until she thought she might never breathe again.

And yet she did. A deep, oxygen-filled inhalation borne of necessity.

"You knew," she whispered on her exhale.

"I knew." His eyes met hers. Apologetic.

Her hand shot out and connected with his cheek. He didn't move, not even when the mark from her hand suffused an angry red. She swallowed hard, her whole body aflame, her palm smarting. He'd known...for how long? How many secrets did he hold? How much more did he keep from her? She'd been very wrong to trust him.

"Secrets do not make a friendship," she said coldly. His face was blank, as if unaffected by her anger. So be it. She was done with this man, with everything. Never again would she allow herself to dream of him, to relive his recent kisses and his tender words over the years.

Shaking, she whirled and forced her trembling knees to march to the train, just as it let out another ear-splitting whistle.

Let Lou seek his revenge. Let him ignore the God who cared for him. Let him reject the woman who would have given him her all.

She was done with him and everything he represented.

Her eyes burned as she stepped onto the train and searched the seats for a familiar face. She had Josie, and she was going home.

She would have a family, with or without Lou Riley.

The heart was the biggest betrayer of all.

Mary discovered that unfortunate tidbit when she couldn't stop dreaming about Lou during the journey home. She'd see him stretching out his hand, asking for help, but her pride kept her heart far from him.

No.

Her broken feelings were the culprit, not pride, for even seeing him in her dreams caused her to wake with dried tears upon her cheek.

The bright spot in her life was Josie. Between her and Gracie's excited chatter, there was little time during the days' travel to pine over Lou. Only at night did he steal her sleep.

Finally, weary and dirty, they arrived at the ranch. Josie pounded up the steps, yelling for James. Gracie bounced around in excitement before grabbing Trevor for a long kiss. He embraced her, the quiet smile on his face testament to his love for his young bride.

God had changed him so deeply.... Could He do the same for Mary? Give her peace with how things had ended with Lou?

Feeling unsettled and scattered, Mary stepped out of

the neighbor's wagon. James had been unable to meet their train due to ranch duties, and so Mr. Horn had come to fetch them.

"Don't forget the potluck next month," he said from his perch on the wagon seat. "It's our last meeting with food before the cold weather shows up. We've got a special afternoon of preaching and then supper and music. Miss Alma has everything planned out."

"We'll be there," Mary said feebly.

Mr. Horn inclined his head and then took off, his team of horses digging up the road and clouding the air with desert dirt. Summer in Harney County was dry and sunny. The climate remained the same. Not like her feelings, which had been flung about in a tornado of change.

Everyone had gone into the house, but she stayed outside, longing for freedom from the cage she'd put herself in. Not only did she feel guilty for saying what she had to Lou, but she dreaded seeing her mother.

It had been easy to forgive her when she'd understood a woman's need to find her husband. It was much harder now, knowing the nightmare of her past could have been prevented if only her mother had kept quiet. Examined more deeply Langdon's inquiry. Anything but flippantly giving out her daughter's whereabouts in exchange for her husband's.

She gripped her luggage and slowly walked to her house, leaving the ranch house behind. She must face her mother at some point. Now, with no audience, seemed best.

And yet her feet dragged. Knowing Trevor's mother had sold her hurt, but she'd been aware of Julia's character and hadn't been surprised. What her mother had done was a different matter.

A strong wind blew at her hair. How she wished it would

also blow away this knowledge of her mother's unwitting betrayal.

Eventually she reached the house. Her mother stood near the gate, hair unplaited, eyes the deep black of the Paiute. Grimness painted her face into grooves and shadows. Her skirt whipped around her ankles and familiarity washed over Mary.

She'd wanted her mother here. Longed to see her restored to the laughing, beautiful woman of her youth. Maybe somehow she'd thought this would do the same for her, that if her mother was healed of her past, then she could be, also.

Did that mean she'd only been thinking of herself? That her motives had always been more selfish than she'd realized?

She stepped forward, eyes on her mother, a frown niggling at her lips.

"My daughter." Rose spoke quietly, and the breeze diluted her words into a faint sound of pleading.

She couldn't do this. She couldn't face her or accuse her. Better to leave things in the past.

"This morning James brought me a telegram from Lou," said Rose without blinking. "He wrote that you know what I never wished to confess. Do you understand his hatred for me now? Can you see why I hesitated to intrude in your home?"

Mary's mouth was so dry she could taste the desert upon her tongue.

"I have packed my bags and stayed only to tell you one thing—I am sorry, with the deepest regret a human can feel. This sorrow is a wound within my soul that does not heal. Nor should it. I have prayed to the spirits that you may have a good life. A blessed life with strong loves and much goodness." Rose blinked and a single tear edged from beneath her lashes. "You deserved more than what I gave you."

"Mother…" Mary dipped her head, hiding from the pain on her mother's face. She wanted to comfort her somehow, to ease her pain. *God help me.*

Seventy times seven.

The scripture reverberated through her. Like a seedling on the wind, dropped into the soil of her heart, and with her acceptance of His words, a new feeling spread through her. She lifted her head, feeling different, alive, helped. She stepped forward and before her mother could respond, embraced her.

She hugged her tightly for several moments, inhaling the wind in her mother's hair and the cedar scent that clung to her skin from her basket weaving.

When she felt able to speak, she pulled back and looked her mother in the eyes. "You speak of spirits and blessing. I am blessed and healed by One, my mother. The One who created me. He also created you, and loves you. Though my life has had pain, it has not lacked comfort."

Rose nodded slowly, her lips trembling. "I have seen the peace on your face and wondered at it."

"Yes." Mary felt the smile start in her heart and work to her face. "My Bible says God is our comfort so that we can be a comfort to others."

"The white man's God is trouble." Her mother frowned.

Mary's smile wavered. "No. He has been my peace. And now, in His name, I offer you forgiveness."

Rose shivered as though the parched breath of desert wind sliced through her very bones.

"Please stay and live with me," Mary continued, feeling the wobble in her voice. "I love you, and though what you did hurts, I know we can be healed."

"How can you forgive me?" Her mother's eyes welled

with tears. They dripped down her cheeks, filling the grooves like flooded riverbeds.

"Because…no one is perfect. Not one person but Christ Himself. I choose this path, Mother. Please walk it with me." Mary held out her hand, afraid, hoping her mother would take it, that she would pass from the shadowlands where she'd lived for too long.

After what seemed an interminable wait, her mother reached for her and burst into tears. Taken aback but feeling weepy herself, Mary allowed her mother to gather her into her arms.

She hadn't known she would forgive her mother, not until she'd seen that pain upon her face. Forgiveness was the right thing to do, and she hoped she would have done it anyway, whether or not her mother felt regret. But she did, and it was as though a piece of Mary's heart finally felt respite.

She rested her cheek against her mother's shoulder, and her thoughts turned to Lou. She hoped he'd find Mr. Langdon, because she had no doubt Josie's uncle would come looking for them at the ranch—it was only a matter of time.

Then perhaps Lou would run to Asia again. Maybe stay there this time, because to face his sorrows, to forgive God for the pain in his life, had proved too hard for him.

She hoped the best for him, she really did. But she also hoped for herself, because there was one part of her heart, a large portion, that might never be free unless she could let him go.

And right now, letting go wasn't even something she could imagine.

Chapter Twenty-Seven

A sea of ebony stretched before Lou. The image altered. A woman, small and gently curved, stood at the door. Glossy strands of her hair glistened beneath a milky moon. Her face… He couldn't see her face. He moved closer, his pulse thumping through him in quick, steady beats.

If only he could see her somehow. It wasn't Sarah. Her hair was blond. And she was gone, wasn't she? Gone forever. He waited for the familiar ache to surge through him, but it didn't arrive. Instead, he drew closer to the woman before him, the one whose expression he couldn't see. But he wanted to. He wanted to touch her skin, to see laughter light her eyes.

Moonlight flowed over her slight shoulders, undulating into the room where he stayed. He moved quickly, needing to reach her, but the moment his hand connected to her sleeve, she vanished and he awoke. He blinked, his eyes gritty and his feelings raw.

Mary's face swam before him, the way she'd looked when he'd kissed her that second time. Soft and dewy. In love.

And she'd said it, too. Said that she loved him, with luminous eyes and trust in her voice. Idiot that he was, he'd thrown her feelings in her face. Remembering how he'd mentioned Sarah, he groaned and pressed his palms against his eyes.

Enough whining. He'd made his bed and it was the best one for him. Common sense told him Mary needed a good man with a whole heart and a spiritual bent. What could he offer her? A house. That was about it.

You make her smile.

Okay, so he could give her some good stories. So what?

She trusts you.

Not anymore. Not since she found out he'd known her mother exposed her whereabouts to Langdon.

Muttering, he sat up and threw the flimsy blanket off his legs. He had a criminal to hunt down, and today was his last day to find him before shipping out for Hong Kong. If he didn't arrest Langdon today, he'd have to leave the duty to his team, and that wasn't going to happen.

This was his man and he'd get him no matter what.

He hurried out of bed, dressed and went in search of his junior agents.

"You're sure he's here?" Lou gazed dubiously at the rickety house in front of them. The structure seemed barely capable of standing against such a steep wind.

"Yep. I've been here several times in the past few years. They let the hooch sit here a spell after the drop-offs and then slowly move it out." O'Leary shaded his forehead against the sunset. "Langdon doesn't usually do the dirty work, but with heat on him, he's probably hiding out here. We've taken down his other spots and put the word out that we're done with the search. He's an arrogant fellow, usually handles the money and the politics. He doesn't suppose we'll keep looking for him now that we've got some success on the table."

"I'll take your word for it," said Lou grimly. Getting Langdon would be a real coup, not just professionally but personally, too. And if they couldn't get him on the shooting charge, they'd have a smuggling charge to put him away for a while.

He eyed the house. "Best way in?"

O'Leary, whom he'd specifically requested work at his side, gestured to the right. "Around back there's a cellar door. We'll drop in there and work our way up."

"Let's go." Lou and the four other men who made up their team followed O'Leary to the back. He located a heavy door set into the incline leading up to the abandoned house. The moan of the wind disguised the hinge's whine when O'Leary and Lou opened the cellar.

"It's not padlocked because the men use it routinely, and they don't expect theft in this place."

Lou glanced over his shoulder as the agents filed in. No other lights were visible on this rugged portion of Oregon landscape. Even the roads didn't come this far. They'd hiked a jagged path to reach the house. O'Leary had done his work well. Lou planned on making sure he received a commendation for it.

He dropped down after the last agent, leaving the cellar door open. The cold damp hit him square in the face and he suppressed a shiver. They followed O'Leary up the stairs quietly, and listened for sounds.

Nothing.

The lights had been on in the upper parts of the house. O'Leary nudged the door open and Lou slid through first, revolver ready, back against the wall. He eased into what looked like the kitchen in the waning light. He cocked his head, listening, but only heard the shushed sound of the other men filtering into the room. They spread out in a tactical offense formation.

Lou used his gun to gesture upward. O'Leary nodded. He gave the other men the sign to scope out the rest of the house while he and Lou made their way to the next set of stairs. Positioned in the living room, the narrow staircase had obviously been built for much smaller people.

Lou semisquatted his way up the stairs, keeping O'Leary behind him. He didn't like casualties on his watch. Knew they happened, but not when he could help it. As they touched the top step, the crackle of a radio reached their hearing. He craned his head around the corner.

Unbelievable.

A short hiss escaped his lips, lost beneath the soft jazz emanating from the room. Langdon sat in a chair, head between his hands... Alone. No one else present that Lou could tell. The closet was open. A single window.

Wait, there might be a hallway.... He shifted a bit forward. Yes. An open door to Langdon's right looked like a hallway leading to other rooms. He'd go around, then, and leave O'Leary here.

He pulled back, motioned for the agent to stay put and went to the right. The narrow hall creaked with every step. He kept his gun ready, his eyes open until he reached a doorway on his left. Peeking in, he caught a glimpse of shaggy brown hair and blankets. Langdon's guard asleep on the bed.

That made things easy. He zipped into the bedroom and took care of the guard. He'd sleep for a few hours and wake up with a headache.

Satisfied, he stalked to the door that led to Langdon's room. He paused in the entry, aimed his gun and said softly, "I didn't take you for stupid."

Langdon startled, whipping his head up and looking wildly around. His eyes were bloodshot, his chin whiskered. Dirty light filtered in from the small window behind him.

"Had a tough time lately?" Lou goaded. "Lost your girl, business is shut down, times are hard all around. Where're your goons? The one sleeping in the bed was easy to take care of. I expected more from you." He showed his teeth in what might pass as a smile to some. "Stand up."

Langdon glared at him but did as he said. "I hope you have a warrant." His sneer was filled with arrogance.

"Got it and more. You're facing quite a bit of time, you know. Your cohorts are snitches, every one of them. Got no loyalty to you."

"You have nothing."

"I've an eyewitness to attempted murder."

"Who?" he scoffed.

Lou's lips twitched. "Me."

Langdon's face visibly paled. His eyes darted. "Says who? I want my lawyer."

"You'll get him. Make no mistake about that. In the meantime, why don't we have a little chat. Off the record." Lou used his shoe to flip the door behind him closed. He stepped into the room, keeping his revolver trained on his quarry. No doubt Langdon had some kind of pistol stored on his person.

"I'm not talking."

"Sure you are. We'll just have a nice little chat about Mary." Lou looked down the barrel of his .38. "She's a special lady. You've had your eye on her for a long time, and the way I figure things, your time is about up. In fact, it's been up."

"I don't know what you're talking about," Langdon said stiffly. His fingers clenched at his side, inching toward a pocket.

"Wouldn't do that if I were you. At this range, there's

no way I'd miss that pretty face of yours. I don't think you'd like that."

Langdon's fingers wavered, then slowly moved into a more relaxed position.

"That's a good smuggler," Lou murmured. "Here's the thing—you'll be done following Mary. You'll leave her alone and never set foot in Harney County again."

"Or what?"

The silky arrogance of his voice set Lou's teeth on edge. He just wanted to shoot this guy, get rid of him forever. He could feel the anger burning through his veins.

"You don't want to find out. I expect you'll be put away for a long, long time."

Langdon's face twisted suddenly. All the smoothness left it, the spoiled surety wiped away by a bitterness Lou hadn't expected to see.

"You think you know everything." Langdon spat on the floorboards. "Mary's nothing to me, but I plan to ruin her just like her mother ruined my father."

Well, this was new. Lou narrowed his eyes. "You're out for revenge?"

"Justice, the kind the law doesn't mete out. The kind God forgets to give. Mary thinks God is watching out for her, but she's wrong. He looks out for no man. Her mother destroyed my father. Stole his money, broke his heart and left him a withered, whupped old man. He killed himself a year later. I was sixteen. Mary's mother, *Rose*—" he said her name with vitriol, his face marred by angry lines "—will pay for what she did to me. God doesn't hand out justice, but I do."

"Why are you telling me all this?" Lou asked in a deliberately bored tone.

"Because I want you to know that I will never, ever give up. Mary is my revenge, and it doesn't hurt that she has a face a man doesn't forget. This will never be over until Rose feels the torture my family experienced. You can put me away—" Langdon's voice lowered to a hiss "—but you will never stop me."

Lou's finger itched to stroke the trigger. A bit of pressure. That was all it would take to make this mess go away.

And then he'd be no better than Langdon. Using his power to get what he wanted. Believing God had no place in his actions, that God didn't care. Lou swallowed, his throat tight.

Right now, with the mustiness of the room in his nose, the impaired light that washed Langdon into shadows, Lou felt as if his soul was being tested. As if his decision at this moment would affect the rest of his life.

He looked at Langdon and saw himself. The anger over his past. Everything that had gone wrong, things he had no control over, things he'd believed God should control. He'd read enough of the Bible as a kid to know it said God gave each person a free will to make his or her own choices.

But Sarah and Abby hadn't chosen to get sick. They hadn't chosen death. It had chosen them.

His stomach clenched, but his aim didn't waver. Langdon watched him carefully, his entire being poised in stillness. Whether they had chosen sickness or not, he didn't want to be like Langdon, letting his bitterness over the past poison him until there was nothing left but evil. Maybe Langdon had been born this way; maybe there was something off with his mind that had nothing to do with his childhood.

Nevertheless, Lou felt as if he'd come to some kind of crossroads. A place to make a choice and to change the course of his life. He looked at Langdon and felt anger and pity. Setting his jaw, he repositioned his weapon and gave Langdon a hard stare.

He knew what he had to do.

"Got a telegram from Lou," James announced, coming into the kitchen where Mary had laid out four pies, a cake and a platter of snickerdoodles.

Despite the delicious scents permeating her kitchen, Mary's stomach roiled. Six weeks later and the mention of Lou's name still unsettled her so badly she couldn't eat. She covered her apple pie with a cloth, noticing how her fingers trembled.

"He's left the Orient. Done with special agent stuff," James added when Mary didn't respond.

She didn't know what to say. She could feel James's gaze on her and ignored him in favor of covering the rest of her dishes. They'd have to hold them tight to keep them from being smashed in the wagon.

"You riding with me to the church picnic?" he asked.

She nodded and handed him her snickerdoodles. "Hold that very carefully."

He balanced the cookies in one hand. "Your ma is staying home, ya know."

While Mary and Rose had gone far in mending their relationship, her mother still felt uncomfortable in church-like settings. Mary hoped someday she'd feel good about joining them, but for now it was a blessing she'd stayed.

"Josie might feel badly that Mother isn't going," she said, stacking a pie gently into a Pyrex storage container.

"Nah." James snickered. "That girl is running all over the place, and Gracie thinks it's fun joining her. I've got the feeling Josie'll be riding with Trevor and Gracie to the picnic. You and me will ride in the wagon. We've got to get a move on to make it in time. Alma don't like it when I'm late." A funny smile crossed his face, and Mary paused with her fiddling.

Was he in love?

He caught her glance, but the mooning look didn't leave his face. "Sometimes it takes an old man time to figure out the important things in life." He winked at her and left, carrying the snickerdoodles with him.

She continued filling her pie holder, but her emotions threatened to overflow. She blinked hard and picked up the carrier. The wagon was parked just outside the front door. Carefully she maneuvered through the kitchen door, traipsed down the hall and let herself out into the warm August weather.

The sun chose to shine today. It was neither hot nor chilly. Perfect for a picnic. She heard Josie's squeals and watched her balance atop a horse, Trevor and Gracie on either side of the saddle.

Smiling, Mary loaded the food onto the wagon and then climbed in. James had thoughtfully left a hat for her on the seat. He must have snagged it from her living room. She arranged it on her head, trying to feel happy about the picnic.

After all, God had heard her prayers. He'd given her a family. Brought her mother back to her, given her a daughter to love. Even James felt like a father to her. With Trevor and Gracie staying at the ranch, she should have felt content with their big family dinners and the long walks they took together.

She didn't, though. There was always this nagging awareness of something missing. When she went to town, her eyes caught on every blond man she saw. She paused at the sound of a man's low tones. Everywhere she went, she thought she saw Lou. She hoped to feel his hand on her shoulder, to see the sparkle in his eyes or the way his

lips turned at the corners when he smiled. His ready laugh
followed her.

James heaved himself into the wagon beside her. The
horses pranced, ready for their jaunt. Their manes wavered
in front of Mary, blurring as an unwelcome stinging filled
her eyes. She blinked again, harder this time.

"You okay, Mary girl?" James patted her shoulder, his
palms an awkward pressure on her blouse.

"I'll be fine." She tried to quiet her sniffle, but it came
out loud and unattractive.

"Anything you want to talk about?" His voice was gruff
but kind.

He hated emotional outbursts. She knew that, but
wanted nothing more than to cry and ask him why a man
kissed a woman, listened to her pain, gave her advice and
then left her for a job across the ocean. Why couldn't a
man say goodbye to a family he no longer had, to welcome
a new family? He didn't even have to say goodbye, she
wouldn't expect that. She just wanted him to be willing to
be open to a new season in his life. To change.

But evidently that was too much for Lou. Frowning, she
picked at a piece of linen sticking out from one of her pies.
"Let's just go, James. There's nothing to change what is."

"Now, now, you never know what's around the corner. Miss Alma surely took me by surprise." He let out a
crackly laugh that tilted Mary's lips a bit.

"I'm sure you must have seen her coming," she pointed
out. "Miss Alma is not a subtle person."

"What I didn't see coming were my own feelings. When
I fixed that pipe at her house while you were making mis-
chief in Portland, why, I stood up, caught a sniff of something baking in the oven and that fancy perfume she wears,
and I just felt like I'd gone home. Like there was something

missing out of my life and she held that missing piece, right there in her bathroom."

Mary bit her bottom lip, torn between happiness for James and sadness for herself. "So that's how she snagged you, food and perfume?"

"Nope. It was that home feeling." He cracked the reins and the horses set off. Mary gripped her pies. "Not that you haven't provided a home, my girl, but I always knew I was an employee."

"Oh, no." She turned to him. "You've been…like a father to me. In so many ways."

His cheeks flushed. "Well, I'm right glad to hear that." He cleared his throat. "Mark my words, Mary girl. If Lou don't get himself home soon, if he don't make right whatever's wrong between you two, then he's a bigger fool than I thought. You deserve better. My Alma told me she's got a surprise for you at this picnic."

Mary stifled her groan. "Don't tell me it's a man."

"Well, now, I didn't say that. I don't want her thinking I ruined your surprise."

"Here's the thing, James." She took a deep breath and suddenly found she believed it. "I miss Lou and hope he'll come home, but I am blessed and filled by the family I have. I don't need a man to make me whole or to give me purpose."

"Nah. I know that." He shot her a grin. "But love, not a man, surely makes a person's life more full."

She looked forward and exhaled her pent-up breath. That might very well be, but she wouldn't put her life on hold, hadn't, in fact, waiting for a love that might never come.

For a love that almost was.

Chapter Twenty-Eight

Lou came home to an empty ranch.

Dropping his luggage in the hallway, he meandered around the empty house before stepping back outside. It was a nice August day, perfect for an outing. Maybe that was where everyone had gone.

Fatigue pulled at his eyelids. He shook his head, ran fingers through hair that hadn't been trimmed in a while. He circled the house and headed toward Mary's home. Flowers bloomed outside her door.

He knocked, and Mary's mother answered. She looked happier than he'd ever seen her, a smile playing on her lips and knitting needles in her hand.

"You are here for my daughter?"

He nodded.

Rose studied him carefully. He couldn't read her dark eyes but somehow felt her disapproval. "They went to Horn's," she said finally. She touched the door, beginning to swing it closed, but he stopped her.

"I've got something to get off my chest," he said. Taking a deep breath, he kept her gaze. "I treated you wrongly. Will you forgive me?"

This time she blinked and it seemed as though her features softened. Then her lips curved again. "*Besa soobeda*. This is a good thing," she said quietly. "You are forgiven. Find my daughter and make things right."

The door shut. Grinning, he pivoted and went to get a horse.

He supposed he could wait for them to get home, but he didn't want to. Mary's mother was right. He hadn't traveled for so long to come home to emptiness.

He was back to do what he should have six weeks ago. No, what he should have done months ago. It had only taken seeing an old friend with his new family for him to realize that he'd made a huge mistake. Interspersed in all his traveling was some Bible reading and serious soul searching.

He readied a horse and within minutes was galloping toward the Horn place. It didn't take long to find the huge picnic in progress. The scents reached him before he could even distinguish faces.

He patted the rump of his roan and tied her up next to the other horses. He spotted Trevor's truck parked next to the few other vehicles some had dared to drive over the challenging roadways.

Sparse grasses flowed with the direction of the breeze. A bird twittered in the oak beside him. He took a steadying breath, surprised by the tightness of his gut. He'd faced down professional killers and never felt this nervous.

Wiping his hands against his jeans, he set off toward the picnic. Children shrieked with delight as a small dog ran in circles around them, yapping and wagging its tail. Other kids were climbing Horn's maple. They'd have skinned shins, no doubt, by the end of the picnic.

He grinned, thinking of his own childhood and all its adventures.

"Mister Lou!" The high-pitched scream barely reached

him before Josie smacked into his leg. He chuckled, reached under her arms and threw her into the air. Her squeal almost shattered his eardrums.

Laughing, he brought her close and hugged her.

"I missed you so much," she said into his ear, her arms a vise around his neck.

His smile quivered, and he hugged her tighter. "I missed you, too."

She pulled back and gave him a serious look. Her purple ribbon hung over one eye. "Are you leaving again? Because I don't think Miss Mary will like that very much."

"What about you?" he teased, tweaking her nose. "Don't you want me to stay?"

Her eyes rounded and her whole body tensed. "Are you teasing me?"

He winked at her. "Let's just say I plan on sticking around, if Miss Mary will have me."

Her face lit up and she wiggled to get free. "Okay, I'm going to get her right now and tell her you have to stay."

"Wait, wait," he said, laughing and putting her down. "Let me surprise her."

"Ooh, I like surprises!"

"Shh." He rubbed her head and she leaned into his touch, beaming at him with such wide-eyed openness that his chest clenched with emotion. "I love you, little Josie. Do you know that?"

She nodded, a very solemn look crossing her face. "I know, Mister Lou. I love you, too, ya know."

Smiling, he fixed her ribbon. "Come back in a bit and I'll get you some chocolate cake."

"Miss Mary said I had to eat my broccoli first. I hate broccoli!" She scampered off before he could respond, which was all well and good because at that moment he glimpsed the shine of black hair moving through the crowd of people.

He moved toward her, his heart racing, his stomach churning. He'd wondered how he'd feel when he saw her again, and the emotions roaring through him proved to be more powerful than he expected.

He stepped over a bush and followed Mary to the dessert table. Of course that was where she'd be. Checking out the goods, arranging them just so. She'd always be a homemaker.

She was quiet and deep, like a refreshing lake in the middle of a forest. Fresh and sweet to the taste, offering sustenance to all those who visited. He'd missed this stillness of hers, the ability she had of setting anyone at ease with her gentle smile.

Even her movements were soft and contained…and yet he remembered her in his arms. Full of passion and energy, giving all of herself to him in the way only a woman in love can do. His throat felt hot and tight as he watched her rearrange snickerdoodles on a plate. Her hair was up in some kind of doodad. Its glossiness beckoned to him. He wanted to pull it down, let the waves flow wild in the breeze, let them weave through his fingers with abandon.

He wanted her in his arms.

His hands ached to hold her, to feel the love she offered. But was he enough? Could he make her happy?

Swallowing hard, he stepped behind her. He saw the moment she felt his presence. Her back stiffened. There was the slightest intake of air, almost indiscernible beneath the noise of the picnic.

Mary swiveled around, her hand against her heart. Lou grinned at her, his lips curving in that familiar way, smile lines fanning out from his eyes, and her breath caught so hard she choked.

Coughing, she put her hand against her mouth. He was immediately near her, rubbing her back, asking if she was okay.

She nodded, face hot. It wasn't fair how he made her feel, these emotions he'd brought alive in her.

"You're back," she managed to croak. Not the most attractive speaking she'd ever done. Her neck felt on fire.

"I'm back." His mouth twisted into a rueful smile. "China wasn't quite what I wanted."

"Oh?" she breathed. Words were forsaking her and she did not appreciate their absence.

"It looks like you've been doing well without me." His hand waved in the air. "You even talked James into attending a church picnic. Impressive."

She swallowed, willing herself to breathe normally when every nerve ending tingled with unspoken anticipation. "That was Miss Alma's doing."

"Ah. Somehow I'm not surprised." Lou's eyes twinkled and he moved closer, edging into her space. "And you? Now that I'm not your employer, how have you been surviving?"

"My mother is with me. She sells her baskets."

"No need to be defensive. I'm sorry about what happened with her, but if you can look past it, I can." His finger came out to touch her cheek.

She shivered.

His gaze probed and she couldn't look away from the intensity in the blueness of his eyes. "What I want to know is how *you* are doing," he repeated in a low tone.

She wet her lips, unnerved and yet strangely alert to his attention. "I'm fine. Besides my selling herbs to him, Joseph at the general store likes me to bring in baked goods two or three times a week. The town ladies enjoy getting fresh, ready-made food. It is enough money for something I enjoy doing."

"Sounds like you're handling things just fine, then. Not needing me, I suppose?"

What did he mean by that? She studied him, her voice coming out stiffer than she expected. "I am content."

"Well," he said, his fingers rubbing through his hair and sending it in all sorts of directions, "wish I could say the same about myself."

Her brows lifted.

"See, this here's the thing. I'm not doing good at all. In fact, I'm miserable." The smile left his face. "I had a girl once, a long time ago, who I loved. She was carefree and opinionated. She was a bright fire that burned out too quickly. And I thought I'd never survive when she took our baby with her."

Mary's heart pounded beneath her sternum, an unsteady beat that matched the pace of her breathing.

"I thought I'd never feel whole again. But when I was shot, things began to change. So before I left Oregon for China, I put in for a different job." He shrugged, a thoughtful look on his face. "And then I traveled to Hong Kong, lots on my mind. I thought I'd left God in the dust, but He's been pursuing me. He's in my thoughts all the time. I think of you and I see Him. So I popped open the Bible and pretty soon I started feeling this change. This remembrance." His gaze turned very solemn. "I never told you this, but Sarah and I were churchgoing folk. I believed in Jesus and followed Him. When she died—"

"I'm sorry, Lou." Mary couldn't help it, the words slipped past her lips and broke his confession.

"But I don't want you to be sorry." His eyes crinkled. "I reached China, and the man who met me was an old agent friend. He'd lost so much, like me, but when he met me at the port, he had a wife and child with him. He'd moved on, and I realized so had I."

Mary glanced around at the picnic. She saw people watching them surreptitiously. James had his arms around a very satisfied-looking Miss Alma. Gracie was giving her a thumbs-up.

Lou gripped her shoulders, forcing her attention to him. His hands were gentle, his fingers rotating in a comforting movement against her blouse. "I visited Sarah's and Abby's graves."

She felt her eyes widen at his words.

"And I was okay. As I knelt there, I thought of how I'd loved them but then I thought about how I love Josie. And—" he trailed off, his eyes softening "—how I love you."

She sucked in air, suddenly feeling fear spread through her. Biting her lower lip, she pulled from his grasp. "But your job—"

"Is nothing without a home to come home to. What I realized is that God is giving me what I've missed for so long. He's been trying for a long time, but I was too dumb to realize it. You're the home for my heart, Mary." He crowded her again, backing her against the dessert table, but somehow she didn't feel encroached upon. Rather, she felt enveloped, hugged…safe. "Whenever I come home from a trip, I look for you. It's been like that for years, but I chalked it up to brotherly feelings. To friendship. What you said weeks ago, about us not being friends, you were right. I don't want friendship."

"You don't?" she whispered. Her whole body trembled. She could hardly think.

His hand reached up and touched her hair, then slid down to cup her cheek. His palm was firm and strong. "I love you so much it hurts to breathe. I want to hold you and be with you, to inhale the scent of your hair while you bake, to watch your fingers works as you knit, to go to sleep with you and wake in the morning, your hand in mine. When I think of you, I think of heat and strength and goodness. I don't ever want to let you go."

Mary pressed her lips together, hardly daring to believe what he was saying, and yet her pulse sped with the honesty in his voice. "Your job?" she ventured carefully.

He chuckled. "You're awfully worried about that, aren't you? Langdon is going to be locked away for a long time. We've got more witnesses against him. I put in for a position with the Harney County Sheriff's Office and was accepted. Turns out they think I'll be good at the job, with a little training. Any more questions?"

She shook her head, wondering in a very scattered way if this was the moment where they'd kiss. Her lips tingled at the thought.

"Good, because I have one more question for you, and I'm going to need a direct answer." His smile spread lopsided across his face and his eyes sparkled. He dropped down on one knee. There was a collective silence, and Mary felt every picnicker's eye upon them.

"Mary O'Roarke, woman I love, the one lady I want to spend the rest of my life with, will you marry me?" He held up a ring. The light caught the planed surfaces of a modest diamond, splaying rainbow glints.

"Of course she will," Josie piped up from beside her.

She hadn't even felt the little girl's presence, but here she was, her back straight and stoic, her tone firmer than a mama with a naughty little boy. Mary couldn't hold back her smile; her lips curved and wouldn't straighten.

"You think so?" Lou asked her, his own lips playing tag with his cheeks.

"I know so," Josie asserted, but there was the slightest tremble to her words.

"In that case, let me present you with your ring," said Lou. He pulled out a tiny diamond solitaire.

Josie gasped. "For me?"

"Yep. It's a symbol of our devotion."

"I'm going to wear it forever! Look, James." She ran off and Lou stood, the ring still in his hand. "What do you say, Mary?" An uncertain look entered his eyes.

Taking a deep breath, smile unwavering, she held out her fingers. "I'd say I'd like to see how it fits."

Laughing, he slid the ring onto her finger and pulled her close. His lips met hers and she felt his smile against hers, and then they were heart to heart, fingers entwined.

When the kiss ended, when the cheers and whoops from onlookers quieted, Lou pressed his cheek against hers and whispered in her ear, "What God has brought together, let no man tear asunder. Here's to our new family."

She giggled and kissed him again. When she felt sufficiently dizzy and slack limbed, she pulled back and winked at him. "To our family on the range."

* * * * *

Dear Reader,

This story was both painful and a pleasure to write. Josie reminded me so much of my vibrant and strong niece. She made me laugh with her antics. After writing *Love on the Range,* I really wanted Mary to have a happily ever after, too, and who better than with Lou Riley, mysterious and charming secret agent? Mary needed someone to trust, and unbeknownst to her, Lou needed a family. Enter Josie, a murderous uncle and some funny side characters like Miss Alma and James, and this story started rolling.

Discovering little tidbits about prohibition in Oregon, the rise of the Ku Klux Klan and how war affected people's health was an added bonus in the writing.

I'm so happy that Lou, Mary and Josie have their family together. Family is one of the most precious gifts a person can have, and thank goodness blood ties are not required to create one!

I would love to hear what you thought of this story. You can friend me on Facebook or visit my website at www.jessicanelson.net. My email is jessicaenelson@bellsouth.net, or feel free to drop a letter to Love Inspired Books, 233 Broadway, Suite 1001, New York, NY 10279.

Many blessings,

Jessica Nelson

Questions for Discussion

1. Which characters can you identify with? What part of their journey mirrors your own?

2. Lou had a past that no one knew about. Why do you think this secret was destroying him? Have you ever felt like God took something irreplaceable? How did you move past that feeling?

3. Mary suffered trauma through no fault of her own. How has forgiveness factored into your life? Especially when you feel someone is undeserving of your forgiveness?

4. Mary's desire to protect Josie caused her to lose sight of how Josie's mother felt. Sometimes good intentions can cause others pain. Has that ever happened to you, and how did you rectify the situation?

5. Josie scared Lou because she reminded him of the family he lost as a young man. Soon he began to see that what he feared was what he actually needed in order to heal. Has facing a fear ever led you to a place of healing? What prompted you to face the fear rather than run from it?

6. James battled alcoholism as a young man. He lost everything until Mary took him in. Have you ever faced addiction or known someone trying to recover from it?

7. Fear can be overcome, but often not without great struggle. Has Mary overcome her fears? How did

she do it? In what ways have you conquered your own fear?

8. Both Lou and Josie's uncle were angry at God. In the end, they dealt with their anger in different ways. Which way do you think is healthier, and why?

9. When trauma or loss occurs, it is natural to question God's love. Have you ever felt angry with God? How did He bring you peace?

10. Josie was filled with questions about God. What kind of questions have you struggled with in your life? Where and how did you find the answers to your questions?

11. Mary told Josie that God loves her and wants to answer her. In what ways has God answered your cries for help?

12. Mary was wary of intimacy with men because of her past, but she trusted Lou. Who in your life do you trust, and why?

13. Lou ignored his own emotional needs for a long time, covering them with an active life helping others, and laughter. Do you think this was healthy in the long run? Is there a balance between meeting our own needs and the needs of others, and how can you find that balance?

14. Reading the Bible comforted both Lou and Mary in many ways. How often do you read the Bible and

what are your favorite passages? Why are they your favorite?

15. Lou was afraid to love again. What would you say to someone who has suffered a great loss? Have you ever experienced trauma and what steps did you take to heal from the pain?

A HERO IN THE MAKING
Brides of Simpson Creek
by Laurie Kingery

Opening a little restaurant of her own—that's Ella Justiss's dream. She never factored in Nate Bohannan or the chaos he'd bring to her life. Though getting to know the handsome drifter may lead her to find unexpected happiness with this unlikely hero.

GROOM BY DESIGN
The Dressmaker's Daughters
by Christine Johnson

Ruth Fox is desperate to keep her father's dressmaking shop afloat while he's ill. She finds herself falling for Sam Rothenburg, but doesn't realize his secret new business could spell doom for hers.

SECOND CHANCE CINDERELLA
by Carla Capshaw

When a maid comes face-to-face with the man she loved long ago, who is now a self-made London gentleman, will her secret keep them apart or reunite them?

THE WARRIOR'S VOW
by Christina Rich

Outside Jerusalem, a hidden princess must put her life in the hands of the warrior who is on a mission to overthrow her mother the queen.

LIHCNM0614

REQUEST YOUR FREE BOOKS!

2 FREE INSPIRATIONAL NOVELS
PLUS 2
FREE
MYSTERY GIFTS

Love Inspired.

HISTORICAL
INSPIRATIONAL HISTORICAL ROMANCE

YES! Please send me 2 FREE Love Inspired® Historical novels and my 2 FREE mystery gifts (gifts are worth about $10). After receiving them, if I don't wish to receive any more books, I can return the shipping statement marked "cancel." If I don't cancel, I will receive 4 brand-new novels every month and be billed just $4.74 per book in the U.S. or $5.24 per book in Canada. That's a saving of at least 21% off the cover price. It's quite a bargain! Shipping and handling is just 50¢ per book in the U.S. and 75¢ per book in Canada.* I understand that accepting the 2 free books and gifts places me under no obligation to buy anything. I can always return a shipment and cancel at any time. Even if I never buy another book, the two free books and gifts are mine to keep forever.

102/302 IDN F5CN

Name	(PLEASE PRINT)
Address	Apt. #
City	State/Prov.	Zip/Postal Code

Signature (if under 18, a parent or guardian must sign)

Mail to the Harlequin® Reader Service:
IN U.S.A.: P.O. Box 1867, Buffalo, NY 14240-1867
IN CANADA: P.O. Box 609, Fort Erie, Ontario L2A 5X3

Want to try two free books from another series?
Call 1-800-873-8635 or visit www.ReaderService.com.

* Terms and prices subject to change without notice. Prices do not include applicable taxes. Sales tax applicable in N.Y. Canadian residents will be charged applicable taxes. Offer not valid in Quebec. This offer is limited to one order per household. Not valid for current subscribers to Love Inspired Historical books. All orders subject to credit approval. Credit or debit balances in a customer's account(s) may be offset by any other outstanding balance owed by or to the customer. Please allow 4 to 6 weeks for delivery. Offer available while quantities last.

Your Privacy—The Harlequin® Reader Service is committed to protecting your privacy. Our Privacy Policy is available online at www.ReaderService.com or upon request from the Harlequin Reader Service.

We make a portion of our mailing list available to reputable third parties that offer products we believe may interest you. If you prefer that we not exchange your name with third parties, or if you wish to clarify or modify your communication preferences, please visit us at www.ReaderService.com/consumerchoice or write to us at Harlequin Reader Service Preference Service, P.O. Box 9062, Buffalo, NY 14269. Include your complete name and address.

LIH13R